Suburbia

Rose and Thorn

Part 1

Christian J. Alecci

DEDICATION

This book is dedicated to riding your bike after dark, keeping your doors unlocked, trick or treating till it's late and breaking bones from falling off trees. This is to dodgeball and the fact that not everyone should get a participation trophy.

This is to the real Suburbia I was blessed to grow up in.

Only Love for Stonewall Ct.

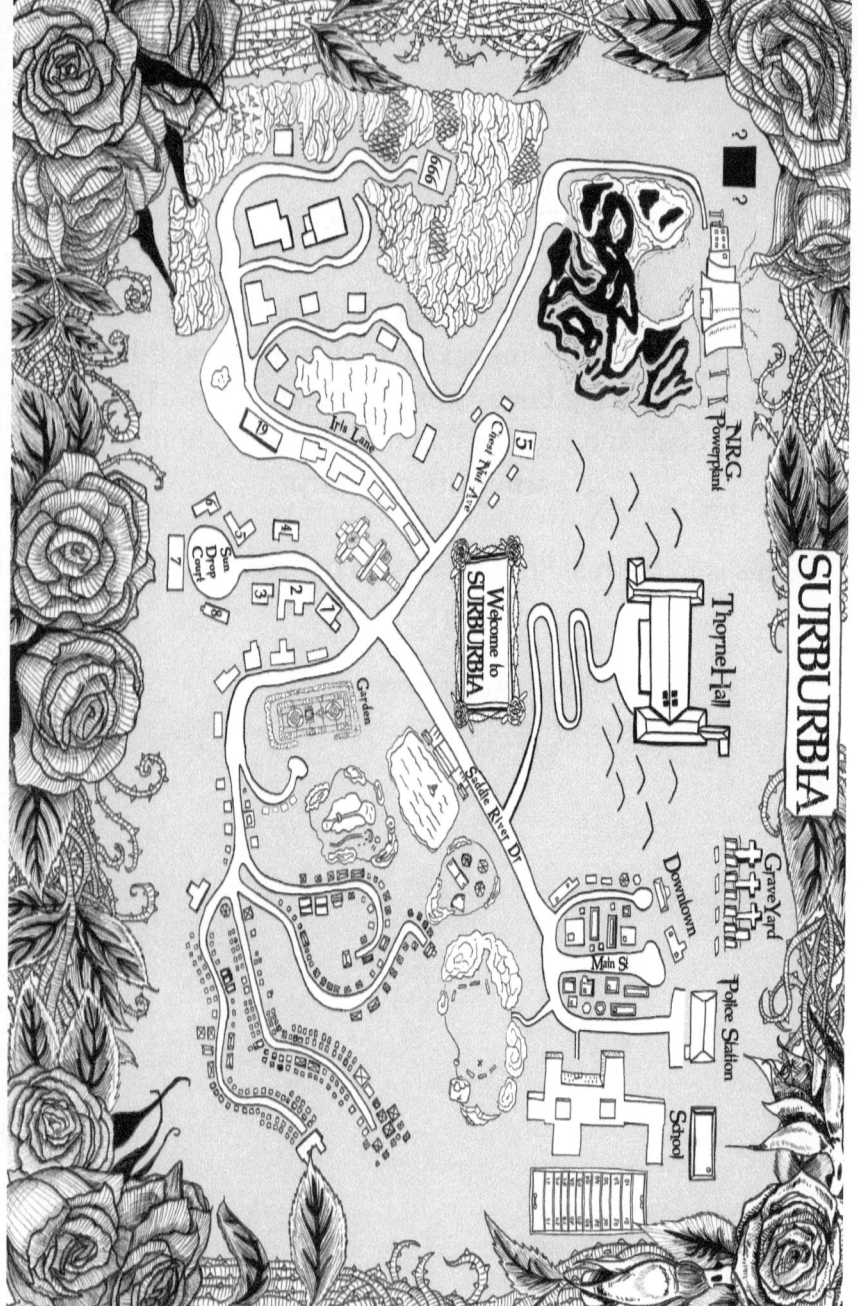

SURBURBIA

Welcome to SURBURBIA

N.R.G. Powerplant

Thorne Hall

Grave Yard

Downtown

Main St

Police Station

School

Sadha River Dr

Garden

Sun Drop Court

Iris Lane

Crest Nd Ave

999

"What you allow, is what will continue."

- Unknown

Maxine Johnson's Personal Diary
Given to her therapist for safekeeping

Spring, 1995

Dear Diary,

Today, I made my first key lime pie.

I digress.

Today, I went out and bought a new diary.

I lost my old diary during my college days. This is the first entry I have made in years. Since…well…since I attended school. A lifetime has passed since college parties and scholar boys. Since badly rolled joints and experimental drugs.

A lifetime has passed.

I don't even know if I'm the same anymore.

I do know.

I'm not…

Can one be aware of something that they are completely unaware of? I actually don't know if that's a question or a statement. A cry out or an inner thought.

I didn't need a diary when I was living in the country. It seemed when Larry left for work in the mornings that my days would be so filled, I just didn't have time to journal. There were friends at every corner, hikes to take, fields to graze, Van Halen and Genesis to listen to. Drink. Smoke. Away.

But now that we have gone *suburban*, I find I have not only the time to restart my writing, but a need to be able to communicate with something tangible. Something I can literally put my hands on and know is real.

We've been living on Sun Drop Court for many years now.

But *Suburbia* isn't as pretty as it used to be.

I've begun…I've begun…

Unable to decipher the light from the shadows. The creatures that are friendly from the phantoms in the dark. Not demons and ghosts. It's the people around who are the creatures, and I can no longer tell the good from the evil.

For I have never made a key lime pie before. It seemed an appropriate choice now that the snow is melting. Buds of spring are popping up in our garden. I wish it could be because of Mother Nature and her will. But here on Sun Drop Court, the gardeners are in before Mother Nature has had a chance to run her course. They make the lawns as perfect lawns should be—not how I would garden; I love gardening. The flowers seem an almost unnatural color compared with the garden I kept in our countryside home. Even if there were still herbs in my garden, I wouldn't use them with the amount of insecticide the gardeners spray. There was something soothing in gardening and quite rewarding about using your own pumpkins for carving on Halloween, or grazing the top of a meal with fresh-picked cilantro. Yet another pleasure that has been taken from me. Yet another joy gone.

I smile. Oh, I make sure I smile. But it's cracking. I feel it cracking.

Little boxes. Colorful boxes. Intricate boxes. Blue box. Yellow box. Green box. All with slate roofs and wraparound porches. Boxes spread out as far as the eye can see. A view of modern colonial styles shooting up right next to one another. White picket fences break emerald-green yards that reach out on perfect acre plots. A gazebo here. A pool there. The occasional tennis court. All the entrances to our homes had white gates covered in various colors of flora that matched the houses.

Oh, yes. In the winter, our town displays matching lights that people drive from miles around to see and gaze at pathetically. Ours are the houses all the parents take their kids trick-or-treating to. Just to get a glimpse inside. Just a whisper of *suburban* life. A peek at what they believe to be perfection.

Perfect. A word around here you are expected to live up to. Perfect. A word that should have never been introduced into the English language.

The grass is always greener. Why is that, dear diary? How is the grass always greener? Someone else is always in better shape than you. Has better hair than you. Drives a better car. Has a more intelligent child. Is a better hostess. Someone else. Always someone else.

April Mayfair says it's not God's will for us to judge and envy others, but how hard it is not to look upon Athena Rose without turning green. After two children—one a teenager, one a child, and no work done—she has maintained a perfect figure. She runs daily, practices yoga in her backyard, even finds time to train for charity races she organizes. All the while never missing a PTA meeting or a book club tea, or failing to host a single one of her parties.

There is an attractiveness in consistency.

I've never seen a golden strand of her perfect hair out of place. A stain on her dress. A tear in her stockings. I swear, the models in the pages of *Better Homes and Gardens* are trying to look like Athena Rose. She is that someone else. She is the greener grass. I do not hate her…I *envy* her. I can admit that. It's not a hateful envy…it's a glow that I wish I knew how to emanate. Being near her just creates warmth. It amazes me, though. Truly amazes me how a family tree can twist and turn.

Just as the Good Witch of the East had a wicked sister deep in the west, Athena Rose has such a relative. A sister who has allowed me not to dislike Athena's perfection, but to appreciate it. For kindness and warmth is so much better than...well...

Cynthia Wolf-Thorne may well have been green. She storms Sun Drop Court on her flying broom in the form of an ever-new Mercedes, as if coming down from Thorne Hall was a blessing upon us all. Her son Dax seems sweet enough and always waves when he comes to pick up Felicia for their dates. The little boy reminds me of a golden retriever—wide-eyed and blond. Though 'dates' is a loose term, as they are both children. We all were somewhat sweet when we were in our innocence. Not my child. My daughter Felicia is prettier at her age than I have ever been. I fear when she hits puberty she'll become more of a monster. Her hair is fire red and her eyes burn. I see the way her amber-gold eyes work...I see her watching...her eyes working the room...that calculated little...

I digress.

I made my first key lime pie today.

Even Captain Thorne seems a pleasant enough fellow during social affairs and in passing. A man who with his presence and laughter alone could command a room. Larry might work endless weeks for him at the power plant, but the Captain returns this hardship by building us a pool, updating appliances, even buying a new car, but all Cynthia seems to do is cast negativity and awfulness wherever she stalks.

When Athena told me she was related to that wench, Heavens to Betsy, I gasped. How two women of such different natures could share blood is beyond me.
Well, if you can believe it, she came uncalled to my house last week.

The rains of spring were trickling down outside, making music while bouncing off my blue gazebo. A gazebo I built, dear diary, something I was actually allowed to do, but the workers had to finish it once I became close to birthing… that thing.

Oh, dear diary, how I love the spring. My garden's hydrangeas are just beginning to bloom. The smells of morning dew. Watching a silver winter melt into a blooming spring. But even Cynthia can ruin that. On that wet day when she decided to grace my door front with her presence. She waved a designer umbrella around like a weapon as she stood proudly waiting for me to answer the door. I asked her if she could believe it was spring already and she replied, "I can because I have a calendar and eyes."

Without invitation, she pushed past me.

Stalking around my home freely, she then had the audacity to announce that she didn't want her son Dax hanging around the 'likes' of my Felicia. My word. She even threatened to have us all sent back to 'where we found you' if their play dates didn't end. That I was no longer welcome at dinner parties and book clubs, that I better find hobbies for loneliness would soon become my only friend.

I had all these things I wanted to say to Cynthia. All these emotions and feelings bottled up inside. As tears came to my eyes, she just stood there with that smug stare while I mumbled pathetically. Apologizes I knew I didn't owe her.

She poked a long nail into my stomach before leaving and warned me again, "You and your daughter are no longer allowed at any social events. I do not want to see you in a dress. Or your daughter done up. Find a social life somewhere else, for your life on the Court is over."

Cynthia swung her mane of highlighted hair and sniffed at the air before leaving, exclaiming, "It smells awful in here. Did you try to bake? Horrid." Her Gucci umbrella exploded open and she proudly strutted off.

Oh, when she left I was so angry. All the things I wanted to say spilled out as I smashed my fists into the wall. All the words I couldn't form came out as my skin broke. The blows became stronger and stronger. The blood didn't bother me. Neither did the bruises. It feels good to feel. It feels good to be alive for a moment.

There is cause and effect. You have to light the candle…it doesn't just burn. The flicker of flame doesn't just catch on the curtain. It is left unattended. Unwatched. In the loneliness…the house burns down to nothing.

Today, I made my first key lime pie.

I digress, dear diary, I digress.

Digression.

Larry works late these days and no matter how many attempts I make at donning tempting lingerie, he doesn't seem to want to make love to me anymore. He sleeps on the couch most nights after giving me my tea and leaves before I rise for the day. Always bringing me tea before bed, watches at the door with this sad look before retreating downstairs. Maybe he's seeking out love elsewhere. I will try harder, for without him I'd be all alone. That is my wifely duty. He needs to want to want me. He needs to want to need me. He needs to want and need and want.

Oh, yes, of course, there is my daughter. That… creature.

Felicia might only be a child, but she seems to know what I'm thinking, so I keep her away from me. Her little amber eyes haunt me wherever I go in the house. Why does she seem to know when I am sad? When I am depressed? Why does she continue to play and laugh while life is crumbling around us? Why is she always watching? What does she want from me?

Things were better before I had her. Felicia was both conceived and born on the Court, a product of *Suburbia,* the little creature was. I can't remember making her, as if the act that caused the thing is something I have completely blocked from memory. Making Larry smile is hard enough, but she always wants too much from me. It's exhausting. She's aging me. Her fault. It's her fault.

I've taken to locking her in her room whenever she's not at school and Larry is at work. It's easier that way. We all need some quiet. There just doesn't seem to be any time to think here in *Suburbia*. Everything is so loud. Everything is so loud.

Can't you hear the screams?

I tossed the key lime pie in the trash.

I began from scratch...that's all we can do, right?

April has tried to relieve my stress with prayers, but why is no one up there listening to me? Returning my pleas? I wish I had something I believed in. The later Larry comes home from work and the more that little creature watches me from afar, I feel myself slipping. I'm scared of the thoughts that cross my mind. I'm afraid of where they might lead me. But I have you, right, dear diary? And together we'll make sure I don't crack. Together, you will help me find myself before I'm completely lost. Before it's too late. Before I pull a trigger that cannot be undone.

April Mayfair stood on her perfectly maintained porch twisting the diamond cross that was always around her neck.

Punctuality is a virtue and, so far, the McArthur family was not faring so well. The moving trucks were late and staring at the beige-and-gray colonial was giving April neurosis. The porch needed work, the window frames painting, and major construction needed to happen in that kitchen to bring it up-to-date. The house stood out on the street—it was the only empty one and every crack and slouched window pane made April want to march over there and fix them.

Cynthia had kept the gardeners mowing their lawn and caring for that end of the spectrum, but April couldn't imagine what the inside of the house looked like now. After so many years…after so much…

April inhaled heavily and exhaled. Not her church; not her pews.

It helped that the town realtor was a gossip. Cynthia Wolf-Thorne enjoyed talking negatively about other people as much as she enjoyed casting herself in a positive light. The minute the McArthur family signed the papers on the old Johnson residence, all of Sun Drop Court knew the details.

Probably the entire town, as Cynthia fed on people who brought offerings of gossip up to Thorne Hall.

The Captain Thorne had hired a new man for his force up at the power plant. Picked this young family from a blue-collared neighborhood in the city and, though Cynthia didn't say it at tea, obviously also offered them one undeniable check. No one had taken Larry Johnson's executive place in years and it looked like he'd finally found a man to fill the spot. They obviously skipped the sordid history of the Johnson house and simply, *beautifully*, offered them a *beautiful* (figurative) colonial on a *beautiful* (relative) *suburban* street.

How many families have they brought in now? April couldn't count. The streets of their town were littered with the Captain's 'workers.' People who were moved from lower-class neighborhoods or cheap country trailers to here…to a place April where and her husband had worked to be able to fit into. To a place many had worked very hard to build their lives and their families around, and not just to be cut a check and get a free upgrade.

Suburbia.

The picture of perfection.

April had felt the glass of that picture cracking, and this was yet another crack. You can't fix cracking glass—you can piece it together, but it will never look like it did when it was new.

The McArthur family, seemingly, would be a pleasant addition to the lane. Gregory McArthur didn't really interest her—some former college athlete who worked for some small bank; she knew how hard the Captain worked his men. It was the wife and kids who concerned her. April would be able to see them from her windows. Susan McArthur had owned her own moderately successful baking shop in the city (yawn) and had produced three children. Matthew, a boy who was, annoyingly, the same age as April's thirteen-year-old son, Todd—can't they just be shipped off till they are mature?— and twin baby girls. Identical twins. Susan's only job would be to repair the damage the Johnson family did to that home. God be thanked that it was still standing after what had happened behind those doors.

Cynthia wasn't one of those realtors who spruced up a house for you and rubbed your back in hopes of a deal. She couldn't care less what you thought about the property. You could fix those cracks on the wall and the creak in the stairs on your own time. As far as she was concerned, it was a blessing to even be considered fit to live in 'her land.'

Cynthia had yelled at her housekeeper, Rosaletta, once, telling her that she would not only kick her out of her 'land,' but out of America as well. April had heard it. April had a tendency to always 'hear it.'

If God could hear everything, why couldn't she?

April didn't truly give thought to how Cynthia treated the hired and heftily paid help—this wasn't slavery; the woman could leave. There was something in the Bible about tolerating certain behaviors for monetary favors... Oh, yes, harlots.

April just cared about... She twisted the cross round and round and round.

Cared about.

Twisted the cross tighter.

Cared.

Wasn't it a beautiful day?

She would give Cynthia one thing; she had her tenants move in on the most spectacular of days. Though if it was pouring with rain, she'd have them move in all the same. Hydrangeas of fantastic colors decorated all of the lawns. Each house complete with an archway at the end of the stone pathway, various flowers flowing up and around them. One truly felt welcome walking under these archways. Some houses had floods of shimmering blues, others rainbows ranging from pinks to purples to yellows and greens. Pastels that caught the light and shimmered. Every porch decorated with an assortment of color appropriate for the house's ambiance, nothing too extreme. All the Callery Pears were in bloom and the street had that special aroma to it... I always hated that smell. White picket fences at their whitest—all paint cracks immediately repaired.

April watched as a couple jogged up the street. A handsome financial advisor from a few streets over was taking his golden retriever for a walk. Smiling politely as he passed by Athena Rose as she made her way down toward the old Johnson…new McArthur house. A beautiful yellow-and-blue sundress elegantly bouncing around her as she balanced a large tray of what April could only assume was her famous shepherd's pie on one hand. April smirked as she thought to herself, *Athena should have just waited on her porch; it's been hours and there's no sign of the McArthurs.* In the midst of that thought, a large moving truck turned onto Sun Drop Court and made its way up the street.

Athena Rose, on point as always. As James 3:16 stated: For where jealousy and selfish ambition exist, there will be disorder and every vile practice.

April let loose of her cross and the smile spread her lips. "Athena! Yoohoo! Athena! Over here!"

Athena's golden locks were fanned out and floated around as her sun-kissed face met April's. We do not envy. We do not covet what others have. We smile and…

"Oh, April." Athena's pearly whites seemed to sparkle off the sun. "What a beautiful day for new neighbors. How is Todd? I see he's returned from boarding school for the summer."

Todd. The kid. Her son. April's fingers were back at the diamond cross. Twisted it again and it became a noose, so she released it.

"Todd's home from boarding school." It wasn't a lie—some called it a boarding school. "We have discussed it and the Catholic school way of life might have worked for my husband, but Todd is of a different nature. I'll matriculate him with the public school this year. Keep him close to home and close to our church."

"Oh, how lovely." Athena's face didn't wrinkle as she held her smile—nothing to do with plastic surgery; just unnecessarily perfect genes. "The McArthur family has a boy around the same age… Make sure to get the boys together so they both have friends when they enter a new school…make the transition easier…no one enjoys being the new kid on the block. Once upon a time, Cynthia and I were the new girls around here."

"Once upon a time…of course." April felt her hand twitching. She brought it to the cross. "As long as Todd sticks to his prayers and the way of the church. He needs to not be influenced by the rabble that attends these public schools. They really let anyone go there. I swear…but Pastor Jefferson thought it best that…"

"Does Pastor Jefferson approve of marijuana?"

"Marijuana? Athena! My word!"

But Athena was now motioning with her free hand, the perfectly manicured nails pointed toward April's well-kept home. Through her own gardening, her own cooking, painting, and projects—her nails were perfect. As April turned, she didn't see her newly painted shutters or the perfect box flowers that sat outside her windows. No, what she saw was a thick, undeniable puff of smoke coming out of Todd's window. Like a dragon in its lair…like a demon lurking in its den.

Damn. Damn. Damn.

"Jesus can see you!" April yelled toward the window. "Jesus sees you!"

"April," Athena said in a hushed voice, "our new neighbors… *Dope* isn't exactly a comfortable welcoming to our street. My word."

Of course. Of course.

April let her church smile beam. "If you would excuse me."

"Of course."

"I'll see you at…"

"Yes, this week's book club."

"It's been lovely, Athena…my best to Benjamin and the kids."

"Yes, we must have you and Leonardo over to dinner before summer begins."

"I'll keep you in my prayers."

They exchanged air kisses. April hurriedly made her way back up to her house as Athena turned to face the moving truck and the car that parked a yard behind.

"I didn't expect this." Susan McArthur let out a breath as their station wagon stopped behind the moving truck. "I know Mrs. Thorne told us it would be nice, but this...I mean...will your new salary cover this? I know we don't have enough furniture to fit in there. We barely had enough furniture for our studio in the city."

Susan opened her purse and took an extra painkiller as her husband, Gregory, silently sighed. He wished he could have the same effect on his wife as those pills.

"Deep breaths, my love." Greg reached over and gently massaged his hand into her tiny ones. "Just relax."

He was secretly hoping he could slip the pill out of her fingers, but the minute he let go, into her mouth it went. She had begun chewing them.

They had driven the entire way like this. Greg was just as nervous as his wife, but there was no time to show it. She would just get more anxious and take more pills.

Support and comfort. Stability and strength. When she let on a frown, he let on a smile, no matter what was going on inside. It hadn't always been this way. On their wedding day he had been terrified she wouldn't show. When he first saw her at the end of the aisle, full of confidence and beauty, he'd begun to tear up. She used to see the glass as overflowing. Had a way of always catching the storm on the horizon and turning it into a sunset. Then she had that terrible car accident and the pills came into the picture. They changed her. Weakened her. It would anger some, but we all go through phases, and that was all this was, a phase. He just wished when he wrapped his arms around her and told her it would be all right, she'd believe him. For he would make it all right for the both of them. That's why he took this job.

"Matthew," Greg shot jokingly back to his son who had no idea of anything beyond his iPod, "what do you think?"

"He's listening to that pod apple thing." Susan didn't need to look back to know that their shaggy-haired teenager wasn't mentally with them. "He's always listening to that thing. Why did we buy it for him? I used to have to give him silent time…I wish I could take all those minutes back and use them now. Having a conversation with him would be nice."

"It doesn't work that way." Greg smiled over at his wife who was nervously looking at their new home. "It's a phase…that'll last till college, maybe a little after. It's a period of time almost everyone goes through. I didn't talk to my parents till my twenties and now we are closer than ever. He'll come back."

Kids hit an age where they believe they don't need their parents anymore; they don't need curfews or rules or guidance. Through high school, through college…then, at some point, they realize their friends won't be there forever. That support doesn't come from their frat brothers or their roommates. Family will be there for them, as they had been since the beginning.

Matthew was at that age and it was okay. Greg remembered being at that age and all it was was a phase. His son was handsome and athletic—a combination of both his and his wife's great genes—though his shaggy hair hid his face and he preferred baggy clothes over collared shirts and khakis. But Matthew was calm and reserved and Greg did have a tendency to be daring…impulsive. Like taking a whopper check and a new house for a job he wasn't quite sure he understood. Moving his whole family to *Suburbia*.

But she had the twins, Kat and Katie, to take care of —they needed her; they were only two. Maybe that would… somehow…bring her back to reality. He had hoped this new setting, plus the girls, would be a way for her to refresh. Plus, the amount of zeros on that check…

From outside the car, Greg heard a…well, he heard their realtor. "A whore ah!" screamed Cynthia in her best Spanish. No doors had opened from the moving truck and

Greg was in such a daydream he didn't see the red Mercedes slither in. Cynthia was in a tight black-and-silver Chanel dress with a belt cinching her waist. Her mass of long blond curls bounced around her thin face like a lion's. "You no work-o for free-o! Unpack-o the *stuff-o now! A whore ah!*"

Startled, one of the baby girls made a crying sound as the other one comforted her and hushed her before Susan could even turn around. Katie and Kat were only two, but twins…no books can really explain their connection. Susan had read them all and each one tended to contradict the next. The girls' bond was truly an enigma.

"I guess we should get…get going," Susan let out with a slight stutter and shake as she folded her arms. Releasing Greg's hand and attempting to comfort herself— great, the pill set in—she put on her best smile for the kids, but Greg could tell she was nervous. For a second, her hand reached back to the bottle of pills in her purse and Greg pushed it away.

"We will be fine," Greg reassured her. "The Captain said we'd fit right in. I wouldn't have moved us otherwise. You know me."

"I do." Susan smiled and reached toward her door handle. "That's what worries me. You're impulsive."

"Well, if we were going to have more kids, *Suburbia* would have been the next move," he began and, as Susan's eyes went wide, he laughed. "I'm joking."

"That's not a funny joke, dear."

A huge diamond ring haloed in smaller diamonds slammed against their window. Followed by the angry face of Cynthia Wolf-Thorne.

"What the hell," Matthew let out from the backseat.

"Language," Susan scolded back at her son. In the second it took for her to turn her head, Greg shoved her pill bottle to the bottom of her purse.

"He speaks!" Greg let out in his clear-the-air voice, but the air wasn't clear...another rapping at the window.

"Are you going to just sit there all day?" Cynthia was still tapping at the glass with her giant diamond ring. "I didn't drive all the way down here to watch you have family time in a...wood-paneled station wagon."

"You ready?" Greg kissed his wife deeply on the cheek. "We can turn around if you want. Go back to the city and hope that our studio will magically grow to withstand three kids."

"That was only half-funny, but better than the first one." Susan took a deep breath, giving the pill another second to settle in, and opened the passenger door. Standing there was Athena Rose. "Wow."

Athena's eyebrow raised and her emerald eyes sparkled. "Well," Athena said gaily. "Wow to you, too!"

"I'm sorry," Susan stuttered, forgetting where she was for a second. "I'm just so..."

"You must be overwhelmed." Athena reached her free hand out, while balancing a covered tray, and helped Susan out of the car. "I've heard the three biggest stressors in life are death, taxes, and moving. I was once the new gal on the block, and if I can help make that transition easier for you…I will. I'm Athena Rose. My family and I live just up the Court from you."

"What is taking your wife so long?" Cynthia exclaimed as she circled around the car. She was strutting proudly before laying eyes on Athena, her posture shifting as she awkwardly scratched a long nail at her nose. "Oh."

"Oh?" Athena laughed as her musical voice filled the air. "Is that how you greet your sister? I wouldn't scratch that nose too hard if I was you. Don't want another rhinoplasty, do we?"

"I…" Cynthia put her bony arms on her waist. "What are you doing down here? I wasn't expecting you."

"Of course not. If you returned any of my phone calls, you… This must be your husband, Susan. Gregory, yes?" Athena floated to Greg and graced a kiss on his cheek. "How handsome are you? Susan, quite the lucky woman you are. I'm Athena Rose. Neighbor up the street. My best friend Maxine Johnson once lived in this house."

"Oh." Susan put a hand on Athena's shoulder. "I'm sorry. Did she move?"

"You could say that." Athena held her smile. "A story for another day, I'm sure. Or maybe one for today…"

"Athena," Cynthia interrupted with force. "You can spew pleasantries and stories from a million years ago later. I don't have all day and I wanted to show them the house. I have other things to do. I'm sure they'd love it if you came back later."

"Of course…dearest sister." Athena motioned toward the house as the laborers were slowly beginning to unload the moving truck. "Maybe I can help you give them a tour."

"You two are related?" Greg inquired with an eyebrow raised before his wife put an elbow in his side. "What? Making friendly talk."

"She just said we were sisters," Cynthia said, exasperated, before turning on Athena. "A tour? A tour of what? An empty house? You couldn't have waited to come down here? I haven't even had their furniture put in yet."

They bought us furniture, Susan thought. *They bought us furniture* and *a house?*

"I'd have missed your smiling face." Athena didn't miss a beat and Greg couldn't help but chuckle. "Seeing you is always so pleasant, sister, even though you haven't let me into this house since the Johnson family left. But, I will return. Here, for the McArthurs. So you don't have to worry about dinner on your first night."

Athena plopped the tray into Cynthia's arms before turning on her heels and facing Susan. "I'll come and visit you guys again, and soon. I'm sure Gregory will be busy with the Captain and one can go stir-crazy without activity. There is plenty of that on the Court. We housewives keep busy. Oh, I almost forgot." Out of her bag she pulled a copy of *House of Leaves*. "We just started a new book for the book club. We meet biweekly at my house to discuss, but Cynthia has the maid read the book and explain it to her."

"I do not!" Cynthia retorted, missing the joke because it was directed at her. "I just don't have time for books."

"Are you sure you don't want to stay?" Susan's eyes were connected with Athena's, which were much more relaxing and comforting than those of her sister. Some people just give off warmth and some make the air turn to frost.

"Oh." Athena drew the word out into a long sound until Cynthia huffed again. "I guess I must be going. Benjamin will be home from work soon and I'd hate for him not to have a warm dinner waiting for him on the table. Plus, my oldest, Lucas, came in tonight from out of town and I rarely get to see him anymore. They grow up so fast, don't they? Oh, who is this?"

Matthew had gotten out of the car and was eyeing the adults with limited interest as he surfed the black-and-white screen of his iPod.

"My oldest." Greg put a muscular arm around his son's shoulders. "Matthew says hi."

"What?" Matthew dropped the headphones around his shoulders.

"Hello, Matthew." Athena's eyes were on him and, for some reason, Susan felt a tinge of envy that they had left hers. "I'm Athena. I have a daughter who I'm sure would love to meet a handsome boy like you. Looks certainly run in this family, don't they?"

"Oh." Matthew looked back at her through the straggles of his hair. "Sure. Thanks, I guess."

"Impressive. Articulate. Isn't he the scholar?" Cynthia was checking the Rolex on her wrist, which sparkled in the sun. "Athena, I mean, what are you doing? Come on."

Then it all changed. Athena's eyes were on her sister's. The air was still as the clouds began to turn pink and dart their shadows off the trees all over the court. Pinks turned dark and light shaded gray. In the backseat, both girls let out a small whimper.

"You will return my calls, Cynthia."

"I've been busy."

"You will return my calls."

"The Captain has been…"

"Excuses." Athena waved her hand through the air. "Susan and Gregory, has Cynthia told you about the former owners…"

"I'll call you tonight," Cynthia interrupted. She was a lion that had been cornered by a pack of wolves. "I promise."

"Good!" Athena allowed the warmth to return to the air and Susan felt herself relax into it like in a sauna. "Welcome to Sun Drop Court! Please don't hesitate to ask for anything. Without good neighbors, where would we be?"

Athena dropped kisses on everyone's cheeks— including Matthew's and Cynthia's—then turned and acknowledged the twin girls in the car with a pleasant glance before breezing up the street.

Susan watched her walk away. She grazed with ease and waved at everyone she passed. Susan wanted her to return, wanted to talk to her and spend time with her. Until now, Susan didn't believe women like Athena existed—the perfect housewife.

Now they were left with...

"Can we get this over with?" Cynthia was ushering them toward the house. "You...Michael...entertain those... adorable...cute...children...in the car. I won't be long with your parents. I have actual things to do."

Matthew didn't even hear her get his name wrong. He went to put his headphones back on when a charismatic voice sprung up behind him, "Hi!"

He turned to face a girl who was about his age, but about three times his size. Where he was lean, she was lard. Her mermaid-blond locks were pulled into pigtails and her fat red face had a great smile spread across it. A pink polo shirt and khaki pants spread across her large body, but her green eyes were what caught him—they were alive and friendly... and fun.

"Uh." Matthew felt his cheeks redden. He had talked to girls before, but this was different. "Hi."

"Who are you?" She beamed. "You look friendly."

"I guess I am." He laughed. "You seem friendly as well."

"Aw. That's sweet. Are you sweet? You seem sweet." She reached a pudgy hand out and grasped Matthew's and shook it firmly. "You just met my mom."

"That...that's your mom?" Matthew turned to look at Cynthia Wolf-Thorne, who had his parents halfway up to the house, but who then stopped to continue to destroy the Spanish language to workers who actually spoke perfect English. The girl laughed—it was warm; it was welcoming.

"No, silly. That's, like, my Auntie Sin." She pointed up the block to where Athena Rose had stopped to talk to a well-dressed couple who were out for a walk. "That's my mommy...er...mom. I'm Sammy Rose."

"Matthew McArthur."

"Oh." She giggled and looked away shyly. "We sound like adults, don't we? With these pleasantries, maybe I should curtsy."

So she did.

He bowed back to her in hopes of…and she laughed and his hopes were filled. What a sound. What a musical sound. The type of laugh that warmed a heart and made you want to laugh as well, whether you understood the joke or not.

"My mom said a new boy came to the street. I was new once. No friends. Didn't know anyone," Sammy confessed, playing with a pigtail. Matthew had been flirted with before, but he liked every moment of this encounter better than any of the previous ones. "But I can be your friend. If you want, of course. Friends make everything better. Company helps it all. Do you miss yours? Did you have many where you came from?"

She reached out for his hand, but before Matthew could reach back, a needle popped the proverbial balloon.

"Oink," said a raspy voice. "Oink, oink, oink."

"No." Sammy put her hands over her ears and her face fell to ruin. "No. No. No."

The needle was a girl who seemed just a bit older. Wet, red hair pulled tightly back. Dark, unfriendly amber-gold eyes staring out of hollow and dark-ringed sockets. Where Sammy had obviously enjoyed healthy servings of cake, this girl could have used a meal or two. Behind her were a couple of brunette girls around the same age—one who had already begun to get her bosoms. The redhead's face was beautiful, but was aged too much for a girl...she had some city miles on her. To boot, she was wearing clothes completely inappropriate for someone who had to repeat seventh grade.

"Little piggy left her house," the redhead spewed out of thin lips, reeking of cigarette smoke. "Little piggy went to the field. Little piggy. Little piggy. Little piggy is about to go crying all the way home. Oink."

"No. No. No. No." Sammy's hands tightened over her ears and Matthew felt an emptiness in his chest that he hadn't experienced before. "No. No. No. No."

"Were you talking to the animal?" The redhead continued as the girls laughed along behind her. "Talking to the piggy. Are you a farmer? You look like you could be a farmer. You going to farm this pig, farmer?"

The redhead's eyes were on Matthew, judging him in a way that told him this was a one-time opportunity.

"No, she just talked to me." Matthew didn't know why he said what he said next. "Oink."

His chest felt even emptier as Sammy, tears filling her green eyes, shot him a look that ate through him. They weren't sparkling and alive anymore—they were broken. He had broken the glow.

"But...but...but...you said you were my friend."
Sammy went to run up the street, but the redhead caught her
claws around her fat arm. "Felicia, stop it. It hurts. I'll tell.
Please, it hurts. Help."

"Oh, yes!" The redheaded nightmare named Felicia
continued, her golden eyes thinning with rage as her nails dug
into Sammy's arms and spots of blood began to slowly form
and drip down her arm. "Go cry to mommy, fatty fat piggy.
Go cry and cry and cry. The more you cry, the fatter you'll
get. The fatter you'll get, the more I'll oink. The more I'll
oink, the more you'll..."

"Notwithstanding, I have a few things against thee,
because thou sufferest that woman Jezebel, which calleth
herself a prophetess," a strong male voice boomed behind
them, "to teach and to seduce my servants to commit
fornication, and to eat things sacrificed unto idols. Revelation,
two-twenty."

While Felicia taunted Sammy, a boy appeared. A boy
who had hit puberty early and was beaming with confidence.
His cheekbones were high and his eyes pale and stern, though
also blurry and hazed over. Wearing a uniform of red and
gold, his collar popped up; he seemed more royal than
civilian. A proud smile spread across his face.

"Excuse me?" Felicia shot a look back before realizing
who was standing there. "Oh...Todd...I..."

Todd boomed a laugh. "I called you a whore."

"The hell you…" Felicia began. She was losing the attention of the girls she was with. Her little gang was looking worriedly at one another. "I…"

"What's wrong with you? Your parents didn't love you enough or something?" Todd continued as he strutted proudly toward Felicia, who was now scratching at the side of her head. "That's what my mom says. Your parents deserted you; no one hugs you before bed. Instead of turning that around and trying to find the sun in the sky…look at you. A creature who roams through the forest unaware of the trees. You are creating storms on beautiful days. An example of where Michael forgot to go right and Lucifer knew where to go wrong."

"Todd." Sammy shot the boy a pleading look as she struggled a pudgy arm away from Felicia. "It's okay. You don't have to. You're just going to make it worse."

"No." Todd Mayfair was firing holiness at Felicia. "I've had enough of watching this go on each summer. It's old, Felicia. The day it's acceptable to punch girls, I'm coming for you."

Felicia shot her squad a look. She had to win them back. "Go back to boarding school, you faggot." Felicia spat at him and it hit him on the side of the cheek. He wiped it away without a thought. "The minute school starts, I'll hunt this piggy down. She'll regret this…trying to make new friends with people moving into *my house*! You'll be across the country and won't be able to guard the fat pig. You won't be able to do anything."

"Well…I should get tested now that your saliva has touched me. That's something I should definitely do. But, I'm joining your…*public* school this year." Todd smacked Felicia's arm that was clutching Sammy's so strongly Matthew thought he heard something pop. "The Lord banishes jezebels like you. In His absence, I will take His place."

"Come on, Todd." Felicia's attitude changed with this new information. "I'm just having some fun. Plus, how is she supposed to meet boys being as round as the world. No one is going to be kissing her; I'm just toughening her up."

Felicia shot the girls behind her looks for support, but she had lost her following. Todd held his smile and grabbed Sammy, dipped her in his tanned arms, and kissed her deeply. He opened his eyes to meet the pack of mean girls who were turning red and uncomfortable. It was obvious none of them had actually ever been kissed before. Felicia had been forced to do other things by one of her foster fathers, but no one had ever kissed her.

"*Jesus sees you!*" April Mayfair came tearing out of her house swinging her Bible like a judge's mallet, catching the kiss. "I might not know how you snuck out of the house! But Jesus does… Out here kissing and carrying on with…oh, my, Samantha Rose…my word….Are you okay? You are bleeding, child!"

"We're all fine," Matthew let out. Todd's eyebrow rose, interested that this was when Matthew decided to speak up, and Sammy gave him another betrayed look. Matthew just wanted her eyes to sparkle again; he wanted her to smile again. That laugh…that beautiful laugh, but he had sided with the enemy in his first moments on the block. He had dug a grave so deep that he didn't know if anyone could help him out of it.

Now or ever. *Oink*. It rang in his head. *Oink*.

"Who are you?" April Mayfair's eyes were the same as her son's, pale and stern. Though not blazed by dope. "The rest of these kids, I know. I've never seen you before. Are you one of those out-of-town boys? I've told Cynthia time and time again that we need a gate around this community."

"Uh…Matthew McArthur…this is my new house."

"My house," mumbled Felicia, angrily. "It's. My. House."

Kids had become kids again. Actual adults were here and the playground antics had ended.

"A pleasure to meet you, Matthew. I've been looking forward to meeting your family. I think it's best if everyone who doesn't live on the Court goes home. It's getting late. Are your parents inside? I'd love to meet them."

Then April's eyes fell on Felicia with a look of grave disapproval. "What are you wearing, child? You are thirteen years old, not an old hooker. You smell like where flowers go to die. I can see your bra strap. If I can see you bra strap, Jesus can see your bra strap. There is no place in heaven for harlots and jezebels. You're like Lola at the Copacabana, and we know how she turned out. I'd think on that next time you wrap a scarf around you and call it an outfit."

"I'm sorry, Mrs. Mayfair," Felicia grumbled. She went to turn on her bike. The awful encounter was over. If only they could have been so lucky. An even more horrifying voice roared in the air. A chill spilled among the entire group. Matthew's skin began to crawl as he realized this wasn't close to being over.

"*Absolutely not!*" Cynthia Wolf-Thorne must have heard the commotion and was storming down the cobblestone pathway, moving quickly and impressively on her high heels. Matthew's parents in tow with looks of worry on both of their faces. "No! No! No! You don't even live here anymore. If I wanted the rabble here I would go down to the ghetto and pick up some homeless people myself. I'd spread them around my yard and feed them as I pleased! But you... you...*you!*"

"I..." Felicia stammered and Matthew, for a second, felt bad for her. Sammy caught him as he gave Felicia a sympathetic look and she frowned at him. How could he possibly make this any worse?

"I...I...I...I!" Cynthia mocked Felicia while waving a diamond-encrusted hand through the air, allowing it to fall onto Sammy Rose's shoulder and hug her close. April Mayfair had the Bible clutched against her chest and an arm firmly around Todd's shoulders, who looked amused by all that was transpiring. Susan and Gregory McArthur were each holding one of the twins, who were reaching toward each other. Sammy Rose's face had ballooned tenfold and tears were clearing up. But Cynthia Wolf-Thorne was staring not only at Felicia, but into her.

"If I wanted you to live on this street, I would have let you. After your mother made those 'great decisions'… If I wanted to, I would have kept you around. But I see you in her. Who are you with?" Cynthia shot looks to the cowering girls behind Felicia who, once in the Wolf's glare, began to whimper. "Aly Bane and Melissa Han—once respectable girls from respectable families hanging out with an urchin? You are even dressed like this…this…missed abortion. Go home, the both of you. Now! I'll be on the phone with your parents before you even get there." The girls turned their bikes and sped up the street without looking back.

Cynthia watched as Felicia went to get on her bike, "Oh. Ha-ha. No. Not you. That's not even your bike, is it? Give it to me. You can walk back."

"Cynthia, is that really necessary?"

"Yes, April. It is completely necessary." Cynthia grabbed the bike and pushed the girl toward the end of the

35

Court. "We are all done here. Do you hear me, you little redheaded shit?"

"Matthew…" Susan called to her son, doing her best to separate him from the drama that deep down he felt he'd started. "Get over here, hon. Come see your room."

With her red head bowed, Felicia shot Sammy Rose one final glare, but Cynthia had that covered as well. "Don't you dare look upon my blood! Look at me. If I ever catch you around this house, this street, or anywhere near my family again, so help me." Cynthia's voice dropped to a silent growl, but Matthew could hear her as clear as day and his skin rippled with goosebumps. "I'll run you over with my Mercedes and make sure it looks like an accident. It'll be easy. I'll buy a new one. I'll have a new car and no one will miss you."

"She's joking, Matthew," Susan whispered into her son's ear, obviously feeling the stress and anxiety coming off him. "Just relax."

Matthew could see the fury building in Cynthia as Felicia, head down, body shaking, tears buckling at her eyes, made her way up the street. If it was a joke, it was not a good one.

"Well," Cynthia turned and, for the first time, spread a smile over her face. A smile she must have used a million times for charity events and grants for the power plant. "Shame on her, huh? A fly in a fine glass of wine. Sorry, dears. Didn't mean for such drama on your first day. Not the picture I have painted of this street, but…history will be history."

"I'm sorry this is how we have to meet." April was looking over each McArthur. Now that everyone else had cleared out, she had the chance to fully run her eyes over each of them. Judgement time. "I'm April Mayfair and this is my son, Todd. I live right across the street, with my husband, Leonardo. He's a doctor; never hurts to have a doctor right across the street. Todd and I are going to read from Deuteronomy. This was quite the rustle, and reading from the good book always calms our nerves. Perhaps you would like to join us? We can start over and put a nice spin on this day. I just made croissants this morning, a secret recipe that maybe I'd consider sharing."

"That's sweet, April." Susan smiled. "But we aren't religious."

"Oh." With that, April immediately looked disinterested in the entire family. She turned with Todd under her arm and headed back to her house, silently scolding verses of the Bible at him. Matthew had felt eyes on him throughout all of this, as Sammy Rose had never stopped staring at him. Her green eyes filled with hurt and confusion, as all she had tried to do was be nice. All she had tried to do was make a friend. Be kind. Be welcoming. Be a good person.

Cynthia planted her red lips on her forehead. "Go home, little sweet." An ounce of kindness offered to her family member. "Don't let anyone tell you what you are and what you are not. Dry those beautiful green eyes. I'm sure your father is home by now."

Greg put an arm around his son while still perfectly balancing one of the girls. "What happened, champ? You okay?"

Matthew just wanted to go to his room. Not this room, a room he had never seen, but his room in the city. It was small—he had to share it with his baby sisters—but it was safe; it was comfortable. It was home. This wasn't home. Before he could respond to his father, perhaps beg him to drive them home, a gunshot, followed by a shriveling sound, tore the air. A scream rang through the trees and sky. It cut through the skin. Matthew felt the scream tear through him, a similarly empty feeling to the one Samantha had given him, but something much more depraved.

This wasn't only a bad beginning; this was an ending.

It came from up the street. Cynthia's mouth fell open. Her eyes twitched as they landed on the house that Athena Rose had swept into.

"Oh no," Cynthia let out in horror. Her grip on her niece tightened as she led her toward her Mercedes, which soon zoomed up the street to the Rose house. You could almost still hear the echo of the shot in the air…and that scream. Matthew watched as Cynthia flew up the steps and into the house, leaving Sammy in the car.

As the McArthur family stood on their manicured lawn, the sun began to set over Sun Drop Court, darkness settling in. This was a moving day they wouldn't soon forget.

Matthew would find out later that night that Benjamin Rose had shot himself.

That night, he had sat at the window in his new bedroom and stared out at the perfect *suburban* street, contemplating why a man with such a beautiful family would do such a thing.

Across the way, Todd was sitting on his window sill, leg hanging over—smoking a joint. Todd was staring up toward the sky, which tonight was sparkled with stars. Matthew stared up at the stars and allowed himself to get lost.

He wouldn't sleep that night.

It wouldn't be the last night Matthew would sit awake in his bedroom on Sun Drop Court.

Nor would it be close to the worst.

Maxine Johnson's Personal Diary
Summer, 1995

Dear Diary,

    I'm terrified of the noises I hear at night.

    Larry claims he doesn't hear them, but he always falls asleep on the couch after he gives me my nighttime tea. He wouldn't hear the sounds around and above. I wouldn't dare ask Felicia…creatures lie. For all I know, she is the cause of the scratching that continues in the dark of the night.

    But in slumber I feel things. Disturbances. Ruptures. Invasions. I don't know how else to describe it.

    I digress.

    The Wolf-Thorne's maid, Rosaletta, took all the kids to see *Clueless*. Some new flick about high-school girls and the hardships of being rich, from my understanding. Who got invites? The Wolf-Thornes' little niece, Sammy, her son, Dax, the Mayfair children, but not my little creature. I've noticed my invites to dinners at Thorne Hall have been cut short since her visit in the spring. Athena was kind enough to attempt to keep me in the book club, but the way Cynthia stares at me the entire time…I dare not show anymore.

What have I done wrong? Why have I been cast out of my social circle? It has to be because of that strange thing that lurks around the house and needs to be constantly fed and paid attention to…my daughter.

As punishment, whenever Larry is away, I just keep Felicia's bedroom door locked. Away. All summer long. It's been quiet. The longer he works, the more time I get in silence from the little beast. It breathes too much of my air. It eats too much of my food.

With her up there, I've been able to breathe.

She had the nerve to say, "Daddy wouldn't like this." Well…I told her that Daddy didn't care. It's not like he asked about her anyway…or me…or anything.

Old Mother Watson came to visit last week. A whimsical Disney name. Doesn't she sound like a fairy-tale character? Well, she isn't. She's black and Walt Disney would never have tolerated that.

We sat out in the gazebo…I made lemonade, from scratch. Something about cutting and crushing those lemons and watching them spin and turn and annihilating the pulp felt so…

The air conditioning needs proper fixing and only certain rooms are cool during these scalding days. None of the bedrooms… But after my tea, I sleep till morning.

Besides, sitting out in the garden gives one's eye a spectacle of color. Nothing is more beautiful than when flora is in full bloom.

There is something therapeutic about gardening. Finite objectives. Easy rewards. Simple satisfactions. Having a gardener on Sun Drop Court was not a choice, but a social obligation. More of my personal therapy gone. I no longer got to waste worries away in the tending of roses. Plus, the last one I picked, a thorn stuck so far into my thumb it scarred.

"You've been missed," Old Mother Watson said after a slew of pleasantries and check-ins of her many, many grandchildren, and her husband, Leroy, who worked for the Captain. One of his original workers, besides the Mayfairs, who were the oldest neighbors on the street. "I haven't seen you out and about this summer. I thought I could be expecting one of your bar-be-cues…three years in a row and this summer…nothing. I thought it had become an annual affair. I still can taste those pastry puffs…you must give me that recipe. I don't believe a woman's place is in the kitchen, but with your skill, you could move right into one. Tell me, Max, where have you been?"

Lost? Confused? Losing time? Losing connections and mind? Oh, how badly…

"I've been busy." As much as I wanted to try to tell her about the horrors that have been running through my head, I didn't yet have words for them. How could I possibly explain that which I don't comprehend myself? "You know, keeping the house clean and taking care of my husband."

Do people actually want to hear the truth when they ask such questions? How are you? How is your day? All they want is a "great" and then to move on. Or do they actually care? Is there genuine care for me or is it a selfish need to know?

"And where is that beautiful little Felicia? Is she at camp with the other children?"

"She's in her room." Before Mother Watson could comment on the heat or make any remarks about my parenting skills of that creature, I steered the conversation elsewhere. "I do miss book club and teas and dinner parties. What are you ladies currently reading?"

The taking of my social life is the slash across the wrist that allows the blood to drip, drop by drop. I'll never die. But I feel the pain. That, I can feel. I can put a word to this emotional tyranny: loneliness.

"Ironically… Is it ironic? Well, "The Yellow Wallpaper." It's what made me come by. It's a story of a woman whose husband locked her in the attic and she…well, never mind that." Andrea then looked me over as if I was a fragile glass she was juggling and was terrified of breaking. "Cynthia commented that Larry had you in a similar state, all locked up over here. Had forbidden you from coming to our book clubs and teas. I know it's not my place, or anyone's place, to meddle in such matters. But, I had to come check on you, my dear. Make sure you were okay."

Oh, dear diary, I don't like the rage that has recently possessed me.

I tossed a chair in front of Old Mother Watson in the gazebo today; it went flying across the lawn. Bringing my fists down on the small table in front of us, smashing the glass lemonade tray I had prepared, and cracking the wicker table in half. My hands and feet covered in blood and glass.

Oh, dear diary, it seems like we are past the point of containment. I am lost.

In her kind nature, she did not judge, but instead helped me clean up and relax. How dare the Wolf-Thorne make up such lies about my marriage... Larry and I are barely communicating these days; he doesn't care enough to 'lock me up in the house.' He brings me tea at night and then he goes to sleep on the couch. Not once has he locked the door; not once has he abused me... But this separation is its own sort of abuse, I suppose. Tea has become a nightly gesture with a kiss on the forehead, then he sleeps downstairs while that little terror probably laughs at me from her room.

I hope it's sweltering in there. I hope she feels the pain she has brought upon me.

How can one grasp their sanity when they can't even hang on?

Old Mother Watson recommended I see the town doctor. Maybe that would help me. But is there help for things that I can't even understand?

Shadows and creaks in the night, feelings during sleep, misunderstood notions of madness and darkness. See? I can't even make sense myself.

At night, the noises continue. A door opening, a creak in the hallway, a shadow over me. Something is coming for me…I can feel it. It hangs from the ceiling. Something is coming for me. Something is coming for me. It takes me places. It takes me away and wraps me in shadows…but every morning I awake, alone in bed, less sane than the night before.

The feelings that have come over me in this nighttime shadow land have made the hate I feel for Cynthia Thorne grow. How I've gone from social club member to forgotten island, I cannot tell you.

But it started when Cynthia Thorne forbade our kids from hanging out together. From her Dax taking my Felicia out on their little kid dates. It must be her fault; she must pay… My…little…Felicia.

Felicia will pay.

The High-School Years
Roses and Thornes
Fall, 2004

"Our Father which art in heaven,

Hallowed be thy name.

Thy kingdom come,

Thy will be done

On Earth, as it is in Heaven.

Give us this day our daily bread.

And forgive us our debts,

As we forgive our debtors.

And lead us not into temptation,

But deliver us from…"

"Todd?"

"No. Sigh. Matthew."

"What?"

"You said my name!"

"You said mine!"

"No?" Todd exhaled heavily and stared across at Matthew. "That was Matthew 6…9…13, I believe. The King James ver—"

"Dude." Matthew made to wave his hands in the air, but obviously couldn't. "What is praying going to do to get us out of here?"

"*Dude*," Todd mocked with that dazzling smile of his. "I'm not praying to get us out of here. I'm doing my penance so I don't have to think about tonight ever again. Also, don't move around so much; you don't want the handcuffs to scar your wrists."

Matthew felt himself turning red and just sat there. In a jail cell. With the neighborhood church boy. Who enjoyed fast cars and, from the reaction of the cops' faces when they searched the car, an apparent desire to be the next George Jung, but with marijuana. Out of the few friends Matthew had made in school, his mother only approved of Todd… His mother. Her moods were so erratic these days. How would she react to…

"My mother," Matthew began, going to put his face in his hands. "Fuck. She's not going to handle this well."

"You forgot you had handcuffs on again, didn't you?" Todd teased. "Neither Mrs. Mayfair nor Mrs. McArthur will be bothered tonight. Neither of our mothers are going to know about this. I gave the cops a different number."

"A fake number? Dude, how much more trouble are you going to get me into today?"

But Todd was giving a look to the grand, golden-embroidered plaque on the police station wall. The one with the crest of a family that seemed to have their name on every building in town…

"Todd…"

"Why the formal title?"

"What?"

"I thought I had become the official 'dude' by now." Todd put his head against the concrete wall. "I can hear his car now. Salvation."

The plaque on the wall read: *Police Station Donated by Thorne Hall* and underneath was the year *1955*. It didn't matter which generation of Thorne built the police building because they still powered it. The Captain enjoyed keeping peace in his little kingdom and had, for years and years, taken care of any matter that might upset it.

Matthew McArthur would be lying if he didn't feel an extreme sense of relief. His mother scolded him if he got anything below a C. Now, being arrested and charged with possession? He saw the pills she slipped into her mouth…he knew she wasn't all there. At one time he could predict what he came home to. Now? He had no idea.

The longer his father worked, the later he came home, the more his mom seemed to stress. It took a few years to figure out that her random outbursts and spouts of anger were not actually meant for him…it was too many painkillers and too many vodka spritzers. His father was a different story. The once athletic man was now skinny, and whatever he did up at that power plant looked like it was sucking him dry. He would never tell anyone, but Matthew had started having nightmares about the cleverly named NRG Power Plant.

Gregory McArthur would get home at night and fake a smile, while his wife, higher than any kite, would serve burnt meatloaf or overcooked pasta, and everyone pretended like everything was fine. Kat and Katie sometimes didn't even talk, as if they knew more than Matthew did. They just sat there, their fingers wrapped around each others, communicating in silence. They had a bond he didn't understand. It was almost like they could telepathically communicate, like some kind of X-Men.

In truth, he was alone at home. He needed an escape. He needed friends. He needed Todd not to mess this up. But…as always…Todd was right…

Matthew could hear the purr of the Captain's Bentley town car pull up outside. It wasn't long before the doors to the police station burst open. In entered Captain Abraham Thorne. All six-foot-whatever of him dressed in a fine black three-piece suit walked proudly, swinging a thick, expensive-looking cane with a marble top and inlayed gold specks. He was a strong man who had spent his years living in excess and who had a healthy belly to show for it. A thick beard laced with gray covered a chiseled jaw and strong cheekbones, while dark glasses covered his eyes. He was partially blind and never took the glasses off. Yet, each stride was confident.

"Gentleman," the Captain boomed as he entered the station. "What a fine night it is. What a fine night, indeed."

The younger of the two police officers went to retort, but the older one pushed past him, a look of slight worry on his face, which the younger officer didn't catch.

"Captain Thorne, what can we do for you tonight? I didn't know you were gonna drop in." The older policeman offered a handshake, but the Captain had his eyes on Matthew and Todd. "You gave us a great donation last year. We are incredibly grateful."

"Of course, of course." The Captain waved past them and walked directly to the cell, a shift in his voice. Hellos and how-do-you-dos turned quickly into a cold demand: "You will let them go and forget you saw them tonight."

"I'm sorry, shouldn't we call the mayor?" the young police officer spoke up, and the older one stared at him with a look that implied he needed to shut his mouth. But law and order was all that was on this rookie's mind. "We caught Todd Mayfair with almost a pound of…"

The black cane came swinging and smashed onto the police officer's desk.

"Who is this guy, Fred?" the Captain asked as, from under his dark glasses, the younger police officer felt his glare. "I haven't seen him before."

"Rookie, sir. The mayor has sent us at least a dozen new officers over the past year.."

"Sir?" The young cop's eyebrows raised. "Who is this clown, Fred?"

Without turning, the cane came swinging again and smacked the golden plaque mounted on the otherwise gray wall. The bottom of the cane was pure gold. He smacked it twice, as if to remind them that that which can be built can also be torn down.

"As I say," the Captain Abraham Thorne boomed, "Life is like a box of chocolates. Do you really want to grab the wrong one...rookie?"

Before either of them could speak again, Fred had the keys and was quickly opening the cell door. The Captain's eyes held heavy on the rookie before he turned and, as if he were a proud uncle, spread his arms. The cane flew around and the rookie had to dodge it.

"Boys! Boys!" the Captain boomed in a jolly tone. "Todd, this *rookie* will take you to the car they found you in. Let us all forget we even encountered one another tonight. Boys will be boys, right, Fred? Can't get the mothers all upset over some youthful spurts. We were all young and naive once. A pass for this night, don't you agree?"

"Of course." Fred looked over to the rookie, whose eyes were raised in disbelief, and firmly ordered: "Get their things and the car out of our lot. I'll finish up with the Captain here. Quick, now. Go."

Todd was already heading out of the cell and through the otherwise quiet police station. Matthew quickly got up and, as he passed the Captain, received a friendly pat on the back and a hold on his shoulder "You have strong shoulders, Matthew!" the Captain exclaimed. "Consider joining the football team… I've been trying to get Todd on it for years! Could use some new faces. We could use a win, isn't that right, Fred? Dax can only do so much to keep that team up… shame, really. I do love going to the games, but I prefer winning."

Fred didn't say anything. The middle-aged cop seemed to have the same look on his face as a kid waiting outside the principal's office. Matthew, though relieved at being set free, almost wished he could stay to hear the conversation that would take place after they were gone.

Matthew watched a lot of TV and read many books. If you get arrested for drugs…this…doesn't normally happen.

The rookie led them outside after gathering their belongings.

"Rich twats," he mumbled as he led them toward the impound lot. "Whole world is going to hell because of people like you. No law. No order. What's the point? The glove never fits when you have money."

"You are very articulate," Todd said in his naturally soothing voice. "Must be why you became a cop, I assume."

The rookie turned and pushed his chest out toward Todd in a sad display of attempted masculinity. "It's douches like you and your families. You might have gotten off tonight, you little twat, but don't think I won't arrest you the next chance I get." The rookie also looked at Matthew. "Even you, quiet one. What is the point of having rules and laws when no one actually follows them?"

"With all due respect," Matthew mumbled politely as they neared Todd's father's shiny new BMW, "I don't think you're going to get the chance, dude."

The rookie stood perplexed, taking in what Matthew had just said as Todd started up the car. Matthew had noticed that anyone who challenged the Captain—or even teachers who challenged Cynthia or Dax—seemed to not be around for long.

Matthew gave the rookie one last look. How long had this guy wanted to be a cop? How long had this guy wanted to do right by society? Todd had enough marijuana in his car, the bag the size of a pillow. All this cop was trying to do was his job. Keep a community safe. Keep families and homes safe, but not a child of the Captain's workers.

Special rules for special people.

Some of us can walk through fire.

"Well, that was fun." Todd switched gears and his car roared out of the parking lot. "Look! Your wrists. I told you not to move so much; you are going to have bruises. I can see them already. Got to be more careful, Matthew."

"I wasn't planning on getting arrested, Todd."

"No weapon forged against you will prevail, and you will refute every tongue that accuses you."

"What does that even mean?"

But Todd just smiled his confident, award-winning smile as his father's car roared into an otherwise silent night. Crunching and spitting back fall leaves, it tore down the quiet road.

"It means everything, Matthew. It means everything."

"Toxic" by Britney Spears was on and Todd began to sing: "With the taste of your lips, I'm on a ride."

Matthew sighed, pushing his head out the window and letting that perfect fall air run over his face and hair.

The rookie was relocated and never heard from again.

A Morning in Suburbia

As roses tend to do, Samantha had bloomed.

Time following her father's death had been fragmented. She remembered parts of the funeral. Moments of sorrow, but mostly of confusion. Her Aunt Cynthia kept her in the car while she ran into her parents' old home.

Samantha had no idea how that scene had played out. She remembered the gunshot. The gunshot that the entire world must have heard. The screams reverberating in her ears —screams of both her brother and her mother. The gunshot seemed to just pound over and over again through her brain, her mind... Even at her age, she could picture her father... raising the gun to his head...

What had happened on the day her father took a gun to his head was a mystery.

No matter how that show went, no matter the mystery, no matter the questions surrounding the day, the bottom line... it was her father.

But she did remember one night not too long after.

Soon after, her Aunt Cynthia came for a visit in the dead of night. After a heated fight between sisters, Athena had made a game with her daughter of moving into Thorne Hall. Her mother had tried to make it seem like this was a good thing, but even Samantha knew it wasn't a choice.

So, they moved from their ideal house on Sun Drop Court into Thorne Hall.

Cynthia would proclaim to anyone in grave overtures that it was a 'grand mansion built with no expense spared.' Samantha had always felt like it was more the house on haunted hill.

To be blunt, Samantha hated Thorne Hall.

It was gigantic, for starters, but not in the MTV *Cribs* way where every room is new and freshly decorated. Though it had been in the Thorne family for generations, it had not aged as well as their fortune. Shadows had settled in and sometimes from the chills she experienced, Samantha assumed ghosts as well.

Renovation was an ongoing disaster.

Putting up-to-date heat and AC into the stone fortress had been a difficulty; fuzz would dominate the television; and, at various times, phone calls would just drop. Logically every time Samantha was cut off on the land line, she assumed a poltergeist was coming.

Cynthia had spent years attempting to warm the house with furniture and beautiful paintings, drapes and rugs of brilliant colors from foreign lands, and various statues flown in from museums in Italy and Denmark. But it was like trying to make a grave attractive.

Something that cold can never be warmed up. You always feel…something else is lurking behind those covers… those masks.

As Samantha was nearing the end of her high-school years, she had grown lean and athletic and had watched her mother wilt.

Athena Rose was still a stunning specimen, but her once long and flowing sun-struck locks had turned dark; she spent most of her time in Thorne Hall. She had stopped her daily runs and outdoor yoga sessions after her husband's death. Even her book clubs rarely met and when they did, it was inside Thorne Hall.

It was rare that she would even be in attendance.

Athena's skin had gone from tan to ivory and she'd wrapped her dark locks into a tight bun at the back of her head. For four years, she had worn black and had shown no sign of changing her wardrobe.

"You have inherited your father's social skills. Don't let popularity go to your head; don't confuse friendship with power," her mother would say without a smile. "But the obvious gift you have inherited from me is beauty. All gifts to cherish and enjoy while you can. Youth never appreciates them, but try. For, before you know it, it will all be gone. All gone."

That morning, as with every morning, a semi-grand feast was spread across the cold glass-and-iron dining table in the great room of Thorne Hall. The second-largest room in the manor besides the ballroom, which was only used every four years for the Thorne Foundation Ball, the dining room had windowed doors from floor to ceiling that opened to the backyard. Two oversized fireplaces with wretched-looking gargoyles seated atop stared across the room at each other.

The backyard flowed down the back of a seemingly endless hill and a pool had been installed alongside a tennis court, but they were literally on the outskirts of *Suburbia* and it was obvious. Just past their backyard was the large swamp that eventually led to the NRG Power Plant.

Oddly, this was the only part of Thorne Hall Cynthia had been able to properly update. The wallpaper was a rich golden red, and a fantastic Baccarat chandelier sparkled over the dining room table. This was a part of Thorne Hall people were allowed to see, but other rooms weren't accessible to outsiders. There were several closed-off rooms and a basement door that had a lock on it.

Anytime Athena mentioned the key to the basement, the conversation was immediately changed. Cynthia scratched at her nose and the Captain went on about privacy and guests.

During the slave days, the house was equipped with various stringed bells so the servants could let you know when a meal was ready or a bath was drawn or your youngest had gotten eaten by a bear—you know, the feral times. Well, Cynthia still had her maid ringing those bells.

The bell had rung in Samantha's room, the same time as it did every day, just as she had finished applying her makeup and tying her hair in a loose ponytail.

As on every morning before school, they sat for breakfast.

"A bell went off in my room last night," Cynthia said to Rosaletta, a maid who had been in the Thorne family for what seemed like forever. She was slowly making her way around the table, filling Waterford glasses with orange juice.

"No. No juice! Do I ever drink juice? Why did a bell go off in my room last night, Rosa-leeeta?"

"I dunno, missus." Rosaletta winked directly at Samantha, who smiled at the maid. Rosaletta was the color Thorne Hall desperately needed. It was a pity Cynthia couldn't see past the fact that she was hired help. "Perhaps a spirit again. The whole place is filled with spooks. Spooks, I tell you. Spooks!"

"I know it's you messing with me…the only bells are up here and the others are in the basement, and that area is locked up, and…" Cynthia began, but from across the table, without looking up, Athena, graceful, raised a hand. Cynthia fell silent.

"Samantha." Athena raised her emerald eyes toward her daughter. Cynthia gazed down at her plate and clicked her tongue against her teeth, the only retort she would give. "What time shall we expect you for dinner? Is today cheerleading or field-hockey practice? So hard to keep up with their schedule, isn't it, Cynthia?"

Samantha knew her mother wasn't waiting for her sister to answer.

"Today is sign-ups for debate club," Samantha politely responded after swallowing her food, dabbing a Thorne-monogrammed napkin against her lips. "I have to make sure the pep squad is in order for the rally. But first we need to organize cheerleading tryouts…"

"Well." Cynthia let her eyes fall on her niece, attempting to be a part of the conversation. "I hope you make the team."

"Don't be a fool," Athena exclaimed cheerfully from across the table, causing Rosaletta to stammer and pour more juice for Samantha. "Tryouts aren't for varsity; they are only for freshman. Try not to interrupt, Cynthia, especially when you have nothing to contribute. I'd think you, more than anyone, would know not to tolerate such rudeness. Mother taught you better."

Samantha could no longer remember a time when her mother was kind to her sister.

Athena seemed to terrify her aunt, and even the Captain avoided her.

Samantha never saw Cynthia bow to anyone like she did to her mother…it wasn't her place to ask. She was a senior in high school and had cheerleading today. These were adult matters. A boyfriend to worry about, a clique to run, and college to consider. She never asked because, at this age, it wasn't on her radar.

"Don't you have school? Dax left before breakfast," Aunt Cynthia shot over at Samantha while keeping her eyes firmly fixed on her sister. "I have to talk to your mother."

That wasn't true. Dax Thorne had failed to come home last night. Samantha only knew this because he wanted to get high at random hours of the night after he came back from drinking, and last night, there was a 3 o' clock knock on her door. Dax had as much supervision as a hooker in a brothel.

Not like the Captain was around much anyway.

Samantha looked at her mother; she didn't want to upset her by obeying her aunt, but Athena Rose smiled kindly. "Yes. You may go, dear."

Samantha went around the table, first kissing her aunt, then Rosaletta, who gave her a big hug, then her mother, on the cheek. Her mother slowly turned her face back around and let out her perfect smile.

It wasn't until Samantha had left the room that the adults began conversing.

"How long will this go on?" Cynthia raised herself from the table with her bony arms and started to make her way around, toward her sister, "Athena, you need to…talk to me about all of this….You need to…"

"When will I see my best friend again? When will Maxine come over for tea, or sit on April Mayfair's porch with me? When will Priscilla Primm throw a dinner party, or Linda Henderson hold a pot luck? When this table is filled with my and, at one time, your friends, that's when." Athena was looking at her hard-boiled egg, which she was slowly cracking by rolling along the table. "Basically, when you can suck up the poison that you have injected into this town, that is when this will end. You get that, Cynthia. That's when."

Rosaletta had stopped clearing Samantha's plate for a second, her eye on Cynthia, who had begun to shake. Cynthia's face was slowly turning red and a vein on her forehead was pulsing, and her ulcer burned as memories and time flew through her head.

The silence in the room was heavy.

"I'd like to have a dinner party."

Rosaletta all but dropped what she was clearing.

Cynthia noticed the dramatics. "Oh, for Christ's sake, go watch a soap opera or something. A what?"

"Oh." Athena smiled, still not looking directly at Cynthia. "You heard me."

"It's been four years and all of a sudden you want to have a social event? Where?"

"Here."

"And who's going to be hosting?"

"You and the Captain." Out of a pocket in her black dress she pulled an envelope and dropped it on the table. "This is the guest list."

"Are you going to give it to me?"

"I just did. Fetch."

Still shaking with anger, Cynthia crossed the room and snatched up the envelope. It was only then that Athena allowed their eyes to meet—a look that told Cynthia she was much too close, a rabid animal that needed to keep her distance. Written in her elegant writing, the envelope read: *Dinner Party, October 15th, Thorne Hall.*

With a nail, Cynthia tore the envelope open and released the guest list.

Cynthia skimmed the names. "Well, this has to be a joke. Are you suddenly a comedian?" Cynthia went over the names a second and then a third time. "Our cousin, the mayor. The Mayfairs. The Watsons. The McArthurs. The Scopellos…and Felicia Johnson plus one? That's slightly inappropriate, isn't it? Girl doesn't even live in my area anymore."

"It's hardly your area, dear." Athena had finished her breakfast and had placed her napkin neatly on the table. "And she does. If you listen, she was on the cheerleading team with Samantha for a brief time a few years ago. Now an honor student…doing quite well despite your attempts to destroy her. Only a wicked witch goes after a child like that; shame on you. You will plan accordingly. You will set the table with your Tiffany china. You will host this event for me. You asked when my hate toward you will end. Well, this is the step in the right direction…sis."

Cynthia kept her eyes on the guest list so as not to give her sister a look that might cause her to dispense more punishment, but the anger was rising, the ulcer in her stomach was burning, the headache was coming. Rosaletta had reappeared and was clearing the rest of the table very slowly; this was much more exciting than her soaps.

"Have a good day, Cynthia." Athena smiled brightly as she made her way through the door that led to the wing of Thorne Hall that she and Samantha had taken over. "I'm going into town to have lunch with our cousin today. Tonight we can discuss the menu for the dinner party, as well as the type of invites you picked out. Since it's in the fall, select more golds and blacks. I miss being social. It's time to begin again. Rosaletta, have I told you recently how glowing you are? I bet in your day, you were a beauty to be revered."

With that, Athena made her way out of the great room, the door swinging behind her and sending a gust of cold wind directly at Cynthia as if it were planned.

"When did she become so…so…" Cynthia fell back in her chair, already knowing the answers to the questions she was asking. She began to massage her temple with a finger. "She really is a bitch, isn't she?"

"Who are we talking about?" Rosaletta said as she looked directly at Cynthia while clearing Athena's plates.

This is the pot calling the kettle black, Cynthia thought. Only in private, Athena challenged Cynthia as the biggest bitch in town. *I need a Xanax.*

"You know, I do want juice," Cynthia spat. Waiting the five minutes it took Rosaletta to go back to the kitchen for more juice and a new crystal glass, she sat and tapped her finger. Rosaletta returned with juice and crystal glass in hand. Cynthia continued her impatient finger tapping while Rosaletta poured the juice. As she left the room and the door was almost shut behind her, Cynthia snapped, "To the top, please."

Rosaletta filled the glass all the way to the top.

Cynthia grasped the full glass and lobbed it against the wall, letting it smash.

Cynthia turned, leaving the room feeling slightly better, before she shot back, "Clean that up."

Matthew was climbing the hill that seemingly led to the sky, trying as he could to reach the power plant that sat at the top, but the farther he climbed, the farther away the towers seemed. Pillars pumping out stacks of smoke caused a massive amount of clouds. The only light was the yellow pollution that turned green, that turned orange, that spun around. Spun around and around, circling out from the pillars in which screams resonated, in which terror sprung. The building seemed alive with breath as the smoke let it stream back out of its windows and pillars before inhaling everything around it like a wild tornado. Trees and buildings and people and children were all being sucked back into the monstrous structure.

The building was alive; he could feel its force as he desperately tried to reach it. It didn't want him. It wanted him to climb to it, to struggle. It took another heavy breath of smoke and let it out, spilling it down the hill and causing Matthew to tumble down.

His family and friends were all falling victim to this mighty structure that he had no way of stopping.

Come inside and see what I see. You won't leave. Come inside and know what I know. You won't leave. You won't…

Awake.

Awoken.

Reality broken.

Matthew McArthur had another nightmare. He was covered in sweat and was breathing heavily. He was in his room. His blue room. His blue race-car comforter that he was much too old for. His blue plush rug. His blue-framed pictures of cars. His. Blue. Everything blue. Just like his eyes.

A room that Felicia Johnson once suffered in.

Unlike her, he was back in his safe blue haven.

But the nightmare.

Always the same nightmare. Always the same.

Always the power plant.

NRG.

Making his way over to the window, he pulled back the blue-striped curtain and took in Sun Drop Court, which was already alive. It was 6 a.m. and along the pristine street,

Linda and Thomas Henderson were out walking their dog—not just a dog, but a groomed and healthy yellow lab. April Mayfair was sitting on her porch reading the Bible. Old Mother Watson was tending her flowers in her garden. His father was jogging up the block and passing another man jogging with his wife, all waving and smiling.

Suburbia.

As safe as these images should make him feel, the dream still lurked within him.

Plus…being a growing man in the morning…he had another issue pop up.

So he switched his computer on, opened Snapfish, and relaxed into images.

Images of her.

Something that had become routine.

Every damn day.

At first he'd felt bad for looking, but why post all these pictures if you didn't want someone to look at them, right?

Every day she posted more…she wanted people to look…to watch…to stare…to admire…

There was a lot to admire.

Samantha Rose had bloomed almost overnight. Puberty had struck her, and the kind, sweet girl he had met on that first day finally reflected on her outside. She was a blond gazelle with her mother's deep emerald eyes and naturally tan skin, her body lengthened and curved at the right points.

He scrolled through her webpage. There were pictures of her smiling, pictures of her dancing at a party, pictures of her cheerleading, pictures of her waving as part of the homecoming court. Pictures of her. Pictures of her in bikinis at the beach. Pictures of her…pictures of…

He grabbed a sock he wore yesterday.

The lotion was in his cabinet next to his desk.

"Are you up?" a voice called out, matching the rapping at his door. "Breakfast is ready. I thought we'd all go on a picnic today. It looks like such a nice day. A picnic would be nice."

He was certainly up.

Matthew jumped up and threw a towel around his waist.

"I have school today, Mom. It's a weekday."

"Oh…I thought it was…Satur… Do you need a ride?"

"Mom." He wasn't 'up' any longer. "I got it."

He heard his mom standing out there for a second, as if she wanted to say something, but then she walked away. How many pain killers had she taken this morning? He waited a moment, until he was sure she was in the kitchen, before closing his computer and sighing.

He aimlessly grabbed a green V-neck shirt, a plaid shirt to throw over, a pair of new jeans, underwear, and made his way to the bathroom. He was lost in thought of Samantha Rose as he pulled back the shower curtain and almost fell over when something small jumped up and went, "*Boo!*"

"Holy hell!" Matthew screamed and fell back, and then another small creature jumped at him from the other side, and he jumped again. He stumbled and fell hard into the bathtub as he grasped at the shower curtain. This would leave a bruise. The little giggles surrounded him. It took him a second to catch his breath and realize, "*Mom!* Why are Katie and Kat up here?"

Because she probably didn't even know they were in the house to begin with.

"You screamed like a girl," Kat let out with giggles, wrapping her hand in her sisters. "I told Katie you'd be mad." Katie let out a tiny grin. "But this was funny."

"How many times do I have to tell you? This is my bathroom!" Matthew opened the bathroom door and went to shoo the little terrors out. "Why are there two of you, anyway? One is more than enough. Seriously, go outside and run into each other as hard as possible. Maybe two will become one."

Kat and Katie looked at Matthew with tiny smiles, their hands held together.

Matthew knew that the looks on their faces weren't welcome ones.

"What did you two do?"

"We were in Mommy's bathroom as well. We poured all of Mommy's vitamins down the drain."

"Her vitamins?" Matthew knew that the only vitamins his mom took were sold on the side by kids at school. "You two are going to be in so much trouble. I don't want to be here when she finds that out."

But Katie and Kat shrugged at the same time.

"We are tired of burnt roasts and her rolling the car around when she drives. We fix some problems." Then the wicked smiles returned. "We make others worse."

As they turned and bounced off, Matthew knew they were right…this wasn't good.

Felicia Johnson was meditating on her bed, Pure Moods playing in the background, when the soft voice called up from the kitchen, "Breakfast, darling."

Her gold-speckled amber eyes fluttered open and she relaxed into her surroundings. She had always loved her bedroom. The pink-speckled wallpaper that was soft to the touch, the cream rug that her toes sunk into, the canopy bed with the sheer fabric that shone in the light. Pink was not her favorite color, but she would never complain about such a trivial thing. There was a time when the bedroom in her old house smelled because her mother had refused to clean, when she would spend her summer days in the heat, locked in. No matter how much she beat at those doors, no matter how she screamed, her mother wouldn't come…her mother… And then the screams…the ones no one heard…her mother would answer with…

Her eyes slammed shut, attempting to meditate once more.

Felicia knew why she had no fond memories of her mother, but what she had done to the rest of the town was somewhat of a mystery to her. Or why Cynthia was still punishing Felicia for her mother's sins. Plus, her poor father…

The last time she was in her house on Sun Drop Court—that now belonged to the McArthur family—was to collect her belongings. Yet she had searched for only one thing, her mother's journal. Cynthia followed her closely and she didn't have much time to search. There was even a police escort there, as if a child was going to steal things. She had covered her old room with blue wallpaper, so the scratch marks and… Well, it was all covered up now.

Felicia didn't think Maxine Johnson loved anything or anyone as much as her journal, and she had spent day in and day out, up till her final moments, writing away in it. It was a large book. Cynthia once joked it was her Book of Shadows, a book a witch writes their evil doings inside.

Eventually that got around town…

But Felicia could not find it, and so the questions lingered. All the questions ended with the same final conundrum: why? Why? *Why?*

Namaste.

Breathe in.

Breathe out.

Namaste.

"Darling," the calming voice called up from the kitchen, "no one likes cold oatmeal."

This was her reality now.

Tying her fiery hair into a tight ponytail, she made her way down to the kitchen.

"Morning." She kissed the cheek of the woman who had saved her four years before. Felicia had been so angry the night after that sunset on Sun Drop Court— the night the McArthurs moved in—that she had returned to her foster home and had taken a hammer to all her foster mom's valuables. That—and a phone call from Cynthia Wolf-Thorne herself—had been enough for her foster family.

Back into the system Felicia went.

Orphanages, foster families, hopes of adoption. The unknowing. The feeling of hope dissipating. If Cynthia could convince a foster family to return her, she could probably make sure she grew up in the worst orphanage possible.

Felicia had mentally prepared for the worst, for spending an eternity in the system of lost children.

That night she'd cried herself to sleep, and had known this would become a normal thing.

Felicia had remembered that night, imagining the rest of her life shoved into those bunk beds filled with children over a certain age who no one else wanted. No one wants a teenager; they want a precious baby, not tarnished goods.

They want a newborn they can bring up as their own…not try to fix someone else's mess. Maxine Johnson had left Felicia in worse condition than any of the other children she'd encountered. One nurse was brought to tears when she saw the…

"I made your favorite. I know how you hate the first day of school. So it's chocolate-chip pancakes till you burst! Fresh-made whipped cream and my famous chocolate sauce. One day before I die, I'll show you the recipe. But until then, secrets are secrets."

At first, when Salome Legree made her way into the adoption home, Felicia had thought her some villain from a Disney movie. Her big gray curls of hair were streaked with what was left of her black mane. Her ancient face, free of wrinkles due to a skin regimen she'd never broken, was generous with dark makeup. Her tiny frame was always wrapped in tight, shadow-colored dresses. Even for her age, she insisted on heels and, due to a slight limp on her left side, walked with a black cane featuring a simple gold ball on top.

Salome could have been sixty or eighty—good genes. Never drank, never smoked, practiced yoga; she was what aging well was all about.

Felicia had remembered cringing when she saw that the number on her old Victorian house was 666, but there were no surprises. Felicia still thought she'd make a fantastic witch in a movie, but had received nothing but kindness from Salome since day one. Felicia had fought this at first—her entire life, up until that point, had been spent first with her infamous mother and then later moving from one foster home to another. One foster father had a drinking problem that had led him to wander into her room...

Namaste. That was the past. Felicia calmed herself. *This is the present. Live here. Be present. Put it all in the box, lock it away.*

Salome had adopted Felicia on first sight. She had taught Felicia how to channel her anger and, most importantly, how to be a lady in society. Salome had a way of being strict without being cruel, and it had paid off.

Felicia no longer punched walls; she didn't attack random girls on the street. Also, the crying at night had ceased. The nightmares would never completely stop, but now Salome was there in her dreamscapes, in one form or another, and there she defended her from her mother.

All in all, she was as adjusted as she could be.

"Did you know that tomorrow is your adoption day? Let me know what you'd like for dinner; I know it's not your actual birthday, but to me it's a very special day. A second birthday of sorts…a day celebrating when both of our lives improved."

"Both of our lives. Of course." Felicia smiled inside and out. Never forced. Always real. Salome told her that emotions should be natural; being fake was an unattractive quality in a human. "I'm ready to leave for school whenever you are ready to take me."

Salome smiled. "Go peek out front. An early present."

Together they exited the grand black Victorian with the dark purple accents that must have been where Salome had lived her entire life, and out on the front lawn sat…

"Is that…"

"For you." Salome pointed with her cane and, from her long nail, dangled a golden key chain with a single key. "I just can't help myself sometimes."

A tan 1990s Mercedes sedan sat waiting, a giant purple-and-black bow decorating it. A tiny dent across the passenger side and the mirror had been replaced recently. But all in all, it was more than Felicia had ever expected. Never in her life did she receive presents from her mother.

So these little gestures—pancakes Salome knew she liked, worrying about her first day of school, and now a car—was more than Felicia ever could have hoped for. Blessed. Truly blessed.

Felicia threw her arms around Salome and planted another kiss on her cheek.

"Well, don't break me in half yet, child. My will isn't complete and the house isn't in your name yet."

Could this woman be any kinder? Felicia was surprised each day and constantly felt more admiration for the woman who'd adopted her.

"I'm truly speechless. I like you so much! Can I take it for a spin before school?"

Love was a word Felicia had issues with… Her mother used to tell her she loved her. Maxine Johnson used the word love a lot. But the way she showed it…'like' was as far as Felicia could bring herself right now.

"I'll write you a doctor's note; you can be a little late today. Anything for you." Salome smiled. "Off you go! I care for you deeply, darling. Know that."

Salome would not use the word love until Felicia was ready for it.

Salome watched Felicia bounce up the stairs to get her school bag, gracefully, like a ballerina.

Felicia inherited her mother's looks and grace, and the features she got from her father, undeniable. Salome thought and smiled wickedly to herself, and isn't that just going to drive *them* insane.

"Jesus knows if you are praying in there!" April Mayfair was outside her son Todd's room. Her hair done; even though it was early morning; she had already showered, dressed, and applied her makeup. There was no reason to go through the day looking like a ragamuffin.

April believed in privacy so she never entered her son's room, but she believed in order and routine and she knew he didn't always comply. This was a happy medium...

If you can't follow a simple regimen, how can you get anything accomplished in life? Teach them now so they remember later.

Teach them now because you might not be able to again.

Teach them now, for they might vanish.

As if on cue, his voice raised louder through the air, as if he was already speaking, and she heard the verses being repeated. But it was muffled and she knew he had just woken up, an hour or so after his alarm had first sounded. Disorder leads to chaos...chaos leads to... Her fingers twisted the diamond cross around her neck.

"You can fool me, but you can't fool Him!" Her hand was shaking toward the proverbial God in the sky, anger taking over her face. "You can't fool him! He sees all!"

"Dear." Her husband was coming up the stairs, fresh from a morning run, sweat breaking on his matching Nike workout attire. "who are we trying to fool today?"

Leonardo Mayfair was a handsome man, but a tired man. One who didn't know the family would assume his exhaustion was because of his wife's obsessive-compulsive nature or perhaps due to his long hours at the hospital, but anyone who had heard their tale knew it had nothing to do with his wife or his demanding job as one of the town's only doctors. Their marriage was as perfect as it could be, all things considered.

"Jesus." April looked at her husband, exasperated that he didn't already know this. "Is it so hard to wake up and pray? How often I worry he takes our surroundings for granted. We have been blessed, and taking an hour or two a day to give back is not only necessary but shows appreciation. Shows appreciation that he is still under our roof, safe and not…and not…"

Leo came forward and wrapped his wife's tiny frame in his arms. His arms toned and muscular; even with the amount of time he spent working, he kept up on his body. Exercise helped him keep the stress at bay and a smile on his face at home.

Being a doctor was hard work, but that wasn't the only reason gray hair and stress lines had formed on his handsome face.

"We were his age once," he said against his wife's ear, rubbing his lips across her lobe in an attempt to…he didn't know anymore. It had been years since they had made love. The last time they'd had sex had been after the incident and it had been angry, aggressive. Not on his part, but on hers… He honestly hadn't known she had that sort of…kink in her. He was scared to repeat the act. "When I was a Catholic schoolboy, I had no appreciation for anything other than wondering what was under the nun's robes. Yah know, Sister Bernard?"

"I'm pretty sure that's a sin." April pushed her husband away. "I was his age once, too. My father had me praying double the amount we have Todd doing. I knew where I came from. I knew what to be grateful for. I didn't have gadgets and gizmos and…"

"Times have changed."

"And you gave him a new iPod." April had her arms crossed. "Tools and trades to distract. The more we distract, the farther we go from He who put us here in the first place. It's a disconnection, a disruption…our Lord is being blocked by all these telephones and electricity and…"

It was a worthless argument, so Leo smiled and kissed her on the lips. It wasn't to shut her up, but it had become a recording and he knew how her sentences were going to end, and he had work soon.

"Of course, dear." His eyes never left hers as he released his lips. "I'm going to make us omelets. Come down when you are ready; I'll handle breakfast and whatever else I can before I leave today."

He kissed her again firmly on the lips and she twitched with the amount of love he tried to enter into her. But that didn't stop him. One day, she'd relax back into him...one day. He had loved her for over twenty years; he wasn't going to give up...after...everything that'd happened.

As he made his way down the stairs and into the kitchen, April took a moment. Her hand on her cross, she again twisted it too tight—the noose around her neck. A deep breath. She turned to the door across the hallway from Todd's —the pink door still covered with stickers.

April ran a hand over the tiny hearts and unicorns and finished tracing along the princess that had been broken in two by accident when she was ripped from the sticker book. Running a finger along each letter on the door: G, R, A, C, and E.

Her hand hesitated over the door handle and began to shake. Her fingers outlined the steel knob and almost tightened onto it. She forced her hand into a fist and released it, returning to the cross. Out of Todd's room the steady verses were still beating into her ears.

Without order there is chaos. When you don't watch…when you look away, even for a second…

She retreated from the pink bedroom door, shaking a tear from her eye and smoothing her dress. Making her way down the stairs, away from the room, and losing her thoughts in…in anything else.

"Jesus knows…" she whispered to herself and to no one. "He knows…and one day I will as well. Since God isn't here to pass out punishments, it'll be my job. I'll avenge you, Grace. I will avenge you. I will avenge you as I've avenged before."

Maxine Johnson's Personal Diary
Late Summer, 1995

Dear Diary,

There's no light during the death hour.

But there is a scratching. A gnawing along the walls. A clawing at the door. Hooks dragging themselves along the floors. Me, attached; my skin broken through; cut through like butter. Wrapping wrists like chains. Burning the skin with hellish pains.

The tickle that starts at the bottom of your spine and spreads throughout your body. The bumps that creep along the skin. Paralyzed to turn to face that which lurks in shadows. I am numb, but I am aware.

I am…aware.

You think you know. Yes, I am alone.

I am Maxine Johnson, and I have not lost my mind.

I am alone.

I am Maxine Johnson, and I have not lost my mind.

I am alone? It's too late now.

Whatever it is. It's hungry. Whatever it is. It takes.

It's taking.

It's taking all of me.

I am Maxine Johnson…and I have not…I have not…

I've lost my mind.

Susan McArthur turned to her empty house.

She sighed.

Matthew had been an easy child and a pleasure to be around. He'd played games and laughed all day long. Kat and Katie were difficult and a handful... Many days ended in extra painkillers and a glass of wine. Sometimes wine became vodka, and sometimes vodka became tequila. It took a little more each time. The mischief they got themselves into.

They could be little terrors, but they were still company. She missed them being home all day. She had taken that time for granted and they'd grown up.

Susan McArthur went for the vacuum, though she'd vacuumed yesterday. The dishwasher was already whirling. The washing machine already spinning.

The vacuum ran through a dust-free house and along previously polished hard-wood floors. Susan had to do something.

The vacuuming took all of ten minutes.

Painkillers.

She went to the bathroom and opened her medicine cabinet.

Every bottle was empty.

Susan froze.

A row of orange bottles that had been filled with white pills…a sea of her dreams that she could relax into every time she opened the cabinet was now empty, and she immediately felt it.

After the car accident her doctor had put her on painkillers and had never helped her to ween off them. He just kept writing her scripts. The thought of stopping them was like being invited to a party on a cloud that offered every cake and every dessert you liked…and then having someone ask you to leave.

Susan had been living on that cloud for the past couple of years.

Each bottle was there… She had hoarded the pills over the years so she would never run out. Some days, she took what the doctor prescribed; on other days, she went a little overboard and was passed out on the couch by midday.

Susan couldn't move.

Gregory hated the amount of pills she chewed down, and had time and time again attempted to help her stop taking them. She saw him trying to hide the bottles in the bottom of her purse and even caught him taking a couple out of each bottle.

Susan had gotten herself down to a dosage where she could still be present, though not always fully there.

The cloud party continued in her mind: a rainy day was nothing more than a rainy day; a stubbed toe was nothing more than a nudge; half her mind was always in constant bliss. Not present. Not aware.

Was she an addict? She had no idea. But sometimes, in the loneliness of her own abode, they were her only company. The tiny bananas with the 10/325 on them.

The twins had a tendency to flush various things down the toilet… If they were home right now, an impulse might have caused Susan to strike them for the first time. Throw them across the room like rag-dolls…she could picture it in her mind.

Maybe even worse, but those thoughts quickly passed… She'd never harm any of her children.

Susan fell to her knees.

She reached in her pocket and found the final bottle. A larger, much fuller bottle than the rest. Her paranoia and reliance on the drug had caused her to always keep a bottle on her. A larger bottle that held triple the amount of her original pills. Enough to get her through until she found another doctor…enough to get her through until…enough to get her…enough for….

Susan, in her madness a voice of sense screamed, *come on*.

To what? Back to that imaginary cloud party in the sky? It took her a moment to respond to people and a few times she had almost crashed her car from zoning out. Get her back to…to that?

The next thing Susan McArthur knew, she was sitting on the couch in the middle of the living room staring out the back window. Somewhere from deep within her subconscious, a voice rang out: *Time to break the chains; time to return to reality.* Time to leave the imaginary cloud party in the sky.

Gazing out at the backyard with the freshly painted gazebo, her heart began to race. Her eyes were beginning to blur into the colors of the flowers when…

"Yoohoo! Susan!" April's voice musically called from the front porch, trying to open the door. "I know you were home! You never go out!"

Who just lets herself in? Why would she assume the door was open? Susan stood and brushed the wrinkles from the bottom of her dress before opening the door. There was a time when none of the doors on these streets were locked, a time Susan knew nothing about.

"That took you a while." April stepped past Susan and walked into her house. "Looks great in here. Maxine wasn't big on cleaning and the dust bunnies were practically eating themselves by the end. But you are pristine."

"That's very kind." A compliment from April Mayfair was one you could take to the heart; she was a woman who said what she meant. "Can I get you some tea or coffee, April?"

"I was actually heading down to the Watsons'. Andrea got some of my mail by mistake… Plus, I owe her a visit." Then her voice quieted as if she was speaking of some demon. "But that Scopello woman saw me. She was out sunbathing on her front lawn; can you imagine? So I thought I'd duck in here. I hope that's okay. I can't bear to be caught in another conversation with her. You look frazzled. Is everything okay?"

April looked Susan over with actual concern.

No, April. My six-year-old twins flushed all my drugs down the toilet and I'm about to go into a withdrawal that will last a couple of weeks.

"Everything is fine. Was just in thought." Susan smiled at her friend. "Tea or coffee, April?"

"Yes. Yes. Either will do. We can take it out back by the gazebo. I always loved that backyard, though it was very rare that Maxine had me over. Maybe the one thing the Johnsons did right with this house… You know she built the gazebo herself? Maybe if she spent as much time inside the house as she did on the outside, she…"

Another knock on the door, jiggle at the handle. April went for her cross and dramatically put her hand to her head.

"No! Heavens to Betsy. She found me."

Lorraine Scopello stood on the McArthurs' front porch checking herself out in the glass. April had referred to her as 'Satan's fruit,' 'Devil Barbie,' 'jezebel whore,' and, most memorably, 'boobs of sin.'

A year after the McArthurs had moved to Sun Drop Court, a year after Athena Rose took her daughter and fled the home in which her husband had shot himself, Lorraine Scopello and her daughter, Lexi, moved in—a beautiful Southern widow and her equally beautiful teenage daughter.

From that day, April forgot about the McArthurs' lack of religious beliefs and had focused her moral compass on Lorraine Scopello. Much to April's dismay, Lorraine didn't want to change, but worse, she just wanted to be friends. Her dresses were always too tight and her blond locks always too wild; you got a sexual vibe just by being near her.

Susan scratched the side of her hip and went to open the door, and heard April inhale as if she was about to let in some rabid beast.

Pushing a blond curl out of her face, Lorraine Scopello smiled her warm Southern smile. "Hello, Susan. How do you do?"

"How can one complain on a day like today, Lorraine? Please come in. I was just making some tea for April. Can I offer you some?"

"I thought I saw her sneak in here." Lorraine bounced a hip, causing the tight yellow-and-white dress to practically bust at its seams. "April, honey, you move so fast. I was trying to catch you on the call-da-sack."

April winced at how the word came tumbling off her drawl. "Just trying to be the early bird, Lorraine."

"That makes me the worm, I suppose!" Lorraine crossed Susan's living room, admiring the home for a second before continuing toward April. "I hear you are on the committee for the Thorne Foundation Ball. I missed this recent one, but they have one every four years, and I'd love to get my name in now to help. I'm sure a lot goes into that. They claimed they lost my application and I'd just love to help out. One could go just crazy around here without projects"

Susan made her way into the kitchen and began to prepare tea. She didn't need to be a psychic to know that Lorraine's application wasn't lost... Cynthia probably saw it and set it to fire and then laughed as it burned.

From the minute Lorraine appeared on the street, it was apparent that Cynthia had an unnatural hatred toward her. April had asked her once why and Cynthia had replied, "I can't trust anyone who's named after a quiche." That had been the end of that.

"Ladies. Tea."

Lorraine and April were going back and forth as the three of them made their way into the backyard and onto the gazebo. Complimenting the flowers that Susan hadn't planted. The fence she hadn't painted. The gazebo she hadn't built.

"If you would excuse me for a second." Susan made her way quickly into the bathroom and pulled the pill bottle out of her pocket. It was filled to the lid. She thought quickly, she broke one pill in half, crushed it, rolled a dollar bill, and put it up her nose.

Susan's mind was far away from teas as she crossed back across the lawn to the gazebo.

"I think my Lexi has a liking for your Todd, April."

"Oh?"

"Yes." Lorraine batted her giant, overly mascara'd eyelashes. "You should hear how she talks about him. Oh, the cute little babies they'd have."

"Oh, for goodness sake." April rolled her eyes. "They are teenagers."

"One can dream." Lorraine smiled. "How about you put a word in for Todd. He turned Lexi down the first time they met; she said he wouldn't even flirt back. Now he's a looker; ever consider modeling for him?"

"A boy who obviously knows what he wants. But no, I don't want my underage son pictured half-naked in some girl's locker or trashy magazine."

Susan listened to the conversation for a few minutes before zoning out. A bee was riding from flower to flower and the humming was melodic. When did a bee know it had enough honey? When did it return to its hive? Did the queen know where this worker was at all times, or was there just a trust in the notion that it'd return?

The sweet smell of flowers could be intoxicating and a person could die from a single bee sting.

Crap, Susan thought as the weight of her pill problem escalated in her head. *Crap*.

"I think I should be going." April checked her wrist, where there was no watch. "Church...uh...stuff."

"I need to finish baking for Lexi. One hundred of my famous cupcakes for this art fair," Lorraine exclaimed as if Martha Stewart had a challenger. "Never a dull moment on the PTA. Good day, Susan."

They exchanged kisses and Susan watched from the gazebo as they made their way through the side of the house, the gate, and then left. She sat down on the wooden bench and ran her finger across the rough wood. The blue paint that Maxine had brushed along the wood had begun to crack. A splinter had slipped into her finger and drops of blood began to fall... She couldn't even feel it...she couldn't feel it...

Her daughters, as mischievous as they were, might have just saved her.

Susan wondered how long Maxine had spent building this gazebo and painting it. How much work had gone into a project like this—would that take up enough time for her to adjust?

A project.

Never a dull moment, Susan thought. How long she sat out there, she didn't know. She watched the bee bounce from flower to flower. Before long, he left the backyard, to return to his queen. Susan felt the tinge of emptiness in her chest.

Her friends, the pills, her pocket. Why did she always keep them so close? As if they were going to get up and run away.

Susan looped that through her mind a few times. Her friends. She had just referred to her drugs as her friends.

Try not to lose your mind, Susan thought. *Try not to lose your mind.*

Suburbia was its own jail. At that moment, Susan decided it was time to break herself free from her other jail.

This would be her last bottle of pills.

In the corner of their one-acre plot was an area… Susan eyed a shovel. Maxine had built a gazebo, but this would be a lovely place for a coy pond. Fish. Some rocks. Maybe a little waterfall.

A project.

Susan crossed the yard, grabbed the shovel, and began to dig.

A Day at School in Suburbia

"Don't worry about you or me
Deep beneath the lemon tree
Where flowers cry and birds will flee
A whisper farther than one can see

I met a girl with ribboned hair
Eyes struck white, with skin so fair
If she could breathe she'd sing a song
A whisper of waiting for love too long

Graves are dug deep in ground
Dancers dance around and round
Mists and fogs, with smoke and steam
Escaping from the dreadful scream

Weeds will grow around your feet
At your eyes bugs will eat
They have tried to drum
But what is coming. Will always come.

Nothing is without a fee
Life is fleeting away from me
Grasp my hand. Come to see.
Our resting place. The lemon tree"

"Woof," Todd let out from the back of the classroom. "The darkness of Felicia Johnson."

"I'll take that as a compliment." Felicia closed her notebook and sat down at her desk.

"I dug it." Matthew smiled over at Felicia. "Kind of a darker twist than Aly's poem."

"Aly's poems have become redundant." Lexi rolled her eyes. "Constantly trying to be cool is a quick way to be uncool. Like, sorry."

"Hey!" Aly Bane called from the back of the room. "That's not what the poem was about. It was about being liked…and having people…"

"Why is she even arguing with me?" Lexi shot Aly a look. "One doesn't just become popular; it's a natural thing."

"Thanks for the lesson, Lexi. Also, thank you, Matthew. But you like everything," Felicia joked, interrupting and stopping the high-school female warfare. "Matthew would like a song about penguins."

"I'd love a song about penguins," Todd let out. "I'd also love a penguin."

"Kinda makes sense," came a foreign voice from the back of the classroom. Samantha Rose was busy diligently writing in her pink notebook with a pen boasting pink faux fur on the top, and didn't even look up. "A lot of sense, actually."

"Sense?" Felicia turned around. Samantha put her pen in her notebook and closed it, giving a look to Felicia that one would give a stray dog on its last day in a kill shelter.

"Forgive me. I mean, you haven't exactly had it easy, have you?" Samantha's big green eyes rolled toward the ceiling as if to remember. "Maybe this is some sort of reflection of your childhood. From what I've heard, didn't your mother keep a journal? You and her are both writers, I wonder what else you two have in common."

"Let me remember my fond childhood," Todd chirped. "Being murdered under a lemon tree."

"That's not what I got out of it." Samantha's eyes fell on Felicia. Felicia felt her blood rise. "Someone so alone they wasted away beneath a beautiful tree. It is very sad. My heart goes out to you. I feel for you. It must be so hard at times, always having to wear long sleeves."

"I think that's enough," Mrs. Tredanari said from the front of the classroom. As a creative-writing teacher, she normally let her class run itself. She gave assignments and then let discussions unfold; she felt it was a better way for them to learn, from one another. But she knew why Felicia wore long sleeves and that wasn't an appropriate topic for school. "That was a beautiful poem, Felicia. Good work today. Aly...it would be nice if you found...something else to write about. Not being popular is just a mental concept; it's not an actual, tangible thing. At seventeen, I know you girls can't grasp that."

Samantha Rose, still looking at Felicia, raised her hand; she hadn't finished.

Mrs. Tredanari saw the hand go up, but wished it would go down.

The bell rang at the perfect time.

"Lunch!" Matthew exclaimed. His favorite period. He looked over at Felicia, who didn't return the gesture. Her amber-and-gold eyes were focused on Samantha Rose, who was swishing her hips as she bounced out of the classroom.

"No…library." Felicia followed that Abercrombie skirt and blond hair as it turned toward her locker. "I need to work on…but, first."

"I'll have lunch with you…dude." Todd was smiling at Felicia. "But I'd like to watch this first."

"Watch what, dude?" Matthew saw Felicia head in the direction of where Samantha Rose went. "Wait, no."

Matthew moved to grab Felicia's arm, knowing what was about to come, but he missed.

Lexi Scopello was waiting for Samantha outside the classroom. Some joked that Cynthia Thorne had the Scopellos move onto Sun Drop Court so Samantha could have a best friend. The two girls shared similar features and each, in their own way, embodied the specimen of high-school beauty. Though Lexi had watched movies like *She's All*

That and *Mean Girls* a hundred times, Samantha seemed to embody the prom-queen mentality more naturally.

"Boo...you whore," Lexi let out as she played with Samantha's hair. They had probably been baking in the radiance of each other's beauty so intensely that they hadn't noticed Felicia approaching. "I hate that Tredanari won't let us sit next to each other."

"If you learned how to pass notes better." Samantha was fixing Lexi's pink bra strap so it didn't show. "We wouldn't have gotten moved."

"Oh," Lexi let out sadly, as if an orphan boy had just come begging for food, "look."

"Hello, Felicia." Samantha smiled brightly. "Come to further discuss your poem?"

"I'd prefer, in the future," Felicia could hear her voice shaking with anger, and was having trouble controlling it. So she counted in her head until her mind was level again—a trick Salome had taught her. Serenity could be focused and rage could be put away into an imaginary box. "I'd prefer, in the future, if you didn't discuss my childhood so openly in class. You couldn't possibly begin to understand what I went through in that house."

But Samantha didn't respond. Her big eyes fluttered downward and her lips pursed into a frown.

"That was rude." Lexi put her arm around Samantha and continued in a hushed, scolding tone. "You know her father shot himself."

"I was just trying to be kind." A tear actually streamed down Samantha's tan face, but her makeup didn't run. Of course it didn't. "My Aunt warned me about how cruel you can be. I just didn't think she was right. Maybe she is right."

"Look what you did!" Lexi scolded, an arm around her bestie. "How mean can you be?"

Felicia was dumbstruck. "I'm sorry... I didn't mean to."

"It's in your nature, obviously," Samantha let out as she wiped dramatically at her eye. "Like mother, like daughter."

"Excuse me?" Felicia went to take a step forward, but Todd stepped between them.

"Okay." Todd smiled at everyone. "Lunchtime."

Felicia took a breath and shut this up in the imaginary box; this wasn't worth it; lock all the rage away.

But before anyone could move, the shadows of muscles and varsity-letter jackets surrounded them.

Dax Thorne and teammates.

The Prince of Thorne Hall.

By name and birthright, Dax would one day inherit the entirety of Thorne Hall, and his family would continue a legacy that traced back to the early settlers. From pelts and fur trading, to railroads and oil, to finance and power plants, the years and times had rolled and changed, but a Thorne had always been in Thorne Hall.

This was their town, their *Suburbia*.

"Figured the faggot would be in between a bunch of females," Dax Thorne let out in a gruff voice, tilting the Von Dutch hat on his head. "Why is it that you seem to be everywhere, church boy? Don't have a priest's cock to suck somewhere?"

"Dax!" Lexi's manicured nails went to her breasts, although she laughed flirtatiously. When she'd first transferred, her eyes had been on Todd; every girl's eyes at some point had been on Todd. But Todd had publicly shot down Lexi, politely, but since then she couldn't even look at him. "Language! Do you kiss your mother with that mouth?"

"This kid brings out the worst in me," Dax growled.

But Todd held his smile. "It's sad that I affect you in such a way. How often do you think about me? Do you lie awake at night to come up with these humorous limericks? I should start carrying around a small notebook to make sure to catch these wonders. A very small notebook."

Dax's muscular arm ejected and smashed Todd against the locker. Quite like the Hulk. Todd waved away Felicia's hand when she offered to help him up.

"How about making some friends and coming out to the field party tonight?" Dax, less flirtatious and more predatory, focused his eyes on Felicia. "Always had a thing for redheads. You were cute as a kid…but look at you now. *Playboy* should do a spread on you. Remember those little play dates we used to go on? You were always so good at playing doctor."

"We were kids, Dax. If I remember from 'doctor,' you had small problems. But, I have friends, thank you." Felicia had gotten over Dax Thorne when he became self-aware. They had once been close childhood friends, but both their mothers had forbidden that they continue their play dates. He had grown into a poster child for high-school douchebaggery. His good looks were destroyed by his attitude…the bigger his muscles grew, the more of a bully he had become.

"What do you mean, small problems? All of me is big… all of me! Plus, you call these friends? This church faggot? And…Abercrombie wallpaper?"

"Thanks, dude." Matthew rolled his eyes at Dax, which angered the animal and caused him to eject his arm again and smash Matthew against the locker and onto the ground. Matthew had to hold back tears from swelling, for that would feed the bully. He didn't expect him to be that strong, or for it to hurt as much as it did.

"Oh," Samantha let out as if this was the worst thing she'd ever seen. She lowered herself like a Disney princess to Matthew and offered a Tiffany-jeweled hand to help him up. "Are you okay?"

Matthew couldn't respond, as this was the first time she had spoken to him since their first encounter. A night no one forgot, yet never spoke about. *Oink* rang in his mind. *Oink Oink.*

"Let's go, Sammy." Lexi couldn't even bother to offer her gaze to Matthew, let alone a hand for help. "Enough charity work for the day."

"It looks like it hurt." Samantha's green eyes were on Matthew; she took his hand and kissed it. "Apologize, Dax."

"Never." Dax, confused by what was transpiring, turned to his football cronies and began to make jokes about Todd and Matthew being gay.

"That wasn't nice." Samantha raised herself and looked at her friends as if she was forced to join them and not able to stay and care for any of Matthew's bruises. "I'm sorry for him. Get some ice on that. I hope my kiss made it better,"

The in-crowd made their way down the hall and Felicia's blood boiled as they laughed at the less fortunate they had left behind.

Matthew was awestruck by what had just happened, as if touched by Britney Spears, which made Felicia even more angry. Felicia felt her body calm down now that it was only her and her friends. *Put the rage in a box.* Salome's words were in her mind. *Lock it up and put it on a shelf.* Matthew was brushing himself off and he forced a goofy smile back on his face in an attempt to lighten the mood. Plus, he had just been noticed and kissed by his crush.

Put the rage in a box, Felicia thought. *Put the rage in the box.*

Todd was fixing his popped collar and brushing back his mane of blond hair. But in his eyes was a flicker of anger. "See, I set before you today life and prosperity, death and destruction. At midday you will grope about like a blind person in the dark. You will be unsuccessful in everything you do; day after day you will be oppressed and robbed, with no one to rescue you…it's one thing for him to mess with me… but my friends… That's where I draw the line."

"Doesn't the Bible talk about forgiveness?" Felicia said and side-eyed him as they began to make their way down the hall.

But the words out of Todd's mouth next spread goosebumps across everyone's arms. "It does." Todd gritted his teeth together. "But there is a whole lot more about revenge and justice."

Maxine Johnson's Personal Diary

Fall, 1995

Dear Diary,

I was drowning.

Then I was pulled out.

████████████████████████████ came by today with a bottle of cheap tequila and chocolates. Out to the gazebo one glorious fall day we took liquor and a plate of sweets. ██████████████ insisted on the chocolates I had to try from the box.

I do love *Suburbia* in the fall, though nothing can compare to the colors we had in the country. A spread of colors of leaves that seemed to flow forever. I used to smoke a joint on our back porch when Larry and I were newlyweds, and we'd watch the sunset spill colors in waterfalls over trees that went on forever.

I digress.

This visit was the most real moment I have experienced in a long time. Odd for ██████ to make a house call, but who can turn away a good neighbor.

Productive conversation, deep-felt laughs, getting drunk for the fun of it. Who knew ██████ could bring such joy when the clouds seem the darkest? She didn't inquire about Felicia, who had been locked in her room all day…. I think she might have had school…but the lessons you get at home trump the ones between academia walls.

A few drinks turned into many. The conversation took a turn. I found myself more drunk than ███████ and my words fluttering in swarms. She didn't have any chocolates and the ones I ate seemed to be complementing the tequila's effects. I was talking about my husband. What I know about his work. About my long days. About the shadow that comes at night. How it scratches and creeps. How it covers me. How it's been covering me for years. The emptiness inside. About my hobbies. About my journaling. About my needlepoint. The gazebo I built. The monsters I fear that lurk in the dark.

We must have had too much fun because when I came to, she had left. The day had long since ended and a cool breeze swept the backyard. The bottle was empty and I couldn't have passed a sobriety test if Jesus had held a gun to my forehead. Cabinets had been opened and papers scuffled about… What had I been searching for? Had it been me searching? ███████ wouldn't have been looking through my cabinets.

Then it came to me. Like a light bulb bursting on. It was Felicia.

I had been using belts and wooden spoons up until this point, but for something of this nature, I felt a metal spatula would work best.

April Mayfair says it often: "There are rules to be followed. Without order, there would be chaos." It's why her children are always so well behaved and so well maintained.

Not mine. Not my Felicia. So she has to learn.

Note: Metal spatula preferable to wooden spoon. Belt on buckle side still favorable.

"Two thirty-nine."

Beep.

Susan McArthur was at an empty beach in Spain.

"Four forty-two."

Beep.

Brilliant white sand between her toes.

"Five fifty-six."

Beep.

The rays of warm sun on her face.

"Five seventy-two."

Beep.

"Ten forty-two."

Bubbles of the ocean waves tickling her feet.

"Eight sixty-four."

Beep.

She had never been to the beach.

Sigh.

"Card?"

Was there a beach near here?

"Lady...?"

What would taking the car and never coming back feel like? Take the last of her pills and just wandering into the water. The weening off had been harder than Susan had anticipated, and her only release beyond sitting in a shower was digging the coy pond in the backyard.

"Susan?" a voice from behind her called.

"What?" Susan's voice was too quick...almost harsh. But the small caramel woman with the heavy lines and white hair just smiled. "Sorry. Lost in a daydream."

"Did you forget your discount card?" Old Mother Watson had the bright orange card between her ashy, aged fingers. "Borrow mine."

"Thank...thank you." Susan tried a smile, but even she knew it failed. "How are you doing, Andrea?"

"I'm fine. But what could you possibly be daydreaming about? Beautiful husband. Beautiful children. Beautiful home. A small, lucky percentage of this huge world gets to live in such wonder. Don't waste it daydreaming of somewhere else. My husband was a dreamer and now he's wheelchair-bound. Can't waste the good days in dreams. Nope."

"Of course." Susan handed the discount card back to Mother Watson. Handed the attendant two twenties. "What a beautiful day."

Susan picked up her grocery bags and went to leave the store, but the attendant called after her, "Hey, lady, your change."

The withdrawal symptoms made even the simplest of social interactions seem impossible. But Susan was out of the store. It bothered her how clean it had been in the Grand

Union. How fresh everything was. Not a single dairy product was close to being past its expiration date. Susan had checked. Not a single fruit or vegetable scarred or gone bad.

Boxes were arranged perfectly in each aisle. Little boxes all arranged. Colors seemingly aligned, a painting one could hang on their wall.

More disturbing than that were the other housewives.

Everyone wore their best. Their hair done and makeup fresh. They seemingly posed as they held an apple out with perfectly painted nails. Turning it in the light, searching for a blemish they knew wasn't there. They then turned on their colorful heels and slowly and gracefully made their way to the next item on their list.

Why did everyone seem like they were moving in slow motion?

Susan had prepped herself before going out—curled her hair and painted her face. What else was she supposed to do? She had put on the heels that hurt and a dress that was hard to move in. But what she seemed to struggle with these women accomplished with ease. After every whitewashed smile. After every pageant wave. Susan tried to catch her reflection. Was her hair in place? Was her makeup symmetrical? Was there a single wrinkle on her dress? Would they know? They would know.

The pills would have hidden these fears. Her mind reminded her and her mind was attempting to adjust. It would take time, she reminded herself, and she put her chin up. This was all psychological anyway; tomorrow would be easier than today.

"Susan McArthur? My word." Soft words sung from a musical mouth. "Over here, doll!"

Susan had walked a quarter-mile from the grocery store and into their quaint version of a town. Into the purple and pink trees and architecturally divine cafes and boutiques. She had the grocery bags in her hands and now Athena Rose was waving her over from Cafe Molfetas, a coffee shop, across the street.

Susan raised a hand and an apple fell out of a grocery bag and onto the gravel, crushing the orb's perfect shape. Leaving it, Susan crossed the street to the busy cafe. Athena's black Versace dress was this-season and a sterling-silver belt buckled at her waist. She donned a diamond-and-silver necklace around her neck while a tennis bracelet sparkled on her wrist. Though, for years, Athena's darkened hair was a direct attribute to the fact that she had become a mourning hermit, Susan could see sun lines had begun to spring back along her long, braided locks. In her face, a tan had returned and her emerald eyes gleamed.

"Neil Wolf." A hand ejected into their conversation and Susan hadn't even realized that Athena had gentleman company. Susan put out her hand and the grocery bag smacked against the waist-high gate the cafe had put out to subtly make sure those who were on the street knew they were on the street.

A very handsome, thin man, with blond thick hair and blue eyes, his bone structure showed through the almost gauntness of his face. Yet there was something endearing about him, in his fine tailored suit complete with a tie clip and pocket square. Something very political about him.

"Susan McArthur. Hi. I was just grocery shopping."

"At the Grand Union?" Athena's eyebrows rose and a bright smile spread her face. Never any wrinkles. Never a single blemish. One could turn her round and round in their hand and never find a single mark. "But, that's almost a half a mile away from here."

How did she even wind up downtown? Her car was still in the grocery store parking lot.

"I felt like a walk."

"How could you not? What a beautiful day." Athena beamed. "I had to take Neil downtown so he could appreciate fall in our community. You know what they say about all work and no play."

"It's hard to get out these days." Neil slyly brought his hand to his nose and took a giant sniff on one side. "Never-ending circus with an untrained consort of monkeys. But it's my zoo, so they're my animals. Even now I'm sure they are flinging feces at each other."

"What is it you do, Neil?" It had been four years. It was sensible to Susan that Athena should get back into the dating world. The way he looked at Athena was hungry...a look Susan had seen in her husband's eyes when she was preparing a juicy steak or putting on a new piece of lingerie. Men.

At a certain level we are primal.

"I am the mayor of this fair town."

"How lucky for you, Athena."

Both Athena and Neil exchanged glances.

"Why, this is my cousin, Susan." Athena's laugh was like music in a silent room.

But Neil's face winced slightly, as if this fact bothered him. "We grew up together and spent a lot of time as kids playing about; what were we, six? He lived with my family for an entire year, but that's another story for another day. But we do need to find you a woman, Neil. A man like this—and the mayor, no less—shouldn't go to waste. All alone in that giant mayor's mansion. Have you met the McArthurs, Neil? I don't think so. Susan moved into the old Johnson house four years ago."

"Oh...Maxine Johnson? A shame what happened there." Neil shook his head as if the memories were hurtful, but did a poor job at acting like he cared. "Normally things are quiet on Sun Drop Court, but I remember calls I used to get from your neighbor, Priscilla Primm."

"I haven't met the Primms yet."

"They live behind you, Susan. Nineteen Iris lane."
Athena took a sip of her coffee and not even her lipstick
rubbed off on the lid. "They've lived in this town for,
what…"

"One of the oldest families here, besides the Thornes."
Neil waved a hand. "It's nothing to get frazzled over. She
called in a few times…someone lurking in the back of that
house in the middle of the night. But we have units that
checks out and patrols the area. I've been hiring more police
staff every year. A little extra security is always a sound
decision. Life is to be safe around here. Community is
everything. *Suburbia* should be idealistic."

"Since Neil has become mayor"—Athena's free hand
went to her cousin's back and a proud family look filled her
eyes—"crime has nearly disappeared from our town."

"I like to keep my police force on its toes." Neil nodded
and sniffed again, as if something was stuck in his nose.
Though Susan couldn't imagine the police force being
overwhelmed in a town like this. "As I tell Athena, if you ever
need anything, a favor, please feel free to call me…especially
if you notice anyone lurking in the middle of the night.
That's just not the type of *Suburbia* we want our children to
grow up in."

Susan felt her skin ripple—something else to worry
about, something else to pay attention to, something else to

smile through, something else added onto the 'everything is okay' list…something else.

"It's been a pleasure seeing you, Susan." Athena smiled and took a look at her Cartier watch, her eyes rising at the time, before returning to Susan. "Keep an eye on your mail. I have a dinner party coming up soon that neither of you are allowed to miss."

Salome Legree was in the local bank. A shawl covered her head and big dark sunglasses rested on her darkly made-up face.

The bank with the art-deco golden walls was tucked between a coffee house and a woman's boutique; it fit the town's needs. Back in her day, lines could be back to the door, but due to ATMs and online banking, people no longer needed to come into such establishments. Still, Salome came in the middle of the day when the place was empty and all the tellers were available. No one else was bothering the bank executives who were at their desks.

"Ms. Legray," the bank teller was able to get out. The teller had tried to hide her face when Salome came in, but Salome went right to her, intimidating people even in her old age.

"It's Legree."

"Excuse me, miss?"

"It's Legree." Salome took off the huge sunglasses to make sure the teller saw her roll her eyes. She had few years left to live and the dramatics were fun. "Not Legray or Liegray...Legree! So either pronounce it right or just keep your mouth shut and do your job. How long is this going to take?"

"Just...just..." The mousey teller looked around for her manager. "Give me a moment. This is only my second day, Mrs. Lagray."

"*Legree!* I've been a client here for well over forty years. They should keep you in the back and let the competent workers out front. Hurry! Hurry!" Salome waved her long claws at the teller with disinterest. The bank was small and it was late in the day...she hadn't been seen. She smiled to herself; didn't need a disguise after all. Yet she still placed her sunglasses back on; it had been almost ten years now and everyone thought she...

"Why, bless the stars. Is it? Salome!"

Salome twitched at the sound of her name and her hand had went to her face too quickly. As the years increased, her reflexes weren't her own...she couldn't calculate like she used to; plan like she used to. She would jump at shadows and quiver when crossing a street—aging wasn't fun.

But now, Salome had given herself away. Damn.

"I knew it was you!" Andrea Watson was making her way across the bank. The little dark woman all dressed up in yellows, complete with a white hat and a large yellow rose pinned on it...probably from her own garden. A small grocery bag was dangling in her hand. "My word, it's been what...?"

"Nine years." Salome had no care for the housewife pleasantry game. "Andrea, it's been nine years."

"Yes, yes." Andrea sat down across from Salome on the chair the teller had been using and placed her purse on the table, resting two gloved hands on it. "It's been much too long. You don't write. You don't call. Nowadays you could just email...are you on the Internet, old woman? I would love to hear the great tales of your adventures since you've left our little *suburbia*."

Salome just sat there staring at her 'old friend,' allowing her to lead this dance.

"So...where have you been, old friend?"

Salome dragged her eyes, luckily hidden by her glasses, anxiously over Andrea Watson, her one-time neighbor on Sun Drop Court.

"Traveling."

"Ah...the life. I bet you could regale me with tales of Europe or perhaps Asia...another time." Andrea waved a hand dramatically through the air. "Are you planning on moving back to the Court? I mean, that would shock everyone. You should wait till Halloween time…especially after everyone thinks…"

"I am perfectly fine living where I am living."

"Is this all I'm going to get, Salome? After all these years, you are going to give me nothing? Quite the conundrum this is."

"Mrs. Legree?" The bank manager had returned with an annoyed look on his face; he'd obviously just spent a moment scolding the new girl. "This is your property."

The manager turned and motioned for the new teller to return to her post, to attempt to do a job she obviously wasn't properly trained for. She pushed the beaten, leather-bound book across the table as if it was any other book.

"Storing a book in a bank, Salome; what are you up to?" Andrea laughed. Salome raised herself off her chair and snatched the book from the table. She let out a slight hiss, sending the teller bumbling anxiously to the back. "Oh no! Don't leave, Salome! We have just begun to catch up…. I must let all of Sun Drop Court you have returned… Must call your family…tell them you are back! I'm sure it will confuse a lot of people…"

Salome turned and bent low to her old friend's face and whispered, "What do you want?"

"Could you not hear me? A hearing aid might be a worthy investment. Tell me, what's in your book…I guess…I can have a senior moment and forget we ever saw each other today."

"Fine. Less of a book…more of a diary. Something I wouldn't want the wrong hands to get ahold of till it's time. A one-time patient of mine gave it to me in confidence, someone who is no longer on this earth. But I still am, and I want justice for her. That's all you get, Andrea." Salome's voice lowered into an almost growl that sent Andrea back into her chair. "You are forgetting some priceless pointers. I wouldn't contact anyone, if I were you. If people start finding out I'm… Well, they will also find out why your husband is in that wheelchair. You've been living quite the nice life, haven't you? Hate for that to end now, when you are so close to the end of it. How old is Leroy now, almost ninety? It would only take a few phone calls and your entire situation would unravel."

"We did what we thought was right back then."

"No." Salome shook her head. "I did you a favor. Do not forget that."

"Oh, Salome." Andrea's smile was carefree, but her small hands were rolling over each other behind the purse. "Just two old friends catching up."

Salome straightened her back as much as she could and walked with pride toward the bank door, leading with her cane. But Andrea chirped after her, loud enough for anyone to hear. "I'd be careful with making threats…neither of us would fare well in jail at our age."

Nighttime

With haste, Samantha Rose made her way across the ancient foot bridge. It crossed from the dirt parking lot over the deep swamp to where the corn fields lay. Her boyfriend had attempted to be a gentleman and go first, offering his arm, but she had no patience for that shit. Also, the party had started an hour ago, and her mother had instilled in her that being late was a social crime. Her collegiate beau had tried to get her to blow him and had then attempted to finger her... She had allowed that for moments before she could feel herself about to vomit. His hands bothered her; touching bothered her. He was to be seen and appreciated. No talk; no touch.

Dating a college boy made her look special in the eyes of her peers—Samantha Rose, untouchable by any high school boy...but she was sure his college buddies thought he was some sort of rapist or pedophile.

"Bitch, where you been?" Lexi Scopello greeted them just outside the beginning of the corn field where the swamp bridge ended. "Bitch, you told me you were wearing jean shorts and a bikini top! I look ridiculous now."

"I said plaid skirt with a matching top." Samantha bobbed her head to the side and twisted a golden strand. "I wish you listened better...bitch."

Samantha cringed as her boyfriend's big hand curled around her exposed stomach.

"I got you a drink." Lexi actually looked sexy in the ripped jean shorts she had obviously made earlier this night and a shiny bikini top. This annoyed Samantha; lately she had begun to grow disenchanted. The social games she had enjoyed so much had become…lame. She craved something more. An exploration throughout Thorne Hall had led her to 'more' and tonight she was going to try out some new games.

The question of the matter, was on whom.

"I got a drink for you." The scruff of her 'boyfriend' rubbed against her ear. Samantha pushed forward toward the drink Lexi had gotten her. As a rule, she never got drunk, but she always acted the part and pretended to be just as blacked out as everyone else. It was fun to be the sober one at 3 a.m. … That's when all the secrets came out. She would sip on a vodka soda while some cheerleader told her about her affair with their history teacher or some lacrosse player confessed that he liked men.

Samantha took the red cup from Lexi and didn't even acknowledge spilling a quarter of it on her overly priced golden string-bikini top before pushing through the remaining tall grass.

There was a party ahead. Maybe that would provide… something.

As the grass spread, the same scenarios, the same party antics, the same everything was all her eyes could see. It had all become so passé and lackluster.

Dax was tearing the white Abercrombie polo shirt off his body in some display of masculinity in the middle of the cornfield. The lights of his prized Dodge Ram illuminated their little high-school gathering of debauchery.

"Fucking loser," he spat at one of his teammates. All of them donning their varsity and JV jackets that, at one point, Dax was layered in. But now the prince was showing off his muscles. He roared, "Next."

This was the in-crowd norm. Packing themselves into the opening of the cornfield across the swamp. Just in the distance, looming ominously on a hill, was the NRG Power Plant glaring down through fog and haze. Its dark chimneys seemingly pierced the clouds in which it spat out colors of yellow and orange that were not pretty or welcoming.

Dax bragged that his father had partied in this opening, and his father before him… It had been one big douchebag fest as far back as the mind could reach. But Dax certainly took the cake. He was muscular, intelligent, and maintained a beautiful physique…and he didn't seem to have any plan but to be awful with the gifts he had been given.

"He's been arm-wrestling people all night." Lexi had her arm wrapped in Samantha's, both of them trailing the outside of the party. Queens observing the court. Samantha's college boyfriend was selling weed to the teenagers like it was going out of business. Maybe she'd call the cops and rat him out. That'd be exciting. But she refrained because of what was in her purse....That was what she was waiting to use on someone.

"Dax does enjoy a good competition." Samantha feigned interest as her cousin paraded around. "I wonder if he's winning."

Lexi's manicured nails hit Samantha's chest too hard, way too hard. Lexi was drunk and had forgotten her place on this social ladder. "Of course he's winning, bitch! He's the best! Duh."

Samantha glared at Lexi for a second too long as she went on talking about the younger girls at the party and how desperate they were. How cool she was. How badly they wanted to be just like them. How they wanted to be just like her.

Samantha's chest tingled from where Lexi had smacked her...and that had been enough to steer her mind toward what fun she'd have tonight.

Samantha turned to Lexi and ran a strand of her highlighted hair through her fingers, smiling that smile she'd learned from her mother. "You're so pretty."

As Samantha and Lexi took their seats atop Dax's Dodge Ram with wheels so large you'd question his manhood, the Prince of Thorne Hall was smashing an empty beer can against a freshman's head.

"That hurt?" Dax roared as the freshman winced in pain. "Doesn't hurt me!"

Dax smashed a full beer can against his own head and laughed as it broke open and the liquid oozed down his sweaty muscles. It was almost erotic, Samantha thought. Dax was like an angry Greek god who had been set free upon the masses to show off his power and strength. Not to mention, the high beams from his truck ignited the opening and made him almost glow.

All bow to the prince of steroids, Samantha thought. *All hail the Prince of Thorne Hall.*

That's why Dax threw these parties below his family's power plant; he wasn't going to wait until he inherited this town by birth right.

As far as he was concerned, he owned it now.

Todd Mayfair was hidden by the tall corn stalks and was watching this display of idiocy with grave disapproval. He flicked the golden cross at his neck and took a glance at his watch. They were never late; he just appreciated being early.

Observation of the scene unfolding in front of him made what he had planned easier to wrap his head around. He had a recording at home of him praying that he played whenever he needed to sneak out; his mother never entered his room when he was praying. He had timed it perfectly to stop around when he normally went to bed. He hated to fool his mother, but sometimes…

Rustles in the stalks and his trusty brethren were next to him. A few minutes early, out of respect. They all sat watching in the outskirts, their feet in the swamp.

He only needed four…he could have had a dozen come…maybe double or triple that, but why waste his favors on something small? Todd was sure that in the future there would be bigger events he would need them for.

While Todd watched from the shadows, Dax paraded around abusing all he came in contact with, pushing a kid here, smacking a girl's behind there, at one point he chucked a full beer at Hottie McHotterson Lexi Scopello's head….

Sick…he is sick.

Dax Thorne favored himself a false idol, something for the masses to worship, delusion mixed with ego. Ego inflated by meaningless accomplishments. A prom king crown here. A football trophy there. He thought himself one of these trophies, sparkling and shining gold.

Dax was born sick—this was not his own fault—he had to be cleansed of his ego.

We are all born sick, his mother had once said. *It is how we handle such a sickness. It's as simple as choosing good versus evil.*

In silence, Todd passed the four ski masks and the four filled water bottles.

Todd gripped his father's hammer as they slowly made their way around the cornfield.

Todd could help Dax.

They pulled the ski masks over their faces.

Todd would help.

We are all born sick, but we don't all need to live as such.

"Bitch. I got you a drink." Samantha handed Lexi the only drink she had in her hands before pulling her golden locks back into a ponytail. A subconscious tick of hers whenever she was about to execute a plan.

"What about yours?" Lexi accepted the drink and took a heavy swig of it. "Or are you drunk enough already? Figures…silly bitch."

Samantha beamed her pearly whites and batted her eyelashes. Her boyfriend was on the opposite side of the field smoking a blunt and chugging beers out of the bottom of the cans.

Perfect.

This was all working out so well.

Lexi was bragging to the younger girls about what kind of car her mother was going to buy her, flipping her hair around and smiling confidently. As if she were the queen and the other girls her subjects.

How comical.

Sun Drop Court knew one queen, and that was me, Samantha Rose thought.

Lexi had inherited her mother's looks. That almost Southern-belle charm and gorgeous flair. Boys watched her walk away in her skimpy outfits, and if she wanted something from you, she would probably get it. But she had learned these tricks from teen flicks and bad high-school movies. It wasn't natural- it was some desperate high school act to be prom queen.

She was no Samantha Rose.

"I…" Lexi slowly brought the back of her hand to her forehead in what one could perceive as a dramatic fashion, but Samantha knew otherwise. "I feel woozy."

Samantha hip-bumped her way past all the underclassmen girls, past the Hollister and Abercrombie skirts, Tiffany bracelets and spray tans, as Moses parted the sea.

Samantha wrapped her hand around Lexi's arm and pulled her down from Dax's Dodge Ram. A little too hard perhaps.

"I think it's best if I bring Lexi to relieve herself," Samantha imitated, putting her fingers down her throat and vomiting as all the girls giggled. Back in control, the sideshow was over. "She's good at doing that."

"Sam…" Lexi whispered in her ear as her feet roughly hit the ground. Samantha led her out of the cornfield opening and into the dark. They made their way down to a small clearing by the beginning of the swamp. "I think…I think…was there something in my drink?"

Samantha turned to her friend and tightly pulled a thick strand of Lexi's hair around her finger. Pulled on it until she heard the hair breaking from Lexi's scalp. "You are so pretty. You know that? So…pretty."

Lexi pushed herself off Samantha before stumbling to the ground. Looking up at her friend, she went to mouth words, but only garbles came out. Samantha smiled down at Lexi and waited until she all but passed out; she wouldn't completely pass out. That was the glory in all of this.

Now it was time to find her horny college boyfriend.

As Samantha Rose led her boyfriend out of the party clearing down to where she had lain Lexi out, another drama was unfolding.

"Go get a beer for me, you queer," Dax was roaring, so drunk at this point that even people who thought themselves his closest friends were not safe from his liquor-induced temper. "Queer. Ha-ha."

In the morning, a few freshmen would have bruises they'd hide from their families, maybe a black eye here or there…. That's what normally happened after a party in the cornfields. That, and one, maybe two girls, who woke up in pain trying to convince themselves they had allowed the beast of a man to get on top of them and have his way. That's how Dax Thorne's parties normally ended.

But this wasn't a normal night.

Before the underclassman returned with Dax's beer, a smash echoed through the field, followed by another, and with that, the high beams of Dax's prized Ram went dark. Then a window was smashed, and another. A hammer smashed into the truck, calling for its master to return to his prized possession.

The beast of a boy turned and let out a roar.

Stripped of sight, shrouded in darkness, a panic broke out in the party. A few dozen of high school's finest attempted to figure out what was going on in their drunk and drugged states. But Dax pushed his way toward his car as all the anger and rage and steroids built up in him.

"What in God's name…" Dax began before a shadow from behind tripped him and knocked him to the ground. A swift kick to his head forced the giant's hands to his head as his Von Dutch hat was kicked away. Then his groin was stomped on and his entire body rang with pain.

Dax felt the liquid hit him before he could smell what it was. That's when he began to twist and turn. But four shadowed figures were holding him to the ground as a fifth straddled him, pinning him down and kneeling on his chest.

"You were born sick." An unfamiliar voice was in his head. Dax was reminded of Pastor Jefferson and Sunday School—the voice was commanding, young but stern. That's when Dax's mind began to race; he was reminded of little league and fairs, girls he had taken and games he had won, late-night pool parties and hand jobs in his truck. The brain will search for the most pleasant of times when in a state of terror. A mind desperately searches for a false sense of reality in order to block out events that are unfolding. "But we can cleanse you."

As the figure rose over Dax, he glimpsed a red-and-gold-lined hoodie. As the match was lit, he caught another glimpse—five figures with ski masks and matching hoodies. The colors of the hoodies and style he knew well. But then the gasoline dripped from his hair into his eyes.

He didn't even see the match fall.

"What?" Samantha Rose put both of her hands on her hips and looked at her boyfriend, exasperated. "You want to repeat yourself?"

"I said." He scratched at his head. "No."

"If you say 'no' to me, I will break up with you. What will you tell your college friends then, hmm? A seventeen-year-old girl broke up with big man on campus, Devon."

"First off." The head scratching was done and he folded his arms. "My name is Josh. Second...I...at least...I thought I liked you. I have never met a girl like you before. But I am now thinking that was a good thing."

"Just have sex with her." Samantha motioned toward Lexi's body, which was fully drugged and half-conscious on the dirt. "No condom necessary. Just pull out. It'll be fine, and aren't you horny? You were basically forcing your fist up my jeans before."

Josh, who was everything a college boy should be, looks wise, just stared at Samantha, as if finally recognizing the answer to a riddle. "You need help." He moved past her and lifted Lexi into his arms. "A lot of help."

"So...what? You are not going to have sex with her?"

"No! I am not going to rape her, Samantha!" Josh's eyes opened even wider, despite how stoned he was. "I'm taking this poor girl to get some help. Far away from you."

"I'll tell people you drugged her."

"Yes." Josh rolled his eyes as he pushed past Samantha. "That's what I do: I drug girls so I can bring them to get help. You are not half as smart as you think you are. Don't…just don't call me again."

"I'll tell my friends…."

But she was at a loss for words as Josh carried away one of her only actual friends.

Samantha stood in the darkened spot for a moment. She was exactly as smart as she thought she was. She let her ponytail down and ran her hands through it. Her mother would never have failed like this. She let out a spoiled growl. Maybe she should have just rolled Lexi's body into the swamp and watched what happened next.

She was bored again.

Dax's scream echoed in the air, but only for a moment.

In moments, the darkened cornfield had burst to light in a small arena. In flames. The entire left side of Dax's body had been spread in gasoline and set aflame. While most of the high-school partygoers had fled when the lights were smashed, the rest now were attempting to smack the fire off Dax, with little success. All had drunk too much and were not sufficiently helping the problem…throwing vodka on him, for instance…. Not helpful.

Samantha stood at the edge of the cornfield and watched as her cousin, all six-foot-whatever of him, swung around like a dying ogre. What did being set on fire feel like? Samantha had run a Bic blade across her wrist in middle school when she saw a bunch of goth kids with cut-up arms, but even that pain had been too much for her to bare. It had opened a void. The emptiness she felt as her skin had broken open had stopped her. This had to be much worse. The lack of control mixed with the foreign element literally eating your body away. Or did shock set in at a certain point? Does the body protect its host from the pain?

From the way Dax was screaming, Samantha doubted it. By her feet was his prized Von Dutch hat he'd had his mother specially order for him; it was a one of a kind, leather with special stitching.

Samantha placed it at an angle on her head.

From the distance, where the NRG plant's chimneys rose into the sky, emergency lights began to swirl and a siren echoed in the air. Just as a group of kids were smacking the fire off Dax with jackets, the sirens grew louder. But not loud enough. Samantha heard him begin to whimper…suddenly he seemed more like a dying whale than a Greek god, and she lost complete interest.

Someone had been watching the party from the plant and had sounded the alarms the minute the flames had started. Police were most likely on their way.

Todd Mayfair stood in the cornstalks as long as he could, watching Dax's atonement. His companion had lit the match and had spoken to Dax. Todd had wanted to be the one to do it, but he couldn't risk being recognized. He had expected to struggle to hold him down, but the giant of a boy was so drunk and so scared at that moment that it was easy. Though it had taken all five of them to actually keep him on the ground.

As the sirens cut through the night and red-and-orange lights seemed like they were coming from everywhere, the scene was coming to a close. It had all happened so fast.

As an artist would have been proud of his final painting, Todd felt so. This had been a beautiful scene. It was as if he could see the tainted ego rising off Dax's burning body. The wickedness rising to the above and being singed away.

All of us are born sick.

But we can all be fixed.

Maxine Johnson's Personal Diary

Late Fall, 1995

Dear Diary,

What does horror sound like?

What does true terror…what is the…what noise does it make?

You hear it in movies. TV shows that dare to dwell in the shadows. But have you ever heard it in reality?

What would it be? Under a different circumstance, would one laugh at the sound? Is it…overacted? Dramatic. Silly in its own sense. A sound that one would hear and not know what to do with?

For example: Imagine you are being chased through the woods, and you know just beyond the trees is someone who can help. What noises are you making? As your pursuer gets closer and closer, you can almost feel his breath; what do you yell? Is it dramatic and overacted?

Or is actual terror? Quite the opposite.

Is it so true and real that the bumps and hair on your skin rise at the sound? It could be something that never leaves you, but keeps coming back to scratch and scratch and scratch.

On those nights, when the shadow comes, when it covers me and blankets me, as its holds my hand against the walls, as it clutches my mind in its snare, I know I make that sound. I know someone else hears it. But I can't speak the words to ask what it sounds like.

All the ones who hear.

My sounds of desperate pleas.

Are the ones involved.

It's so cold in horror.

It's so cold in horror.

April Mayfair, Susan McArthur, Lorraine Scopello, and Cynthia Thorne were in the principal's office.

All had been called in for a meeting that afternoon, before the end of the day—it hadn't taken long for the entire town to hear that Dax Thorne had been maimed and set aflame. Everyone had heard about Lexi Scopello being roofied as well. But that was completely overshadowed...this was Dax Thorne, after all.

Prince of Thorne Hall.

"Todd was in his room all night reading the Bible aloud. I came by every twenty minutes to make sure he was doing that...and not fooling about." April was sat perfectly in her chair, legs crossed tight, hands on her skirt that ended at just above her knees. For a church girl, she didn't mind showing off her God-given form. "You haven't accused any of the other mothers in the room. Are you accusing me of... just because my daughter... my Grace..."

April's hand began to shake and Susan quickly reached over and grasped it. April looked at her, shocked, but an instinct had come over Susan. April relaxed into her comfort.

"No one is saying that you are anything but a fantastic mother. Please forgive me for these questions...he was there all night, Mrs. Mayfair?" The principal leaned back in his chair and ran the pencil between his middle and pointer fingers.

There were easy parents to deal with and difficult parents to deal with. He might as well have let the parents of dragons into his office this morning. Behind him the most wicked dragon in the lair was currently storming. He secretly admitted it: yes, he would rather accuse a woman who 'lost' her daughter over what was roaring behind him. "It was the gold-and-red uniforms of the reform school Todd was in before he joined us here that were seen in the field. That is all Dax says he saw before…well…before… when…"

"He was set on fire?" Cynthia spat from her position pacing behind the principal and his chair. She turned to the window and slammed her hands against it powerfully. When you wear that much jewelry, you tend to be able to get a good hit in. Cynthia would take four steps to one side and then turn on her fire-red stilettos and take four steps to the other. She was even in a tight-red Dolce dress that looked like the Devil itself made it for her. Her pacing was utterly unsettling, as you could feel the anger rising off her. Susan was thinking the same thing as the principal; she almost expected her to sprout wings and burn the place to the ground.

"Cynthia, why don't you sit down?" Susan McArthur motioned to the chair next to her. Would she burn or was there a calm to this beast? Cynthia's fired-up eyes met Susan's soothing gaze for a second and she then nodded. She made her way around the principal's desk and sat down next to the rest of the mothers. Susan went into her purse…hesitated, then motioned to Cynthia. Cynthia bent over and watched as in her purse, Susan opened her medication bottle and passed two pills over to her. "Here. Take one now and then one later with a glass of wine; it'll calm your nerves."

Now only fifty-nine pills left, you idiot.

"Thank…thank you?" It was obviously a phrase she didn't get to say a lot. Was Cynthia a beast…or just unloved?

Wow, Susan thought. *Detoxing off the pills has really freed my mind.*

Cynthia's face would have been full of surprise at this act of kindness if not for the Botox. "Really, thank you."

"Scone?" Lorraine Scopello, donned in a tight blue 'dress' that her cleavage was popping out of, had brought scones. "I made them this morning…thought we would be hungry in here."

Cynthia's anger immediately began to rise again.

April Mayfair neatly placed a napkin on her lap and motioned for one. "Not an appropriate food for the principal's office, but…you baked these?"

"Yes. Would you like my recipe?"

"What did you do to get them shaped so perfectly."

"Scone?" Lorraine smiled her Southern smile at the principal. "Have you even eaten today? You must be such a busy man."

"Scone!" Cynthia roared and mocked. "Scone! Scone! You brought scones?"

Lorraine turned slowly and smiled at Cynthia, wrapped one in one of the blue napkins she had brought that matched the basket and her dress, and went to hand it to her.

"I don't think she wants one." Susan took the scone and put it in her lap, giving Lorraine a side look. This wasn't the time to campaign for Mayor of Stepford.

"Ladies." The principal let his hands fall onto the desk to command attention. "If we could finish this up. Mrs. Thorne, what happened to Dax is an absolute tragedy. But drugs and liquor were found in the field last night. Things looked like they got pretty out of control. Now, no fingerprints were found on the water bottles with the gasoline in them, but..."

"Am I late?" A breeze came into the room as the principal's door was quietly opened. It was almost as if the room got brighter. "I apologize..."

"Mrs. Rose?" A shocked tone to the principal's voice. "What a pleasure! It's been...years at this point! I didn't expect you. Please, join us. We are discussing the events of last night. I was not expecting you."

"You said that already. No, we were not expecting her." Cynthia swallowed and went to scratch, with a bony finger, her nose. "You've been leaving Thorne Hall a lot lately, Athena."

Athena just turned and her bright smile, which was like a weapon against her sister, turned away from the comment.

Athena Rose's hair was almost completely blond again and tied in a single braid that swung down her back. A darkened gold dress from Nordstrom's fall collection, black boots, and a loose scarf around her neck completed her ensemble. In her hands were cups of coffee for everyone.

"That's more appropriate," April whispered to Lorraine. "Coffee makes sense. Scones make a mess. I give you a C for effort."

"Susan." Athena smiled brightly as she handed Susan her coffee. Susan could live in Athena's smile. It was true warmth. "I know you are taking a break from caffeine, so I brought you a pumpkin drink I concocted myself; I know you love the flavors of the fall. For the rest of you, I brought pumpkin-spice lattes. They only came out last January, but they are all the rage."

"Thank you for thinking of me." Susan meant it. In a world where being overlooked by selfish needs was paramount, it was the small things that mattered. Athena always remembered she liked oatmeal raisin cookies, what her favorite colors were, and now the type of hot drink she took in the morning. "You are truly…"

"Why are you here?" Cynthia snapped at her, tossing her long mane, which was badly in need of updated highlighting. "I told you this morning I'd come."

"That's reassuring, but as this matter seems to concern my daughter as well…"

"We are here to talk about Dax!" Cynthia slammed her hand on the principal's desk, shaking everything on it. She turned her eyes on Lorraine and smiled the smile she used to get donations. "I'm not minimizing Lexi's ordeal, but being roofied is not uncommon…being set on fire is not the norm."

"Of course, Cynthia." Lorraine tried to cross her arms over her enormous bosoms. "I. Completely. Understand."

"Maybe," Athena took a couple strides to stand next to the principal's chair, "if we had a list of all the boys and girls Dax has bullied over the years, we could narrow down his attacker."

"My son is no bully!" Cynthia went to rise from her chair, but Athena shot her a look that had her back in her chair with her head lowered. Susan never understood, for as wild and untamed as Cynthia was, the fear she had of Athena was troublesome. Someone like Cynthia Wolf-Thorne didn't just fear for no reason.

"Mrs. Thorne." The principal removed his wire glasses and sat back in his chair. He opened a file cabinet, removed a large file, and dropped it on his desk. "This is the file of complaints against your son. I called the Captain and that was the day he renovated the gymnasium; the next time I called him about the matter of Dax bullying, he built us a theater."

"My husband is a philanthropist, and a very busy one at that." Cynthia's face was turning red. It was obvious she had no idea of her son's bullying. It was hard to tell her emotion because of the work she'd had done, but one could see her shock. "Your phone calls to him must have reminded him of his charitable desires toward your school. May I see that folder?"

"This is all confidential information. If a child complains to a teacher or counselor, it's kept private. I would have thought, forgive me, your husband would have let you in on Dax's...reputation. A couple of students switched schools, even some who are still in the hospital. We are, of course, very grateful for all that your husband does, Mrs. Thorne."

Susan could see it: Cynthia had no idea her child was the school bully.

"How long have my friends been bugging you?" Athena laughed, carefree, at the principal, who relaxed slightly. She loosely dropped her manicured hand on his shoulders.

At this point, Susan had almost forgotten what they were discussing. Athena was working some magic on the air and making what was a terrible situation into lightness.

"Over an hour."

"Ladies." Athena turned her eyes on her friends, the emeralds glowing. "I'm sure there will be a proper investigation by both the faculty and my friends on the police force. I was on the phone with our mayor today and he promised me that both Dax's and Lexi's attacks will be handled. Since he has personally hired every officer we have, I'll make sure this is his stop priority. We will stay strong for our children and get to the bottom of this. A cop was here this morning interviewing students, yes?"

The principal nodded. Two cops had come first thing in the morning to talk with various students. None who admitted to knowing anything about a party in a swamp.

"Thank you, Athena." Lorraine smiled gratefully. Cynthia was holding her breath. April looked around the room, displeased at how messy the principal's office was. Susan was just ready to go and dig her coy pond.

April clicked her heels.

"I have to go to the church. Are we done here?"

"Yes." The principal replaced his glasses. "As Athena said, there will be a thorough investigation into these matters. Both for you, Mrs. Wolf-Thorne, and you, Ms. Scopello. The police and the school are working together. In the meantime, if you ladies hear your children say anything, please let us or the cops know. Don't interrogate them; that tends to make them shut up like vaults. Talk to them with care and openness. Children only lie if they are scared about how their parents will react. It's a tough line between being a parent and a friend, but a child should be able to talk to you...without fearing you. We all make mistakes as youths; the only way to not repeat them is to learn right from wrong."

They all exchanged farewells and pleasantries before exiting the principal's office.

April and Susan left to go to the church for a bake sale.

Leaving Cynthia, Lorraine and Athena headed toward their cars together.

"Such a shame." Athena opened her purse to remove her car keys. "I can't believe Rohypnol is going around the school."

Cynthia was too angry to speak.

"That's not what the doctors found in her system." Lorraine's normally beautiful, made-up face looked exhausted from being in the hospital with her daughter for most of the night. Worry and stress—and children—age you. "They found a decent amount of ketamine in her, as well as other drugs that were most likely mixed into her drinks."

Cynthia and Athena stopped her in her footsteps, as Athena blurted, "What? I thought she was roofied."

"She was." Lorraine attempted to keep the carefree song in her voice. "But one can be roofied by GHB and ketamine, as well as plenty of other things. The knowledge you wish you never have to know, right? Good day, ladies. Looking forward to your dinner party on Friday night, Athena."

"Yes, yes, bye," Cynthia snapped before turning toward her sister. "Athena, I swear…"

Athena turned to her surroundings and smiled at a teacher she knew who passed by. The slap she brought across her sister's face was seen by no one.

"We'll speak of this later." Athena's long strand of blond, braided hair swinging back and forth. "Where is my daughter?"

"It's last period now...she should be in science, no? Do you want me to come with you...I swear, Athena...I'm still trying to make amends for..."

"No, no, no." Athena smiled and wrapped her scarf around her neck. "I'll handle this." And she turned and made her way back into the school to find her daughter.

Cynthia scratched at her nose, removed her keys for her brand new fire red Mercedes, and went to walk across the parking lot, but was stopped in her tracks. She shivered as if a ghost was whispering in her ear.

A chill of nostalgia mixed with the horror of déjà vu.

Impossible.

But.

It was impossible.

An old, tan Mercedes sat in the parking lot. One with a scratch along one side.

"It's just impossible." Cynthia tried to laugh it off, but couldn't take her eyes off the vehicle. A vehicle that was so similar to a car she had a while back. She stood frozen for a second and, as the bell sounded, she jumped and dropped her purse. As she gathered her belongings, she whispered to herself, "This is foolish. The dead are dead. The dead are dead."

If only she had taken a look inside the car, she would have seen the same specially ordered plush white-leather seats and their unmistakable stain that had discolored the backseat…one she had made so many years ago.

- -

Samantha Rose was gracing the hallway with her presence, as usual. She was dressed better than everyone else in school, as usual. Her natural golden hair and bright jade eyes were made up to perfection, as usual. But…the looks she was getting…were unusual.

Did some volleyball dyke just sneer? Samantha held her gaze and confident air, but something was off. She began to feel fat again…like a child again…she felt a sound coming that she hadn't heard in years.

Lexi's last class was study hall and they were in the lunchroom now…

Samantha strutted right by her science room and ignored the bell; it would be the first time she'd ever missed a class…and that was okay, right?

Oink.

Samantha pushed into the lunchroom and Lexi was at their circular table in the middle of the room with her usual companions. A table over sat the jocks, seemingly less robust, as their leader was missing…. Samantha didn't care enough to ask her mom about Dax, but he was still in the hospital.

Samantha's table was the prized social table. Only the most beautiful and rich girls got to sit at it. If, for any reason, your outfit was off that day or you had upset Samantha, you sat in the hallway. They had taken *Mean Girls* and one upped it.

But even these rulings were off today.

Lexi's hair wasn't done and she was in sweatpants and an old cheerleading sweatshirt.

"Bitch." All the eyes at the table turned to Samantha. Her seat was taken by some sophomore cheerleader, but no one made to move. *Oink. Oink. Oink.* "I…I thought we always dressed up on game days, and you are in sweats. Guess you can't sit with us."

No one responded. Lexi stared at Samantha with a look Samantha had never encountered from her 'best friend' before; it was as if she didn't know her.

"Josh took me home last night, Samantha."

She had never used her full name before.

"Who's Josh?"

One of the girls at the table snorted and another flipped her phone open and began texting. Gossip was flying around the school and Samantha's phone has been silent all day. They didn't even look at Samantha. They watched Lexi, their new leader.

"Josh…your college boyfriend." Lexi let her eyes flutter back to her new court of followers. "He told me she didn't even remember his name. Called him Devon."

"One of you, get a chair for me."

"No." The youngest girl at the table turned her eyes on Samantha, a freshman Samantha had personally put on the cheerleading team. "No, you can't sit here."

"Is this slut kidding?" Samantha tossed her mane and flared her eyes. "I'm going to…"

"What?" Lexi dangerously growled in her direction. "Roofie her, too? I could have died if Josh hadn't taken me home; you were planning on just leaving me out there…and you asked him to rape me?"

"I…" Samantha stammered. "No. He's lying. You drank too much and…"

"The hospital ran a blood test, Samantha. You're the one who got me the drink. I watched you pour it yourself. You're…you're…" Lexi began to tear up and the two closest girls put their hands on her in support. "…supposed to be my best friend."

This wasn't an act; Lexi was actually upset; these were real emotions. Real tears.

"You should go."

"Don't bother showing up for the game tonight."

"You should move out of town."

"Samantha Rose is the witch of *Suburbia.*"

The bell rang for the end of the day, but Lexi and the girls stayed seated, holding their ground. All were now staring at Samantha. No more words were needed—she was being cast out of her own circle. The circle that she had built. A group of beautiful girls like no other, girls who would join sororities and grow up together and forever hold a bond. It was planned out. She had handpicked each one of these girls to be her friend.

Samantha felt her eye twitch as she turned on her new Gucci heels, stumbled slightly, and made her way out of the lunchroom in a skirt that cost more than what some of these kid's parents made in a week. Her hair was Japanese-straightened, her purse straight from the latest Juicy Couture line, diamond necklace, naturally tan skin, makeup done to perfection... *Oink.*

Oink. Oink. Oink. Oink. Oink.

OINK.

Todd passed Matthew the joint.

They were both seated in the back of Felicia's new-to-her tan Mercedes. It was after school and they had hidden as their parents left their meeting and headed off to their various *suburban* housewife activities.

It had been a stressful day, so why not get high?

"This is called Heller Kush, literally the best grass I can get." Todd coughed. "I have a connection across state who ships it. I have it sent to Old Mother Watson's house…we made a deal."

"What kinda deal?" Matthew blurry-eyed, looked over at Todd, who was messing up his own hair. "With that old woman?"

"I know things; I used to mow her lawn. The kind of deal that keeps us both out of trouble." Todd kept a watch out as Matthew took a hit off the joint. "I heard Samantha Rose drugged Lexi and tried to kill her."

"Dude." Matthew rolled his eyes. "That's ridiculous. They are best friends. Sam would never do that."

"Sam?" Todd laughed and choked as smoke puffed out of his nostrils. "Come on. You might as well call her Ms. Rose, for how close you two are."

"You don't know her." Matthew pushed a strand of hair away from his face. "Dude."

"God be blessed." Todd took a swig of Gatorade. "I bet you a hundred dollars if you got to know her, this huge boner you carry would be gone."

"I bet you're wrong, dude."

"Shake on it, then."

"Fine!" Matthew put the joint in his lip and shook Todd's hand.

April Mayfair had approved of this friendship from the beginning. The two boys couldn't have looked any different. Matthew with his shaggy dark hair, big lips, and blue puppy-dog eyes, and Todd with his golden mane, light pale eyes, and naturally tan skin. She was grateful that her son had a friend from a good family, even if that family wasn't attending church.

For not even Matthew knew that Todd wasn't in his room reciting Bible verses last night.

"Why did you get kicked out of your old school?" Matthew's head was against the back of the seat cushion and he was watching as the smoke and sun spun together. Like dancers in the sky. "What did you do wrong there?"

"Kicked out?" Todd laughed in shock, took a long second, looked Matthew over. Weighing the weight of this conversation. "I didn't get kicked out. Do you really...okay... Matthew, this is...there was this teacher who..."

The back door opened and, in a breeze of Dolce and Gabbana Light Blue perfume, Matthew and Todd found themselves completely shocked.

"Can I get a hit, please?"

"I...I...I...I...I..."

"Absolutely." Todd passed the joint across the car and hit Matthew in the chest. "Forgive my buddy; he gets a little high and words are lost to him."

Matthew would have been grateful that Todd had covered his tracks, but he was in absolute shock. Sitting next to him, grazing up against him with her bare leg, was Samantha Rose.

As she inhaled the joint between baby-pink lips and exhaled like a pro out of her nose, she placed her matching nails over her lips and coughed politely.

"Sorry." She giggled—a magical sound. "Beginner's lungs."

Todd never took his eyes off her face, following every move, every emotion and trying to catch the falter…the lie. But if she was pretending, she was in a league comparable to his. This wasn't the fat girl he saved from bullying so many years ago; this was a calculating machine.

But Matthew had no idea. She may as well have been the goddess of love to him. Aphrodite herself who had just sat next to him. Fool.

"I decided to let Lexi take captain on the cheer squad tonight," Samantha said in a sad voice, pouting her lips perfectly. "I feel so bad that one of the older guys at the party last night drugged her. Let her feel special tonight; I get to lead the squad all the time. I felt it was only the right thing to do as her best friend."

"One of the older guys, eh?" Todd retorted between inhales of smoke. "Is that the story everyone is telling?"

"Well, it's the truth. I had thought I loved my college boyfriend, James, but he not only drugged my best friend last night—he tried to rape her! Then placed all the blame on me." Samantha's hand went to her chest and a perfect tear rolled down her face, "Why would I drug someone I care about so much? Why are guys so mean? Telling lies to keep themselves out of trouble. People can just be so cruel."

"Oh, yes." Todd knew what he was up against now. "People can just be awful, can't they?"

Her blond locks fell onto Matthew's shoulder and she rubbed her head just enough into his neck.

Bravo, bitch. Todd was loving the performance, but Matthew couldn't see past his own desire.

"You can hang out with us tonight." Matthew looked hopefully over at Todd, who nodded slowly in approval. "It'd be our pleasure.

Sure, Todd thought *Why not see where this is leading.*

"Yes." Todd grabbed the joint from her hand. "Our pleasure."

"Oh." Samantha wiped away the tear. "You guys are so sweet. It'd be fun for all of us to hang out before my mother's dinner party tomorrow night. Have a kid's night out. There is this club that has teen nights on a Thursday called Illusions. Or this party just on the outskirts of town; it would be so much fun. Oh, can we go, Matthew? I would love to dance my night away...with someone."

Todd could have sworn Matthew's pants grew nine inches in that second. Yup, Todd had seen Matthew naked once and he had a Pringles can in his pants. Matthew's face was brightening up so much he could have produced light in the dark.

"I'd love to, absolutely, yes. Whatever makes you feel better."

"Let's get out of here." Felicia opened the driver's side door of her car and looked into the back. *Oink*. "Oh...uh... what's...did I miss something?"

"Oh, Felicia," Samantha chirped as if the two were the closest of friends. "The boys invited me out for a night of dancing. I'd love if you came! I don't even need to go home; let's just go to a diner and get some food and head out. I've had such a hard day."

"Please." Matthew's eyes were looking desperately at Felicia, who let out a sigh.

Why is he so blind? The answer: because he was so kind.

"Yes." Todd's eyes never left Samantha's. Such a hard day...you poor girl."

"Right...I have a lot of homework to do, though." Felicia slowly got into her car that had been invaded. "But... sure."

"Oh fun!" Samantha laughed. "A new night with new friends. I'll get in the passenger seat! Shotgun! Shotgun!"

Samantha bounced out of the car, pleased with herself, and opened up the passenger door and got in, grazing her eyes over the lovely girl Felicia had grown into. When she was a bully, she'd almost looked like a drug addict. Underfed orphan full of rage. But now...she was this perfectly structured redhead with skin that needed no makeup. Samantha hadn't forgotten, and today was a reminder above all else where the taunting had come from.

Felicia was the one who set Samantha's entire clock into motion.

Felicia was the first one to ever *oink* at her.

Karma comes to all. Samantha paid today...and tonight, Samantha would pay Felicia back.

OINK.

Maxine Johnson's Personal Diary
Winter, 1996

Dear Diary,

Today, April Mayfair's daughter vanished.

Grace. What a beautiful name.

She was there one second and gone the next.

I was lying down after a small cup of afternoon tea—does that tea knock me out—when I heard the pounding on my door. Heavens to Betsy. I thought it was a fire.

But this…this is much worse.

Have you seen Grace?

Have you seen my Grace?

Have you seen Grace?

April Mayfair, the most frazzled I have ever seen her. One can hide if they are having a bad day because of superficial reasons, but when something actually happens that will change your life? You can't hide that.

I had not seen Grace. I had been home all day trying to write poetry and half-attempting to clean the house.

Have you seen Grace? Over and over she asked. Have you seen Grace? Have you seen Grace?

Grace, only a few years older than Todd, is (was?) such a beautiful little girl. Pale eyes and messy gold hair that runs in the Mayfair family…dimples on the girl's cheeks, a skip in her step, and a sweet smile on her face.

Gone. Just gone.

What would that sensation be like?

I've known death.

I've known tragedy.

But I have never had a child lost to me. It's not a necklace that your grandmother left you that was misplaced; it's not a dog that runs off in the middle of the night…

When I was a little girl in the country, Mama bought me a puppy. I foolishly let him off his leash and he ran and ran. Much faster than I could. Ran right into a car's rolling tire. I remember that feeling of emptiness.

But your own flesh and blood…something you created…

Would I care if my little girl vanished one day?

After all I have done to her…

Would I experience the same terror?

Felicia, whose creation is a blank space in time for me, whose amber eyes flicker with gold that resemble neither mine nor Larry's.

My little monster. Why a monster? Why do I continue to refer to her as a monster? Why not my little girl? Why do I constantly hurt her…praise the Heavens she was not taken.

As I write, dear diary, there seems to be missing time. The anger that comes to me when I think of her…why can't

I place its origin? Lapses of moments and blurred reality. The amount of haze that clouds my mind from unfounded sources. A pregnancy I can barely recall, a conception I have no idea of, and a child that I…I…that I…it had been a curling iron the last time. A cheese grater. A…

What would be next.

Why am I doing this to her?

Seeing a doctor was always considered a sign of weakness in my family, but I do feel weak. I'm ignoring something. Something has been lost and it must be found.

Have you seen my Grace? April was going door-to-door asking the same question. What if that was me?

I will call my neighbor; I'm lucky to have a renowned doctor living right on our street, one who is a friend. I'll call ██████████████████████████. I hope as much confidentiality holds true and the doctor won't tell anyone when I reach out, but ████████████████ reputation is stellar and most of the townspeople are clients of ████████████ ████████████████

Perhaps it can help answer my questions. Maybe that will put names to what comes scratching in the night. Maybe. Just maybe. I will understand why I do…what I do to a child…whom I can't recall why I hate.

Diary, we have reached that point. I am asking for help. We are lost together, but let's be found.

The Night before Athena's Dinner Party
Late Fall, 2004

"What's your name...Hasheem?" Cynthia took a long step out of her brand-new red Mercedes SL that she had roared all the way around town before pulling up into her endless driveway to Thorne Hall. The giant diamonds on her ears she had bought today hadn't been enough; she had bags filled with expensive dresses. Shopping kept her mind from... from...

"Jesus Christ! Can you put someone whose name doesn't sound like a sneeze on the phone?"

Dax, her son, the bully of *Suburbia*. Why hadn't the Captain told her? They had made an agreement to always tell each other everything. Putting kids in the hospital? Forcing families to move out of town? This wasn't the son she raised.... was it?

Cynthia always felt like the Queen of Thorne Hall. It never gave her more pleasure than to scorn and command people from her castle. The stone walls rose high and the windows always seemed dark; it was not a happy castle. Castles weren't meant to impress, but to intimidate.

Roses and thorns covered most of the exterior and it seemed, as the years passed, the closer they wrapped.

Cynthia remembered the day her mother had brought her up to Thorne Hall as a teenager; Athena hadn't bothered coming. She had met Benjamin at a young age and it'd just happened. He was attractive and successful and she was set. But Cynthia had always had trouble making friends, and boys had been scared of her. She never cared, but her mother did. So she brokered the arrangement between Cynthia and Abraham…and it had worked out, right? One of the many things she would like to scorn her mother about—it was a pity how she died—but that old crone was better out of the picture.

Cynthia had been so nervous her first day at Thorne Hall; it was the largest home she had seen in her life. It rambled for tens of thousands of square feet on a hundred acres and overlooked the entire town as if it owned it. And, it just so happened, the inhabitants of Thorne Hall had worked hard enough to ensure they did.

Now it was hers. Cynthia let her spine straighten as she headed for the front doors, returning to roar at the man on the phone who had answered the wrong call that day.

"Aunt…Cynthia?" A strong voice came from behind her. Turning, she almost dropped her purse, flipping the phone shut without ending the call. She hadn't seen her nephew, Lucas Rose, in four years, since that terrible day his father had committed suicide.

"You've grown!" Cynthia strode forward and embraced her nephew, whose hug was cold. Pushing away from him, she smiled naturally. "You look just like your mother. Perfect at every corner, in every corner, in every annoying way."

He didn't smile at the joke.

Cynthia took a long stride backward to get a look at him.

The last time she had seen him, he was a pot-smoking collegian at some Ivy-League school studying law or psychology or justice or whatever. Now he was a young man, gifted with his mother's looks. Samantha had all her father's features and they made her beautiful, but this boy was singular. Trouble. Intelligence and beauty mixed together were dangerous.

"Where is my mother?"

"Why, dear?"

"I'd like to have a few words with her."

"About?"

"You are very inquisitive today, eh?"

"I am your aunt."

"Yes…yes, you are. How is my sister?"

"Blossomed."

"I figured as much by now. Hers was always destined to be that of the tale of the ugly swan. Though my mother would have loved her if she'd had a hunchback and a lazy eye. Would you? Probably not."

"That's not a nice thing to say about your aunt, dear."

Lucas smiled handsomely at Cynthia, who returned the smile. Dressed in a fine gray suit jacket, expensive-looking jeans, and a green shirt that made his emerald eyes pop, he smiled politely and handed over a business card for the local hotel.

"I'm staying just down the road."

"You are more than welcome to stay here, nephew."

"Oh no." Lucas gazed over Thorne Hall with distaste and faked a shudder. "Place is creepy and I would require a priest to perform an exorcism before I stepped inside. Please, tell my mother to come visit me. I wrote the room number on the back of the card. Maybe in another four years I'll see you again, Aunt Cynthia."

As Lucas Rose strolled casually away, Cynthia Thorne let all her breath out.

"Shit," she muttered too loudly. "Shit. Shit. Shit."

Cynthia, as fast as her stilettos could take her, made her way up to the enormous mahogany doors of Thorne Hall and let herself in. The doors opened up to an unnecessary large entrance foyer anchored by a floor of black-and-white cut French marble in a distressed design that circled around itself. Above, a magnificent crystal-cut chandelier exploded the otherwise dark entrance with light.

"Rosaletta!" Purse!" Cynthia tossed her purse at the stairs as the maid scurried out. "Quicker next time. Ridiculous. What am I paying you…"

But even this wasn't cheering her up. Was he home? Could he possibly be home? She made her way up the large winding staircase and across the open hall lined with the cold ivory rug to the west wing of the house. A golden fire's glow was coming from underneath a set of double doors, the only light in an otherwise darkened hallway.

Cynthia Thorne pushed opened the doors and entered her husband's office. Abraham Thorne was reclined in his large plush leather chair, smoking a large cigar, the fire bouncing off his dark glasses. He held up a large finger to keep his wife silent so his call wasn't interrupted.

He continued with his call. "Neil…"

"I prefer Mr. Mayor."

"Yes, of course, Mr. Mayor…if I may just…"

"It'd be like someone not referring to you as Captain. You didn't work all this way doing what you have done to be called otherwise. Though…" a long pause hung heavy from the end of the mayor's office line, "…are you a boat captain? A plane captain? Or do you captain an air balloon; could a hot-air balloon even lift you up. You are one heavy man for…"

"It's a title my father held, as did his father beforehand, and his father… What is the relevance, Mr. Mayor?"

"Oh, you are being very disagreeable today." A long, drawn-out silence from the other end of the line as the Captain's hand tightened until his entire fist turned red. "I have another appointment. We will touch upon this matter another time; you will see the light, or I will not help you on that night. A poem! Farewell."

Click.

"I had to lie about who I was to get him on the phone." The Captain turned around in his chair and slammed one hand against the table as he forced a pleasant, charming smile that beamed through his beard. "Your cousin."

"I know." Cynthia slumped down into the chair across from her husband. "Pour me a scotch."

"Of course, my love," Abraham smiled and poured from the crystal set on his enormous mahogany desk. A desk fit for a warrior or a captain. "You look troubled. Why are you troubled?"

"Lucas Rose… Three fingers, Abraham, not one. I'm not a teenage girl. I know how to drink, for God's sake." Cynthia snatched the glass and downed it. "Our nephew is back in town. Looking for his mother and being inquisitive."

The Captain Abraham Thorne let out a ho-ho-ho and pushed himself up from his chair. With his golden cane in hand, he walked proudly to the window that overlooked the front of Thorne Hall's massive lawn. From the window, you could see the tops of all the houses in the community, little boxes all laid out before Thorne Hall. Little boxes of various colors. Little boxes that he owned.

The Captain tapped the expensive cane against his hand. "Lucas smokes too much marijuana. Paranoia. No need to tell your sister he's back in town. I'm sure he's just here for a family visit. I'll...I'll visit him."

"You don't need to." Cynthia could not protest fast enough. "He is harmless. A child. I'll handle him."

"Then you shall visit him tonight after you go to dinner with your sister. Athena invited you out. I need this cousin of yours back under control. He went wandering around at our last foundation ball."

"What does that matter?"

"Just something...something has changed."

"Well, I'd rather serve Rosaletta a home-cooked meal than go out to dinner with my..."

"Cynthia." Abraham turned and snapped, the fire bouncing off his dark glasses, then it was back to a gleaming smile and grace. "I can't get a handle on what your sister is still doing here. We've offered to buy her a house. Build her a house. Nor has she discussed what was in that will her husband left her. She makes me uncomfortable. A widow wandering the halls watching me."

"Watching you? Now who's paranoid? Athena makes no one comfortable; everyone..."

"Yes." Abraham brought the cane around and smacked it against his desk, as if he was testing its sturdiness. "Everyone loves Athena, but I don't fall for that perfect housewife routine. Your sister is up to something, Cynthia. In the past few months, she's begun to bloom again. I've noticed she leaves the mansion more and more. She is up to something. Make sure your ducks are in a row. Mine are. Dinner tomorrow night should be pleasant, and if you go to dinner with her tonight, you can ensure that. Get a grasp on what she is still doing here, have her call her cousin…tell him I'll…do as he requests, as long as he continues suit at our next foundation ball."

"What do you need him for, anyway?" Cynthia looked her husband over. "Also, why did the principal need to tell me that Dax is the school bully? Apparently you have received a ton of phone calls."

"Cynthia." The Captain again hit the cane against his desk. "So much goes on between these walls, and outside them. It's hard to keep up with all the details. Dax just got back from the hospital and is pretty broken; not a time to discuss his bullying. Also, don't bother yourself with my deal with your cousin; just make sure Athena tells him…I'll do as he requests."

Cynthia swung the rest of the scotch down her throat. "Lets go over my checklist. I will be going to dinner; see if I can't convince Athena to have the mayor continue our foundation tradition. After, I will visit Lucas. Have I covered enough wifely duties for this year…husband?"

"Yes, love." Abraham smiled and sat back in his giant leather chair. "Aren't you forgetting something?" Abraham pointed to his cheek.

"You are joking, right?"

"Right." A wicked smile spread across the Captain's face. "Why should we bother with marital duties now? As I say...life is like...life is like a bar of soap. Once you think you've got a hold of it, it slips away."

Not one of his best analogies.

"As you say, husband." Cynthia was out of his office and closed the wooden doors, shutting out the fireplace light that was igniting the cold hallway. "Rosaletta! Rosaletta!"

Cynthia had some time before dinner with her sister—why not torture the maid a little?

"Why won't you do anything?" Lexi screamed at her mother in their newly remodeled kitchen. "She drugged me in front of the entire school, tried to have me raped. I have a witness! She can't get away with this."

"Your wailing is exhausting, Alexandra," Lorraine snapped back at her daughter, a mother dog biting at her pup when it chews too much of the bone. Lorraine was tapping her nails on her new granite counter and looking at her daughter with a look that she would never allow anyone to see in public. "Get over it. It's technically your fault, anyway."

"How…why?"

"You were honestly dumb enough to think that girl was your friend?" Lorraine laughed at her daughter and lit a cigarette. "I saw the way she's been glancing at you. For missing that, it is your own fault. Get a grip. It is you and I in this world and if we are going to make it, we have to be tough."

"Tough?" Lexi coughed at the smoke being blown her way. "You've been acting like you are running for the Mayor of Stepford since we got here. You never baked, cooked, cleaned, or dressed up like that before. You look like some overly polished doll that…"

The slap came full force across the table, sending Lexi tumbling. Lorraine stepped like a general around and over her daughter on the floor. "If I had ever spoken to my mother like that, she would have washed my mouth out with soap then smacked me around." Lorraine took a long inhale of her cigarette, her eyes squinting. "We all have to play our parts. This isn't the old lot. You were no prom princess back then. Now you are prancing around like queen of the crop, spreading your legs…"

"Mom!"

"…for every varsity jock. The Captain has been very generous, without asking for much, or for anything I'm not

168

willing to do. So I will continue to bake cookies for luncheons and Bible study and," she placed her hand on her chest and swooned back. "Heavens to Betsy, not speak poorly of our fine neighbors in our fine town."

"But we are losing who we are. None of my friends from back home would've ever tried to drug me at a party. For how much nicer it is here, the people are not. If this is *Suburbia*, move us back to our trailer park."

"Never. I will never return to a one-level house on wheels." Lorraine walked toward the window and looked over at Mother Watson's house, which was across the street. Mother Watson was outside, in an adorable old-lady gardening outfit ripping the weeds from her large lawn. She immediately saw her and waved politely, and Lorraine hid the cigarette behind her and beamed her dumb-blond grin.

"I'm enjoying these games much more than the games I had to play to keep us afoot in the white-trash disaster we came from. You'd be lying if you told me any different. Do you want to go back to sharing a bathroom? Not having enough food on our plates?"

"But…" Lexi was flustered. "What if Mrs. Mayfair or even Mrs. Thorne found out…"

"I don't think we have to worry about Cynthia for much longer." Lorraine smiled, overconfident. "I think the Captain has a place for us up at Thorne Hall, as I have been giving him a place to put other things."

"Mom!" Lexi put her hands to her ears. "You are disgusting."

"I will give him what he wants, Alexandra." Lorraine put the cigarette out in the sink and turned to get a cake mix out of the newly refinished cabinets. That's all that lined her shelves, mixes and boxes of stuff that required some water or an egg. None of these 'real housewives' would ever bake from a box; everything of theirs is homemade. They had never tasted mixes before, so Lorraine got away with it. "Now, go fix your face and act like a lady. I have to bake a hundred cupcakes for Jesus or some shit. Plus, we have dinner tomorrow night at Thorne Hall—don't mess this up for mama."

"I'm not hungry," Kat McArthur chirped cheerfully and very quickly Katie's mouth opened with a, "Neither am I. Peas. Bleh."

Susan McArthur smiled warily at her two daughters and took a long sip from the giant coffee mug she had filled with gin. The withdrawals were almost gone at this point, but, boy, did a little gin help it along.

"Go to bed, then, girls."

Both girls looked at each other and spread those smiles. The same smile her son Matthew had, the same smile her husband Gregory had…not her smile. Their eyes were all the same. Her husband's genes were stronger. It showed. As if she hadn't even had these children, but this was the physical. The mental was there. The internal was there. The love and what mattered was there. Susan got up and went over and hugged her two beautiful girls, who awed and hugged her back.

"We love you, Momma."

"We love you so much."

"I love you, too, girls." Susan whispered into their ears. Little innocent angels with beautiful faces and the smile of her beloved husband. "I love you so much."

Matthew was always off with his new friends now, which was fine. Her husband was right. He was a teenager and teenagers should be off with friends.

"Don't leave me," she confessed, though she was unsure whether these words were for her girls or her husband or what. But she had been so lonely.

"You can stop hugging us, Mommy."

"It's starting to hurt, Mommy."

"I'm sorry, dears." Susan kissed them both on their foreheads before wrapping up their perfectly good steaks and the homemade mashed potatoes, all of which she had shopped for that day and prepared herself. "Go run along. Tomorrow I will take you both to the park before I go to Athena's dinner party."

"Thanks, Mommy!"

"So much fun!"

Kat and Katie grasped hands, giggled to each other, and ran off talking about who would swing first or push first tomorrow at the park. They would always have each other, no matter what, and there was a comfort in that that Susan could never describe.

Susan stood at the sink and began to clean the dishes. Looking out at her acre of backyard. The summer flowers had all died out by now and mums scattered her view, the leaves had begun to turn. A cascade of crimson-and-pumpkin-colored leaves which would soon spin down from their branches and cover the grass in a blanket of fall's spectrum of color. Soon they would carve pumpkins and the twins had come to love shopping for Halloween costumes.

Susan gripped the sink for a moment.

Why was it so painful being here?

The front door opened and her husband was home from work. Pale, but a bright smile on his face. "Well." He came and kissed his wife hello. "Your husband landed a big check today. Got a promotion. Maybe we can hire someone to finish the coy pond you are trying to build."

"Not trying." Susan put a hand on her husband's face, though it wasn't his face. It wasn't the face of the man she'd married; the face of the man she went to college with. This was a new face, and a face that made her sad. "We will have fish in there by next summer; I'm seeing this project through myself. Buy something for Matthew, or the girls. Sit. I saved you a dish. It's heated."

"If it's okay," Gregory said and smiled, but it was too much. It was forced. "I'm going to shower. I'm not really that hungry."

Susan noticed that under his collar was a large bandage, blood seeping through it. She went to remove the bandage, but he firmly moved her hand away.

"A little accident at work today. I just need to change it. Don't want you to get your hands soaked in blood."

"What kind of accident?"

"For Christ's sake, Susan," Gregory McArthur snapped at her in a tone she had never heard. "I'm bringing home money; I'm working long hours. When I get home, just have dinner ready for me and be pleasant; is that too much to ask?"

"I said I had a dish prepared..."

"I'm going to bed."

She met his eyes and they were looking everywhere but at her—he wasn't angry at her.

"I can't come to the dinner party tomorrow night; the Captain has a job for me. I'm sorry," Gregory said as he turned from her.

Her eyes were now open; her brain was now clear.

"Go to bed, love." Susan smiled comfortably at him, her insides twisting. "I'll be fine at the dinner party myself."

Looking around the interior of her house, her perfect *suburban* residence. The new kitchen, the oriental rug, the brand-new furniture, the 65-inch TV…it all began to look so ugly and feel dreadfully unsafe.

Gregory had left his suitcase at the door. Susan quietly went over to it. Locked. She tried both the twin's birthdays, then her own, then tried 1234. The Gregory she knew couldn't remember his own phone number, let alone a suitcase number. The suitcase popped open and a thick blue folder sat there.

Inside was a list of women's names. A folder she didn't know what to do with, but maybe Athena did. Susan slipped into the office and made copies while peeking out of the room to make sure no one was coming.

She put the blue folder back in his briefcase and put her copy in her purse.

As Susan went to her phone to text Athena, she turned to her perfect home and hated every inch of it. Something terribly wrong was going on here.

"I can leave my car here?" Felicia asked for the third time. She was scratching at her right arm. "I mean...is it safe?"

"Of course, silly." Samantha's smile never faltered. "Why wouldn't it be?"

Samantha was pulling her long golden strands back into a ponytail and tying the pink tie around tightly. She bounced off in her pastel Abercrombie plaid skirt with the white top that let her boobs bounce freely and, Felicia noticed, wherever her boobs bounced, Matthew's eyes followed.

Matthew's eyes were so busy watching the way that Samantha's waist twitched from side to side, he didn't seem to notice what a terrible area they were in. Felicia wasn't one to judge. Not everyone comes from means and, for a short while, she was in the foster system; she knew struggle. Plus, it wasn't about mansions versus shacks. Her weed dealer lived in a tiny trailer with his entire family and was more welcoming than the richest family in town. Thorne Hall may just as well have been a work camp for the vibes that place gave off. In Felicia's experience, it wasn't brand-new Mercedes verses twenty-year-old, barely starting minivan. It was the type of person you were...but that wasn't the point.

This was a scenario that portends tragedy.

Felicia's first clue was when they turned out of town into an area she had never seen. It left a pit in her stomach.

They had driven a couple miles down a dirt road with no lights when they pulled up to a small house that was situated right against the forest. It was a small house that no one had seemingly taken care of since it was built. The shutters were cracked, the windows dusty, the porch falling apart, and the door looked like it needed to be moved physically to get in and out of.

Also, the crowd wasn't one Felicia had ever seen before. That said something. Back in her early teenage years, she had run with the questionable kids, then with the kids who weren't just questionable, but forbidden from house parties. These weren't just other-side-of-the-tracks kids…these were kids who were banned from *Suburbia* and regular humanity altogether.

This was the end of the road.

"How many times are you going to lock your car, silly?" The 'silly' was dragged out by Samantha's valley-girl accent that Felicia had decided long ago could not be real. She had a hand on her hip and was taunting her… Felicia was slowly putting all the rage in her rage box, but she felt like once she reached 'one,' she would open it just an inch and punch Samantha directly in the…

Put the rage in a box, Salome's calming voice was in her head. *Put it in a box and lock it up there. Lock it up there and be the bigger person. This is one night; just get it over with.*

"Well." Todd didn't look fazed in his forever boarding-school attire, a red polo with the gold accents, his golden hair perfectly pulled back. "This looks like it should be fun."

Samantha twinkled and grabbed Todd's and Matthew's hands and began to sashay her way up to the house. No, this wasn't a house...a shanty would have been a nice description...it was a dump. Felicia followed closely and felt the eyes on her. The hungry eyes of men without a care.

They entered the party. A white substance that normally Felicia would know as coke was laid across the table, but...these kids couldn't afford coke. Giant trash cans were filled with a murky liquid.

"Devenio!" Samantha called out to the roughest-looking man in the room, one covered in tattoos with juiced muscles and a face that looked like a crater. "I'm here."

The entire room's eyes were on them. As if a homeless man had entered a black-tie affair. They were too clean. They were dressed too nicely. Their hair was cut. Not one of them had rips in their jeans. Felicia even felt it, and she had once been the leader of the rough crowd, but that's when they were kids... The older you get, the more dangerous the games you play.

Toy guns become real guns.

But there stood Samantha Rose. Proud. Like the prom queen she believed she was destined to be.

"I want to go," Felicia whispered to Todd. "Now."

But Todd ignored her, his eyes on Samantha.

"Damn you," she whispered to him. "For once, forget your obsession with the demented and deranged and…"

"You brought these people?" Devenio was eyeing them with displeasure. "Why?"

"I'm allowed to have friends, silly." Samantha was filling up party cups with her back to them in the decaying kitchen. The stove seemed to have never been cleaned, the fridge never wiped down. "Here…friends."

Felicia heard the tone she used. Why did she allow this to transpire? Samantha had two blue cups and two green ones. Specifically handing a green one to Matthew, one to Todd, and one blue cup to Felicia, taking a proud sip of her own.

"Let's get this party started, guys!" Samantha turned to the room and tossed her hands in the air. "Let's have some fun!"

Clouds were gathering above the old black-and-purple Victorian on the other edge of the forest. A home that had sat on the edge of town for as long as the Thornes had held their rule.

A house that was no stranger to horror.

Mailbox number 666.

Don't trick or treat at that house.

No solicitors came here.

A house that knew fortitude.

Sufferance.

Temperance.

Salome Legree was in her living room staring at the invitation to Athena Rose's dinner party she had found in Felicia's room. A crooked smile on her face.

"What will I wear?" Salome chuckled to herself wickedly. "What shall I wear?"

Samantha grabbed Felicia's arm.

"Let us girls have some fun," Samantha whispered right into Felicia's ear. "Shall we?"

"Sure," the redheaded bitch from Samantha's childhood said with a confidence that made her stomach churn.

You won't be so proud of yourself for long.

Not for long.

"Boys, play nice." Samantha winked right at Matthew, who literally hadn't said a word the entire night because of his obsession. She would deal with him later. Wait until the drugs kicked in from the spiked drink and either kiss him until he felt like she loved him and never call him again or just tear his heart right out.

He was such a weak puppy dog; whatever she did would destroy him forever. It all depended on her mood. But first…

"Did you notice we are the only girls here? These guys must feel so lucky to actually have some pretty faces around for once." Samantha had her arm wrapped in Felicia's as if they were the best of friends. "Finish your drink, silly. It's a party!"

"I wasn't in the mood to drink tonight."

"Drink." Was the word forced? Was it too harsh? Careful. This has to be done just right. "Try and have some fun…hun!" Samantha swallowed the entirety of her drink to make Felicia feel comfortable. It must have worked, as Felicia followed suit…only a few more gulps…drink the drink. Drink it.

Felicia smiled. A pretty smile. The girl was beautiful. Red hair. Fair complexion. Beautiful amber eyes with golden sparkles. Samantha paused. Only one other person she knew had those eyes, but, at that moment, she couldn't place him or her. A promising body that would only become more desirable as the years progressed. But the girl didn't try to look good. For her, it was au-natural.

Oink.

"Where are you taking me?" Felicia asked as she finished her drink and left the blue cup on a broken nightstand cluttered with empty syringes and cigarette butts. It wouldn't be long now.

Down a twisted, dark hallway they went. Closed doors with ominous lights came out from under them. A black light from one, red from another. But Samantha led her to the end of the hallway and opened the door.

It was a dirty room with a single light bulb hanging from the ceiling. Red swinging back and forth.

No. This was the end of the road.

A carpet stained with time and mistreatment.

Samantha had waited almost five years for this.

A dirty mattress thrown on the floor.

Samantha swung the door shut and tossed her giant purse into the corner. She pushed Felicia, who stumbled over her feet, onto the mattress.

"It's Devenio's birthday. I brought him a few presents. In my bag is enough ketamine and the other drugs to put down a hundred orphans like you. He's going to pay me for them. Then he'll pay me for you." Samantha laughed, not the girly, ditzy wail she let on, but something dark. "Oink, bitch. You are about to be the pig for this entire party. Oink."

Felicia put a hand to her head. The drugs must have been sinking in already.

Looking around terrified, she let out, "But why?"

"Why? Really, ginger bitch?" Samantha got on her knees and brought her face so close to Felicia's that she could smell her, so that Felicia could take in Samantha Rose in all her wonder. "You were the devil of my youth. You bullied me the minute you figured out how to. I was a fat little kid and you took advantage of that and made me cry more times than I can count. I took shit from you for years! Now who's the pig? Now who's…who's…my head…my…"

In a swift move, Felicia grabbed Samantha by her shoulders and swapped their places. Raising herself up to her full height, she glared down at Samantha, a look of pure hatred in her amber-and-gold eyes.

"I was willing to give you the benefit of the doubt today," Felicia began, each word pointed. Each word perfect in its use. She pulled up on her sheer, long-sleeve shirt and revealed an arm covered in various bruises. A cigarette burn here, a knife cut there, and other wounds that one could only imagine how were formed. "Do you know what happened to me in that house? Do you have any idea what I went through before my mother…vanished from my life? I served as an outlet for this unknown rage she possessed. Have you ever had a cheese grater taken to your skin? Have you ever been locked in a room while it is over a hundred degrees outside with no food or water for days? If Matthew removed his wallpaper, he would see *help* scratched in by my fingernails, just hoping my father would stop this madness. But he didn't. No one did. From birth till my parents' disappearance, I was a punching bag for rage. So…I was a bitch at thirteen and took some of my anger out on you. You were a fat, spoiled little girl and I was cut and beaten on every inch of my body. I loved my mother. When she took the cheese grater in her hand, I was saying 'I love you' over and over, hoping she would... I love you mommy, I said... she didn't stop...and... I have repented for my sins. When I was adopted, I was also saved. I was taught kindness, tenderness, love and compassion. I grew up. I've make amends for my actions and the person I was turned into. I didn't ask to be brought into this world; I didn't ask to be tortured and abused for the first part of my life. But you. What happened to you? As beautiful as you are on the outside is as rotten as you are down to that charred core. No, no, no. This isn't how life is going to be for you. I won't allow it. I won't allow you to prance around with that fake valley-girl accent and your mother's beauty tarnishing your family's name. No. You are not going to go around drugging people. Hurting people. Hurting Lexi. Hurting me. Hurting Matthew. I **love** him. At least, I think I do. My mother screwed up that emotion for me years ago, but regardless, whatever I feel for him is purer than any emotion you have ever had. So, let's play your game."

Samantha felt the ketamine drug mix kicking in. Mentally there, but physically uncontrolled. She couldn't move. She couldn't speak. She had lost all control of herself for the first time in her life.

"Now. Is this how we play?" Felicia pulled off her long-sleeve shirt, took off her glasses, let down her hair, and shook her gorgeous fire of a mane out. Her tight jeans and tank top were enough to show off her body. She went over and picked up Samantha's huge purse and pulled out Samantha's phone. "Look, Devenio texted you. 'Ready?' Oh, yes, we are ready."

Felicia shot a text back. In minutes the door burst open and Devenio, along with three of his gnarly-looking followers, entered. Big guys who had never seen the gym, nor under a girl's skirt.

"I thought the redhead…"

"Devenio." Felicia's hand fell onto his chest in the flirting way Samantha mastered so well. Tossing her hair about, she let out a valley-girl laugh. She opened the purse. "A gift from me to you…keep your money. Do what you want with this one. A birthday present should be a present. Maybe throw some dollars at her, make it rain. Ha-ha."

Felicia looked at Samantha once more, a look of pure disgust. "*Oink*…bitch."

Felicia sashayed out of the room the same way Samantha had walked into the party, slamming the door shut behind her. Devenio turned his drugged and hungry eyes on Samantha, as did his friends.

She gagged as they literally tore her clothes off her.

It didn't matter.

She couldn't have screamed even if she'd wanted to.

Susan McArthur's twin daughters were watching her from their bedroom, which overlooked the backyard, digging the coy pond she had so diligently been working on. It was night, her husband had taken a few of her last pills, and was passed out on the couch; Susan assumed her girls were asleep.

She knocked her shoe into the shovel and scooped out another large chunk of dirt. She was almost there. In more ways than one, she had begun to sleep again; her moods were leveling out and she, though it was a struggle, resisted all cravings. The pills were out of her system and, for the first time in a long time, the woman her husband married was back.

But now he was no longer the man she'd married. *What went on at that power plant,* she thought as she struck the ground and pulled up dirt.

From a window, the twins watched. Kat on one side, Katie on the other. Gregory hated to admit it, but he sometimes confused the two. Their personalities were so similar and they looked exactly alike. Sometimes twins have some similar traits, but even when these two spoke, it was in unison.

"Mommy seems to be better."

"Seems, yes."

"Projects are always fun for us."

"She's found a project of her own."

"Maybe we should flush more of her vitamins…"

"…and get a pool instead of a coy pond."

The girls giggled to each other and hopped down to play in their room. They picked up their dolls and began to act out adult themes. Playing house like adults, kissing the husband and wife together. The family had two children and in their giant dollhouse one was on the roof and the other the floor.

Little girls, naive and happy in just being alive.

Oh, what a far cry it is from the worries of a child to those of an adult.

Susan was lost in thought as she dug up more dirt.

Moving here was not a sober choice, and was one she was beginning to regret. Matthew could finish school here; they could send him to college. Then take the girls, flip the house, and move somewhere far away.

More dirt thrown. Another kick into the ground.

Drugs were no excuse to be the poor mother she had become. With a clear head, she needed to move, before her husband completely vanished, so she could find a way to fix their reality.

More dirt thrown. Another hard kick into the ground.

Maybe her husband understood. Katie and Kat only understood games and Matthew was busy downloading porn and watching girls' skirts twitch. She had to force him to do homework…school; what a joke. All their phones had calculators on them—at what point in life would what happened in 1661 matter? When did one ever use advanced trigonometry in their life?

Children. They should be taught morals. Taught how to balance a checkbook. How to get a job. Support a family. Be decent human beings and express love. These should be the lessons of their early years. No one needs to know all fifty states and their capitals. They need to know how to protect themselves when life hits hard. Schools keep them young, keep them pure, keep them naive. Children. If they could only know.

"You make a lot of noise." A half-pleasant voice startled Susan, who almost swung the shovel around, but they were in *Suburbia*. Before her stood a woman dressed in a dark orange dress with a spider web-like shawl tossed over her shoulders. "At first I thought you were burying a body, but after the eighth night of watching you out here, I figured otherwise. Pond?"

"Coy pond, yes. When I lived in the city I always wanted one, and now that I have the chance and time….I'm sorry." Susan wiped sweat off her brow and quickly ran a hand through her hair. "I'm Susan McArthur. I didn't mean to disturb you…You live…"

"Iris Lane. The street behind you. Well, the house behind you. Priscilla Primm." she held out a hand and Susan quickly rubbed the dirt off her dress and shook it. Priscilla's hands were soft and so were all her features. Soft and kind eyes, skin that looked like silk, and a wrap of dark red hair pulled back tight, a long, red metal stick holding it back.

"Funny." Susan rested her arm on the shovel. "We've been here for years and never met. I moved in in 2000."

"I remember that day. I was baking tarts for the school fair. I meant to drop over, but one of my children we thought had pneumonia and needed constant care. Then, honestly, it slipped my mind. That is the funny thing about *Suburbia*, isn't it?" Priscilla smiled. "You can go a lifetime without ever truly knowing your neighbors, even if you do meet them. But alas, we are meeting now. You seem like a hot-chocolate girl. I'm assuming adding a little Irish to it wouldn't hurt?"

"I do love chocolate." Susan laughed. "With three children, the Irish part definitely doesn't hurt, either. But I don't want to trouble you. It's late. I should be asleep, not outside digging."

"No judgment here. Please." Priscilla waved her hand at the coy-pond project. "Come, let's sit on my back porch. Take a break from all your hard work. I think you have earned a special chocolate-liquor combination. This isn't just hot chocolate, the cheap stuff. This is actually hot chocolate, flakes from France. It's the difference between Perrier and Pellegrino. Some just don't understand."

"I'd love that. I don't know if I've ever had a cup of 'real' hot chocolate before. My mother was big on the powder kind."

The cheap kind, Susan thought, and hadn't any idea of the difference between Perrier and Pellegrino.

Susan McArthur had been living on the Lane for almost four years at this point. She had never noticed the house that her oak trees only slightly covered and the gazebo obscured in the back. But she noticed it now.

A larger home than her own. Painted in a grand gold with ivory accents, columns lining the back porch and covering a stone area with polished silver furniture and plush eggshell cushions. A marble fireplace sat at the corner and one could entertain, read, or just relax out back.

"Magnificent job, Priscilla. I mean, if this is what your patio looks like, I'd hate to see the rest of your house. Makes me feel like a pauper."

Out of seemingly thin air, Priscilla had handed Susan a gold-tinted mug filled with hot chocolate and the right amount of liquor. She smiled pleasantly.

"We have lived in this town for so many years. Some people bounce from house to house, from town to town. State to state, in some cases." Priscilla looked over her two-and-a-half-floor magnificent house with pleasure. "But my family and I have remained here; we've had time to perfect this place. We bought this property in the early eighties, but have been blessed to be able to constantly keep it up with the times. Please, Susan, sit anywhere."

Susan sat in a plush chair next to a fireplace. Priscilla walked over to it and pressed a button and the fire exploded on. Sitting across from Susan, Priscilla's eyes flickered with the fire as she sipped on her adult hot chocolate.

"My husband is in finance and spends most of his time in the city. Our children are all grown and it is just us. But why move? Memories and happiness have filled these walls. I picked every stone for this patio, every marble for that fireplace, and every single light fixture, rug, and shower head. Moving seemed…silly. I brought five children into this house and when the holidays roll around, they bring their children."

"You don't ever get bored or lonely?" Priscilla had definitely added enough liquor to the hot chocolate. "Just with you and your husband in this house?"

"Lonely? Never. I am a constant babysitter with the gaggle of grandchildren I have. Plus, on this street we don't lock our doors. My friend, Amanda Snow, comes over at her will to gossip about her sister…various other neighbors and housewives fill our nights with dinner parties and afternoon card games. Things are different here on Iris Lane; it's not unusual for a neighbor to just pop in. But you…you live on Sun Drop Court come year 2004."

"What does that mean?"

"I've been watching you dig for weeks. I honestly thought you were going as mad as Maxine Johnson did in her final days, but I like to think of myself as a good judge of character and what I saw in your eyes was loneliness. Pain, suffering, and a need. A need that at one point that beautiful *suburban* street was able to provide. It all ended in the mid-nineties. I'm sure April Mayfair isn't coming by with baskets of cupcakes. I'm sure you never heard of the Bixby family that moved right around when your house came up for sale. And Mrs. Watson can barely make it down the stairs, let alone the street. Lorraine Scopello was brought in by the Captain, but the first was Maxine Johnson. You see…at one time, Athena Rose had all these streets connected. That woman was the leader of the pack, if you will. Perfection blossomed from her smile and she was the most honest person, to this day, I have ever met. This entire spider web of roads used to have block parties and all the housewives were close. Things changed…and they changed in 1996 and then again in 2000. Terrible what happened to her husband and terrible she has to live with the Wicked Witch of the West up in the Towers of Hades."

"Thorne Hall," Susan replied and laughed. She had heard that mansion called many things. This was a new one. "The Captain doesn't seem too bad."

Priscilla sat there for a second and ran a nail over the tip of her mug.

"I promised myself if I saw it happening again, I would do something. My husband was firm on the fact that I wouldn't get involved over something I thought I saw. But I like to read, so I sit back here a lot. That house has been my screensaver, if you will, for a long…long…time."

"Why are you telling me this now?" Susan ran her eyes over Priscilla Primm, who was perfectly poised and positioned.

"We don't exactly have a wall between our houses." Priscilla turned her head to look over at the McArthur house; she looked through the hydrangeas, through the windows, and through the house. "I tried to talk to Maxine…that had to be 1995. The same year, poor April Mayfair's daughter Grace went missing. Oh…your hot chocolate is empty. Come in—let me refill; I also have fresh cookies. Let's indulge a bit."

Priscilla slid the glass door of her house open and let Susan in first. Fine rugs, a crystal chandelier in the dining room over a fine wooden table, fantastic artwork from various countries decorating the walls, and appropriately placed and expensive-looking statues set the scene for a house that screamed the money that was put into it. Susan and Priscilla's houses were set up similarly, but it was like being in a different world—this family had money the McArthurs never had.

They had Thorne money. They'd built this house and had moved in on their own, weren't handed a check and moved. Susan withstood a shudder—did she even belong here?

Priscilla was in her kitchen that looked very European and caught Susan's eye. Even in the light, Priscilla's skin was perfect. She must have been almost seventy, but you'd never have thought she was a day over fifty. Susan knew she had no makeup on, nor did she need it. There was more than one Athena Rose in these webs of roads.

"Thomas had each piece of this kitchen flown in from Rome, some old aqueduct; they re-painted and set it. I thought it would be too much, but the entire house has turned into the collectables of our years of traveling and our family growing." After pouring more alcohol than chocolate into their gold tinted cups, Priscilla led Susan into the living room, pressed a button, and the fireplace exploded on, a little more intensely. "Please, Susan, take a seat."

The couch was of a leather so fine that you unknowingly rubbed your hands along it. Susan eyed the room: the gorgeous paintings on the wall, the magnificent fireplace, and then the table beside the couch. It held pictures of her children, pictures ranging from when they were kids to wedding photos and then to grandchildren. There was a photo from the eighties with two adults: Priscilla smiling with her beautiful husband and their five children.

"Maxine Johnson was quite a different neighbor than you," Priscilla said between closed lips. "She lived in that house very happily for a few years before things began to go…sour. I'm sure The Wolf, Cynthia, doesn't flash this, but back in the nineties they made some bad investments with my husband. Terrible market choices; the Captain never knew when to sell or buy. Lost a lot of money. Rumors had it they were going to start selling their properties around the country, even Thorne Hall. Those were pleasant years, for they stayed locked in their fortress and doors on your street remained unlocked. Neighbors would come with cobblers and trays of cookies for fun. For a couple years that witch wasn't riding a brand-new Mercedes around. Humbled, really—the diamonds on her ears didn't weigh her to the ground, and she didn't own Versace pre-sale collections. Things only greedy people care about. Things that truly don't matter, and really aren't products of actual happiness."

"I've always struggled with financial problems. Maybe your husband can talk to me." Susan took a healthy sip from her cup. "I owned a small baking shop in the city that never seemed…"

"Let me finish, dear." Priscilla crossed a leg and leaned forward. "1995 was the Thorne Foundation Ball; one every four years. A tradition started by the original Thorne family and that has carried on since. They invite everyone from town, we give a donation, Cynthia takes a small percentage, and the rest goes to charity. A grand event, you know, as I am sure you attended the ball in 2003."

"I did." Susan remembered Thorne Hall lit up like a Christmas tree, the rooms flowing in decorations and her convincing Gregory to buy her a dress with his bonus that she floated around the room in. She had taken a few too many pills and drank too much. "But I was quite intoxicated. I...I struggled for a few years....I..."

Priscilla held her hand up. "I am not here to judge you, Susan." With a loose hand, she pointed across the yard to Susan's house. "I saw you the first day you were out there digging. You looked crazed. I thought, like Maxine...it had begun again. But your eyes are calm. You are not...have you been...are you...what does your husband give you at night?"

"Give me?" Susan laughs. "A kiss if I'm lucky. Sex if I'm really lucky."

Priscilla sat back, tapping her finger on the steel of her chair, causing a noise that ricocheted through the house. "One night, I was outside reading by the fire and when I looked up I saw Benjamin Rose and Leroy Watson drag an unconscious Maxine Johnson out of her house. This didn't happen just once, but six, seven, eight times. This went on for almost a year. Stop your thinking—of course I went to the cops. By then, Neil Wolf sat on the throne of our town and each report I made got thrown away. I'm no fool. The Captain and his family funds built half this town; they own the power plant that runs our electricity. But they also own the police, and the mayor, and the Scopellos and the Johnsons, and now they own your husband. Your family.

"Don't you see? In 2003, a small boy went missing playing on the playground. In 1995, Grace Mayfair went missing. In 1995 Maxine Johnson vanished and, soon after, the Captain bought up the rest of the houses on that block. His spread went a street over and he tried here on Iris. But all of us got together and put an end to that." Priscilla looked at the fireplace and her eyes flickered angrily. "If I was Athena, I would be planning. I would be digging, and I would be planning. Getting all the queens in my corner, gathering all my resources, and plotting revenge. She is the queen of every hive at this point. Every call I make to her is blocked. The gates of Thorne Hall have been closed to me for years. The secrets they are hiding up there...what goes on during their foundation ball? Where is Maxine Johnson? Where is Grace Mayfair? Where are these women and children going?"

They both allowed silence to fill the room. It started as a lonely energy. Something without answer; something that had no response. But Priscilla felt it coming from Susan and turned to her.

"What?"

"I'm going to a dinner party tomorrow night at Thorne Hall. Athena invited the entire street. She...she looks like her old self again."

"Then you must find out what fly got tangled in our perfect *suburban* web. You need to figure out the spider that is cutting cords and destroying a community that once didn't need to lock their doors."

"And then?" Susan looked over at Priscilla, who turned her head and smiled.

"We take our community back." Priscilla held her glass up. "To Athena Rose."

"To Athena." Susan drank her drink down.

She spent another hour at Priscilla's trading friendly dish about the neighbors on her street and about the utopia Sun Drop Court once was. Laughter turned into secrets and before they knew it, it was midnight.

Priscilla led the way with a flashlight back to the gate that connected their backyards. As the flashlight flashed over the hole, something glinted. Something was buried there.

They looked at each other.

Susan said, "Let me just grab the shovel."

Susan made one more kick into the dirt and what she scooped out…was meant to remain hidden forever.

"Dear, do you get a plus one for tomorrow night's dinner party?"

Susan, flustered, looked over at Priscilla. "Yes. I was planning on having Todd watch the girls and bringing Matthew. Gregory has to work."

"Bring me, dear." Priscilla was staring at what they had just uncovered. "Let your son watch the girls. It's time we start making these streets safe again."

"Good evening, Mrs. Wolf-Thorne." The valet opened the wrong side of the Mercedes. "How are you tonight?"

"Don't talk to me." Cynthia opened her own door and pushed it with her long leg and Dolce and Gabbana heel. "You are not my friend."

"I have the door, Mrs Thorne." The valet scurried around, to the other side of the car, but Cynthia was not having it.

"Too late. You work for tips?" she snarled, eyeing the teenager up and down. "Move faster next time."

The Palm was the most happening restaurant in town. If celebrities ever came to their little town, it's where they would go…but celebrities don't visit *Suburbia*. This is where you'd find the mayor having a business lunch or April Mayfair bringing Pastor Jefferson out for their weekly meal. The Captain himself even made appearances at the bar to order one of many drinks that were named after him and his kin.

"Hello," said a voice Cynthia never heard before. "Can you take our picture?"

Cynthia turned. A middle-aged couple was behind her, posing at her brand-new Mercedes. Cynthia would never have noticed them if they hadn't spoken to her. The old woman had her hand on the car. Cynthia twitched.

"What?" This night was off to a rough start. But the woman removed her cell phone from her fanny pack, her husband's hand now on the car. The older woman flipped open her phone and made a comment about the buttons being so tiny, until she found the camera button.

Is this reality? Cynthia thought. *God help me.*

"A picture, please?" the woman pushed her cell phone into Cynthia's newly manicured nails. Literally pushed the phone, as if she were a hired photographer and this was a common thing. "Hold on. Let us get ready."

Cynthia watched them for half a minute as they posed around the car. She raised the phone and smiled pleasantly as one would on vacation, taking a picture for another traveler. They stood posing. Smiling. Chunky arms around each other. Lines of wrinkles bringing down their faces. Old, married, and happy in their elderly years. Happy in their mediocrity. Cynthia let the phone fall and smash to the ground.

"Whoops!" Cynthia watched their shocked expressions with a sense of pleasure for a moment, before turning on her heel, on the phone. "That's what you get for trusting strangers. Touch my Mercedes again and I'll tear your soul out of your body, old woman."

Since finding out that her son was a bully who was set aflame and that not a single student had visited him at the hospital, Cynthia had been on high bitch alert. She didn't know why the Captain didn't tell her that her son sent a kid to the hospital almost monthly, and when she searched his room she found steroids.

It hurts somewhere deep when you realize you aren't raising the child you thought you were.

The interior of The Palm was a spectacle. Trying to be like Vegas. Or something. A Tropicana feel. The ceiling covered in fake palm trees decorated in glittering diamond hanging lights. Above, the ceiling painted black and sparkling with stars. All the furniture of deep burgundy leather, which reminded Cynthia of a cheap French brothel.

"Do you have a reservation?" the hostess asked. A scrawny thing who could have been eighteen or twenty-five. Those annoying youthful years where age doesn't matter as much as the perkiness of your breasts.

"What?"

"A reservation?" The girl looked at her like she didn't speak English. "To...eat here?"

"I know what a fucking reservation is, you dumb cow," Cynthia spat. "Table for two. Athena Rose should be here."

"Oh, yes." The girl's eyes lit up. "Athena Rose. Of course. One moment, please." The girl vanished behind the velvet curtains to gather menus, Cynthia assumed.

That was the summary of life right there. It didn't matter what Cynthia had accomplished as a child or what accolades she was awarded in school—her parents' eyes were always on Athena, always. All the boys in school. All the men in life. Cynthia's mother had to basically arrange the marriage between her and the Captain. Even in that, there was no love. No desire. No passion. While Athena married the love of her life—many suitors claimed priesthood the minute she was off the market—no one was knocking down doors for Cynthia…

She hadn't always been like this. She hadn't always been miserable and unhappy. There was a time in her life when she'd been a dreamer. But watching dream after dream after dream being crushed under the raging fist of life…that changes you.

"Athena hasn't arrived yet. If you'd like, you may sit over there until she comes." The hostess motioned to a crowded area where people were sitting around while waiting for their tables. "It seems there might be room at the bar if you'd like a cocktail before Athena Rose arrives."

She even used the full name, as if this housewife was some sort of celebrity.

"Just seat me."

"I'm sorry, but until your full party is here we just cannot."

"I'm here," Athena's voice fluttered.

"Oh, Mrs. Rose." The hostess beamed with excitement. "You look fabulous tonight. As always. Your friend is here, waiting for you. Are you ready to be seated? Your table has been prepared for you."

"What the fuck," Cynthia mumbled. The hostess gave her a look and Athena beamed her smile.

"This is my sister...not my friend."

The hostess looked in shock, as always, as everyone did, that these two were related. Cynthia scratched at her nose. Nothing changes. Nothing ever will.

"Are you ready?" Cynthia turned toward Athena. "Sister."

Ever beautiful. Ever pristine. Athena Rose, from appearances, had overcome her years of mourning. Donning a light pink-and-black lace dress that perfectly fit her athletic body, her long mane of blond locks tied in such a way that they whipped about her back like a predator's tail. Her face had seen sun and the lines of her cheekbones were apparent.

Cynthia turned green inside. A sick, subconscious part of her had hoped that Athena would remain in mourning... eternally. But, even in mourning, the dark colors suited her.

Without waiting for a reply, Athena turned and motioned to the hostess, who led them to the best table in the entire restaurant. One that could hold six, but the great Athena Rose was present and, for that, they pulled out all the stops.

"How kind of you to come, sister." Athena's eyes were running over Cynthia, as a parent might judge a daughter before letting her out for a night on the town.

"We could have just eaten at Thorne Hall. I would have had Rosaletta prepare something."

"Oh." Athena was eyeing the room casually to see if there was anyone she must greet. "I felt it necessary that we spend some quality time outside those cold stone walls. I had an encounter earlier. Seems Susan McArthur is worrying about her husband. Déjà vu. Reminded me of how my handsome husband faded under your husband's iron fist."

"Don't be dramatic, Athena. The Captain is well known for taking good care of his employees."

"Oh, yes." Athena still had her large purse on her lap. "Builds them pools, puts in new kitchens, even buys them new cars. But Susan had something very interesting to show me…"

"Am I interrupting?" the waiter, another high-schooler or college kid, said. "Or do you ladies need more time to decide on what to order?"

"Of course you are interrupting!" Cynthia snapped, never taking her eyes off Athena. "When two people are talking, you are always interrupting!"

"Of course not, Christopher." Athena ran a hand over the waiter's chest, causing his face to turn red. "A bottle of your best wine, please; we are here to celebrate!"

As the waiter walked away, Cynthia knew anger was written on her face and the ulcer in her stomach burned. But Athena was poised and still smiling. "What in the hell are we…"

"No, no, wine first. Ah, here it is! Thank you, Christopher." Athena winked at him as he poured a glass for first Athena and then Cynthia. "How kind of you. Give us a little to decide what we are going to eat. The Palm just has so many great choices, don't you agree, Cynthia?"

"Keep my glass full." Cynthia swung the entire contents of her wine down in one gulp. "Another, Christian. Another."

"Oh, sister. It's Christopher. He's been here for ages." Athena waited till he walked away. "Cute, isn't he? I'm not in the mood to drink. What do you do all day? Manicures. Massages. Luncheons. Shopping. Searching out your next Mercedes?"

"Your point? Shouldn't you be focusing your clever energy, say, on tomorrow night's dinner party? Shouldn't you be preparing with Rosaletta at Thorne Hall?"

"Oh." a folder appeared on the table; Athena dropped it in front of Cynthia like one would swat off vermin. "Because of this."

"What is this?" Cynthia felt her ulcer burn as she stared at the blue folder, a folder from the NRG plant. A folder that had the name *Larry Johnson* written across its side. Cynthia flipped it open, skimmed through a couple of the pages, confused.

"It's only a list of names, Athena." Cynthia kept her composure, trying to understand what she was looking at. "A list of female names and what looks like their profiles."

"You haven't seen this before, have you? You always scratch at your nose when you are caught off guard." Athena reached across the table and flipped a few pages. The names were in alphabetical order and she stopped at *Maxine Johnson*. "Why is my best friend's name on this list? Most of the names are Russian or…I can't even pronounce them…but I can tell by your face…you have no idea what this is about."

Cynthia finished another glass of wine then took the folder and put it in her purse.

"I'll find out," Cynthia slurred, a bit of the wolf in her voice. "We might be at odds for things that happened years ago, but I will find out what this list means."

"Chugging wine. How…college sorority of you. But you weren't in a sorority, were you, Sin-thee-ah?"

"No. They befriended me to…get to you." Cynthia looked up from the empty wine glasses and now the empty wine bottle. "Red. Red. Wine…"

"Goes to your head." Athena was becoming blurry to Cynthia. But that damn smile on her face. "All you can do… you've done. But memories won't go. No…memories will not go. I have copies of that folder. So please keep the original, return it to the Captain's files in the power plant for all I care. But…this is just a Band-Aid, Cynthia. One I plan on ripping off. Between this and the night my husband left this world, a call to the mayor and the police would be enough to start an investigation."

"Athena," Cynthia slurred out. "I've never seen this before."

"That was all I needed to hear. One thing about you, once you become drunk, the secrets come flying out. You really don't know what this is, do you? Or why the dates all follow your foundation ball?"

Cynthia and her sister sat staring at each other for a moment, as if somehow silence would give meaning to this. But, being drunk not helping, Cynthia couldn't figure it out. She knew the Captain got into some shady business up at the plant, but the new diamonds and preseason gowns had stopped her from ever asking what exactly. Her son, the terror bully; her husband….what was her husband up to?

Another wine bottle finished, Cynthia was beginning to lose track of time; a plate broke. Athena had left. Cynthia had found the bar. The blue folder with the name *Larry Johnson* written in his now basically forgotten handwriting. As he himself was all but forgotten, slipped in her purse.

It's a lie we tell ourselves to sleep better at night. To trudge forward throughout the days. We shall be remembered. We shall be celebrated once we are gone. A legacy shall be left and our time roaming this planet won't have been wasted. It's a lie we tell ourselves to keep our heads up during the day.

In truth.

The world moves on and, as kids become parents and parents become grandparents, we are then lost. A plaque on a wall, a statue in a park—no one actually cares. For humans are selfish and this is the nature of the world.

Another glass of wine down.

There was a boy.

A glass broke in her hand and the boy had wrapped it up for her.

Words exchanged. Whispers and flirts traded.

Cynthia had pushed the valet. The boy had driven her Mercedes for her as she opened the window and put her head against the side, letting her long mane of extensions and dyed hair flutter in the autumn breeze.

That night, sex occurred in her own bed in Thorne Hall. The first time Cynthia had felt the touch of another man since the night she and the great Captain had decided to make Dax. For social reasons. Nothing to do with marital love.

No wonder the boy was so screwed up.

Cynthia awoke to an empty bed in her grand bedroom. The giant bed that was not a king, but as the Captain had called it when ordering it, an emperor mattress, one in which they would never accidentally roll into each other in the middle of the night.

A bedroom fit for a lord. The bed was raised high and dark, twisted tentacles wrapped together to form a headboard. A chandelier of darkened colors hung from the ceiling and emitted what appeared to be candlelight. The floor in front of the fireplace was covered in an actual lion's skin, complete with the head—a trophy from the Captain's great-grandfather. The fireplace took up most of the wall and roared. One could easily be thrown into it.

The space next to her in the bed was wrinkled, not the Captain's space, that felt like a mile away, but as if someone had shared the bed with her. A small smile spread her face for a moment. A single moment when her forehead almost wrinkled with what some call 'expression lines,' the lines given to those who laugh the most and smile the brightest.

Maybe she was beautiful. Maybe she was desirable. Maybe…she remembered her wallet was emptied and, as it tends to do, the night came back to her. She had paid this boy for sex. Her ulcer roared and her head ached as the bells of Thorne Hall, bells that should have died with the slave age, began to clamber. A light flickered.

"You are awake." The Captain was sitting across the huge bedroom in a large plush leather chair beside the balcony. A balcony that had enough room for a ten-person dining table that had never been used, except for Cynthia's morning coffee before she entered the world below. He was tapping the cane against the floor and was already dressed in a fine black suit with a green stripped tie and matching pocket square. "I tipped the boy more after her sobered up and... fled. Got to keep these things hush-hush, my dear. Got to have a way about it that no one will ever know. Can't be sloppy. Our walls are thick and the ceilings high, but there are still weapons that can break them all down. He was very handsome. Did you have fun?"

It was an honest question. They may not have been lovers, but they were friends. Cynthia managed to bring her body out of the bed. Naked still. She grasped at the sheer gold silk nightgown the Captain had carefully laid out for her.

"Abraham, some privacy please."

Cynthia waited until her husband was out of the room, and even another minute to ensure he was elsewhere. She removed the blue folder Athena had tossed at her last night. Glancing at Maxine Johnson's husband's handwriting on the side, she began to flip through it. Names of women, numbers next to their names, all arranged in order of age.

If the walls had begun to fall, Cynthia thought, *she would make it her mission to find out why.*

Matthew McArthur woke up in Todd's bedroom. In his bed. Todd was lying next to him in his boxer briefs. Matthew was also down to his boxers, not his own, but Todd's.

"Dude."

"Matthew."

"Dude."

"Relax." Todd rolled onto his side and smiled at him. A smile that could sell ice to Eskimos. "The love of your life drugged your drink. You vomited all over yourself. I cleaned you up and brought you here. I wasn't going to take you home. Your mother would have flipped; she seems a lot more lucid these days. My mom, at least, doesn't enter my room without asking permission. She believes in privacy, which is very ironic. But that's not the point."

"Dude." Matthew sat up in bed; his head was rushing. He had been hungover before, but this was something else. The last thing he remembered was her smile. Her beautiful smile. The smile that was perfect. Too perfect. "She's not the love of my life."

"Wow." Todd threw his toned arms over his head dramatically. "In the wake of evil, he speaks sense!"

"She drugged me? Why would she drug me?" Matthew scratched at his messy hair. "Where's Felicia?"

"She helped me get you home. Get you in my shower and clean you up. Now she knows what swings between your legs." Todd jested before he got up, and Matthew couldn't help but notice the bulge in his shorts.

"Now that's someone who really cares for you. I'm not saying marry her. I'm not saying anything. But if you are going to focus your energy on someone, she's the one. Not someone who drugs people and hides behind a fake smile. Steer clear of this... Samantha Rose. She was a nice kid when she was fat, but this monster she is now...she's not someone I recommend bringing home to Susan and Gregory. It's okay to stare. It's natural. I'm not only blessed by God above the belt." Todd winked at Matthew and Matthew turned bright red.

"You going to Athena's dinner party tonight?" Todd dropped his trunks and Matthew had to look away. He grabbed a towel and wrapped it around his waist.

"Yah...dude."

"Wanna jump in the shower with me?"

"I..."

"I'm joking." Todd smacked Matthew playfully across the face. "Relax a little, dude. It's not like you got drugged or anything last night."

Matthew looked around Todd's room; it was neurotically clean. A hamper in the corner stood empty and a desk in the corner had two medals he must have won at his reform school, along with a picture of him and a few dozen kids in their gold-and-red uniforms. Smiles on their faces, painted smiles.

"Todd," Matthew said, wanting to distract himself. "Why did you switch schools? I mean, why did you get thrown out?"

Todd turned and for a second held the smile, then let it dissipate. "Are you sure this is the time to go into the deep?" Todd sat down on the side of his bed. "Yes or no, Matthew."

A silence held them.

"I'm your best friend, aren't I?" Matthew put his arm around Todd's shoulder, but it was shrugged off.

Todd beat his hand against his knee for a second, then looked over at the picture of him and his former classmates when they were young. Before he could drive. Just as puberty was hitting. Those awkward years. A time when Samantha Rose was fat and Matthew knew nothing of Sun Drop Court.

Todd stared at the picture of him and the other boys, all in their matching school outfits. All with smiles plastered on their faces. "My mom sent me away not long after my sister was taken… I think a part of her feared she'd mess up again. The thought of losing one child must be awful, but two? I wasn't exactly the easiest child to put up with. St. Sebastian's Academy for Boys was a reform school more than a preppy boarding school. When I was young, I would play with magnifying glasses to set ants on fire, and my mom once saw me shoot an arrow at a neighborhood cat. All early signs of being a serial killer, according to her. So—and I can't blame her—she thought I would learn order and respect at that school, and not be lost down some dark path. In a way, she was right.

"There was a faculty member who had been there for over twenty years. The assistant dean of students could put on a smile like the rest of us, a short fat hairy man, with hair coming out of his nose and ears. He would cater all the parent weekends and gather donations for the school. A very pleasant man, well liked, had been interviewed on TV for his grand charity and contributions. Also for with his work with youths across the globe.

"My roommate was a beautiful boy. Dark, messy hair like yours, but he had these big gray eyes and dark skin. It was hard to deny that, even at his age, he was one day going to be something special; he had that spark, that personality, that glow in his eyes that shined and could make you smile even when you were down. I loved being around him, just for the energy. Some people just have that…thing about them.

"Then, one day, the spark was gone. He became quiet and would spend his time curled up in his bed. I thought nothing of it till I noticed the same lack of sparkle in a few of the other boys' eyes. At that age, you're supposed to feel invincible. At that age, your only worry should be about not feeling the need to worry.

"One day, I noticed a boy leaving the assistant dean's office and I followed him. He was limping slightly and he made his way into the stairwell of the library before he broke into tears. My mom had always been good at comforting when necessary, so I wrapped my arms around him and after a good hour he told me what had happened.

"You don't take advantage of the youth. You don't take the sparkle from someone's eyes. You don't put your hands on children who are just beginning to understand their bodies and confuse them forever. You don't ruin a life before it even has a chance to begin.

"That night, I curled up next to my roommate in bed and wrapped my arms around him. We laid there for a good few hours before he broke down and told me everything, everything that Dean had done to him…. repeatedly. We formed a plan. I had my father send me his video camera… I made up some story about having a project I needed to complete.

"It took a few days of planning, but the next week, my roommate hid in the assistant dean's office closet, leaving the door slightly ajar. I spoke back to one of the nuns in a way that would only be appropriate for me to have a speaking to. A lovely C-word that—at least on my list—is the worst word you can say. So, I was sent to the assistant dean's office."

Todd walked over to the picture and picked it up and rubbed his finger across the faces of the smiling boys. He gulped and a tear rolled from his eye, but all he did was turn his back to the cabinet and slide down to the floor, the picture in hand.

"The assistant dean was all smiles as he went over the whys and hows of the appropriate ways to speak to the nun. Then he dove right into psychological sabotage by telling me, 'What would Mrs. Mayfair think if I called her on this? What would your parents do if you got expelled from here? What college would ever take a kid who was expelled from a highly respected reform school? What would your future hold if I made sure you didn't have one?' The type of threats that get to kids, you know? The type of warfare lawyers and prosecutors use to turn minds."

That's when Todd's face broke and he began to cry. Matthew instinctively went across the room and sat next to his friend and wrapped his arm around Todd's shoulders. Todd looked back at him as the tears continued to roll down his face. "He began by touching me. Rubbing his old man hand across my face and through my hair. I remember the stubble of his hand as he went to my pants, a smile on his face the entire time, as if he was reassuring me that my future was safe with him. Then he removed his pants and my own. He roughly bent me over a chair and turned me around. He spat on his hand and…my roommate and I knew we needed actual proof. We knew. We thought. We were young and this was the best plan we could muster."

Todd shook his head and all the tears fell from his face and he wiped the rest of them away.

"The tape got played for the dean and when word began to spread, more students than you can possibly imagine came forward with similar, if not worse, stories. He had been at that school for twenty years, Matthew. Spent his summer with youths in Uganda and Ethiopia. How many…how many…

"He'd have been in jail for the rest of his life. The parents came together, as well as the alumni; the amount of people who showed up for his hearing made me sick. His lawyer didn't even attempt to give him a good defense. My mother and her friends…well…they made sure he never made it to jail. The police are still looking for him…but they will never find him. My mother finishes all projects she starts.

"She immediately pulled me from the school and I was hailed as a hero by all the parents and kids. If I ever need a favor, I pick up my phone and can have a hundred at my side. But…this was only one man. I don't dream, Matthew; I have nightmares. How many people are out there doing stuff like this? How many… Between that and my sister…my poor mother. I'm happy the rumor around town is that I was kicked out of St. Sebastian's, 'cause that's a lie I can live with. If…if I ever find out who took my baby sister, we will avenge just as we have done before. Our God is forgiving, but He also punishes."

Todd turned his heard toward Matthew, his eyes puffy and his smile weakened.

"Kinda makes you forget you got drugged last night, right? The games we, as kids, play are nothing compared to what an adult's game can do to you."

Matthew wrapped his arms around Todd and hugged him for what felt like an eternity. They sat in Todd's OCD-cleaned room and Matthew understood his best friend better than he ever had, understood why he'd kissed Samantha on that day in 2000, and why he threatened Felicia if she continued her bullying.

All he wanted was to be there for him—all he wanted was to hold him, for he felt, through Todd's body, the pain.

"I'm always here for you, dude," Matthew finally let out. "To talk about this or anything. Always. If you ever need anything. If you ever need anything. I'll never let you down. Never. I swear. You are a hero."

"But at what cost?" Todd smiled and shook himself again, as if shaking off the memories and secrets he had buried so deep. He rubbed his head against Matthew's for a second. "Listen. I'm going to go distract my mom. Go home and shower and clean yourself up. Think long and hard. If you can do anything for me, think about what appears to be good and what is actually good. Samantha Rose is no good for you. Even if you don't have feelings for Felicia, give her a chance. Maybe now you can see the way she looks at you."

Todd opened the door to his room.

"When did you get home?"

"Mom!"

April Mayfair was standing in the hallway behind Todd's door, her arms folded, looking him up and down.

"Late. I went to a party."

April got close and sniffed at Todd's breath. "You know what Pastor Jefferson says about parties."

"No, I actually don't know that one. You know I don't imbibe, Mother."

Her hand hit him in the back of the head, not hard, but enough to get the point across. "Do you know what today is, Todd?"

Yes, he knew what today was. He stared across the hall at the pink door with the stickers. With its Comic Sans-lettered *Grace* in wooden blocks on. He wrapped his arms around his mom and brought her close.

"It's been…it's been…" she began. "Are we ever…will I ever…"

"Together, we will," Todd whispered into his mother's ear. "A day doesn't go by that I don't think of Grace. We brought God's wrath down on Dean Thomas. We will find out who took her. We will find out what happened to her. We will. I promise you. Stay strong with me. Together, we are an unstoppable force. Plus, the minute we find out who took her, we make one phone call and we have an army at our door. I love you, Mom. But, for now, today has to just be another day. Tonight we go to church together and pray."

In between a sob, April Mayfair backed up and straightened herself, wiping her tears away. "Go shower. Jesus knows you're unclean."

But before heading down the hall, she gave him one final look. "I love you, too, son. Don't you ever vanish on me. Or else Jesus and I will find you."

"I don't know who I'd be more scared of." Todd dropped his head and his blond hair fell with it. "Do you still dream about her at night... I mean...do you still have nightmares?"

April went to her cross and looked at her son. "Probably as many as you have. Stay strong, son. We've taken down one monster. We will also take the one who took your sister."

Todd could add Dax to his list, but there were still people out there, people with brilliant smiles on their faces, but who had char for insides. The demons that are portrayed in movies—those murky, dark, liquid creatures that growl and hiss—are simply what lay in the darkest of hearts.

April Mayfair smiled before dropping her head, just like her son had, and made her way into the kitchen. It was time to make a key lime pie—it was her first time making a key lime pie, but a long time ago Maxine Johnson had given her the perfect recipe.

End of Winter, 1996

Dear Diary,

Did I see a doctor or did I see a magician?

Only five sessions in with ███████ and we've decided to give hypnotism a try. A joke I've seen done on TV where people quack like ducks and pretend to undress. A joke…but this was no joke.

This was years of ████████████ abilities learned at schools and academies; this was true science and psychology at work.

My mind has been blocked, barricaded.

By tea. We connected the time and we talked about the breaks, my moods, my symptoms. It all led back to the tea my husband gave me at night.

How can something so horrific…

How can something so macabre…

How can a mind block out…

Why blind me? Why take these memories away? Hidden beneath my mind and in my deepest of moments, fractions of figures are coming back to me. But just fractions. I was being drugged at night. For what purpose?

More importantly, what have I become?

What have I done to my child? ███ said the withdrawal can cause rage and that the mind may do things it normally wouldn't do. Will Felicia's scars ever heal? Can I ever be forgiven... No, I can't.

Felicia is my own and the things I have brought upon her are unforgivable.

My darling daughter.

My sweet angel.

How have I let my mind twist in such a way...

I can never take her scars away—no—but I can attempt revenge.

The tea he brings me at night will go in a plant next to our bed. The next time the scratching comes to me in the night, I will be ready for it. The next time the shadow covers me, I will handle it.

It's become obvious. More of a fool than I have ever been. My husband serves me drugged tea.

I promise you, my love, I will die making this right. Neither mine nor my husband's nor any other monster's death will make any of this right. But it's the best I can do; I don't deserve to live after what I have done to you.

I am done with my writing for the moment, for my mind no longer needs to escape on the pages. No. It's time for action.

My next entry will tell you everything. My next entry—if this diary ever falls into your hands, my dearest Felicia—will be about how I made this right.

For tonight I will not drink the tea my husband has always served me.

I will go where the demons have been taking me.

The Night of Athena Rose's Dinner Party
Late Fall, 2004

Thorne Hall was exploded in light. What Cynthia had failed to do for years, Athena had accomplished in a night. Warmth roared through the hallways, light lit each corner, fireplaces were ablaze, chandeliers sparkled.

A cornucopia of pumpkins and gourds here, long candlesticks properly placed there, a few items moved so that crystal caught mirror and sparkle shined throughout. Thorne Hall actually seemed like it could be habitable—Athena had even shined the suit of armor that stood under the main foyer staircase till it looked new.

Some of us lack the natural ability to create warmth, but Athena thrived in it and there was a time where that was known throughout *Suburbia*.

Around Christmas, Athena used to throw a plethora of Christmas dinners, all featuring different menus and various dishes that most couldn't begin to master; different couples from different streets on different nights. Since her husband had lost his head, this was the first one she was throwing.

Thorne Hall had seemed like a prison to her from the moment she entered it up until she received a phone call over a month ago. An old, old friend had found something that could bring laughter back to the streets if executed properly.

Athena wasn't alone—someone out there wanted to uncover and answer the same questions she did.

Tonight there would be some answers.

Rosaletta was rubbing down the silver in the dining room. The table was set magnificently. Athena had done it herself. As it was fall, little pumpkins with each guest's name sat at their table setting. In the middle was a harvest triple candelabra; she decided on autumn berries and a few differently colored pumpkins instead of flowers. But to keep it traditional, the finest white tablecloth was spread over the table and the fine Tiffany china was set. She had even turned each autumn orange napkin to resemble a fall leaf, something she'd caught in the latest edition of Oprah's magazine. Athena could have done this all on her own, but Rosaletta had insisted on helping…

"Why do you work here?" Athena stood at the dining-room door. Her hair on top of her head and a fluffy white bathrobe wrapping her body. "Why do you put up with them? You have a kind energy, and this…this isn't a kind place."

"Missus…" Rosaletta looked at her with fear as she peered about the dining room. "I love working here. I work nowhere else. Ever."

Athena studied her for a second, looked around the empty dining room, and when she was sure no one was lingering in any shadow, she approached the maid. "Do they have something on you?"

Rosaletta's eyes dropped for a second before meeting Athena's in sadness. "Don't they have something on everyone?" Rosaletta saw Athena wasn't pleased with her answer, so she went back to shining silver. "I wasn't what they ordered, so they kept me as a maid instead. I lied on the list to get out of my country, I would of done whatever they wanted…but they didn't want a fat girl. So I write I in shape. They only want the most beautiful ones for their games."

"What does that mean?"

"No." Rosaletta, put a hand to her mouth, shocked at all she had just said. She shook her head furiously. "I've said way too much."

Athena placed her warm hand on Rosaletta's face; Rosaletta shivered from this simple act of kindness. "If you ever…you can always come to me. Always. Do you hear me? I can send you to an island or anywhere you wish to be."

But the maid didn't respond and quickly turned her face as if to hide tears. She began to scrub at the silver with intention. How many thorns had the Thornes stuck into people over the years?

Athena turned and stormed through the fire-lit corridors of Thorne Hall. Making her way down one hall, she stopped and looked at the locked door at the end. One that had always been locked, that Athena had thought had not been entered since 1995…but the ladies' visit to the principal's office had changed that. It had been opened, and finally she knew who had the key.

Enough, Athena thought. *Just enough.*

Enough.

It was time to drive her finger so far into the Thornes that she'd suffer blood and pain while doing so.

- -

The Captain was dressed in a fine suit with a glittering diamond pendant tie clip, a red tie with a matching silk pocket square, and a vest that needed to be let out half an inch. Making his way past his office and down to the wing of the mansion past where their master bedroom was, he rapped the cane at his son's door.

"Dax," the Captain called. "May I come in?"

Silence answered him from behind the door.

"Dax?" The Captain opened the door and the room was completely dark; his glasses didn't help at all. The wood-colored drapes were completely drawn and his king-size bed was made. Years and years ago, Athena had helped decorate this room, to keep a masculine feel while bringing elegance to... The Captain really didn't give a shit. Let the women busy themselves with color schemes and decorating. If their eyes were focused on their projects, they were less likely to notice what was going on around them.

Dax had a two-room suite. The first room was his bedroom and bathroom, complete with a walk-in closet. The second room was his gym. It housed a fridge at the end filled with various supplements, a weight set that ranged from ten to four-hundred pounds. Barbells. Bench press. Stacking weights. Treadmill. Elliptical. The walls were completely lined by mirrors. The Captain didn't exactly know what kind of workouts his son did, so he just bought every piece of equipment a gym could need. The lights were out in the gym as well. But as the Captain's eyes adjusted, he saw the outline of his brutish son sitting on the bench with two-hundred-pound weights on either side of him.

"Son?" The Captain put his hand on his son's massive shoulder, which felt like stone. "Working out in the dark is a quick way to drop a weight on your face or get hurt. May I turn a light on?"

"No," Dax half-growled. "The dark is fine. I could work out with my eyes shut. I could toss a fridge across a lawn. I could lift a car."

The Captain hadn't seen his son since the hospital, hadn't checked on him or even known if he had left his room since returning home. Running the types of business the Captain does makes you lose track of time, and sometimes yourself. But Dax wasn't brought into this world to be weak or sit in the dark while the world was turning about him.

"Dax." The Captain leaned against the cane. "What happened to you is awful and…"

"Don't want to talk about it, Father. Nothing I can do about it now; it's over. I can't go back to that school. I can't even look at myself in the mirror. No one can love a…"

"Silence!" the Captain roared and he felt his son shift. "Life isn't fair, son. For eighteen years, you've had it good—great, in fact—and better than most others ever have it. You've had plenty of girlfriends and been lucky enough to parade around like you have. Guess what. Life has now actually thrown fire at you and you sit here brooding in your gym like a puppy dog who doesn't get played with. Are you a puppy? Are you? Does someone need to pet and pamper you?"

"No."

"You are a dragon," the Captain boomed. "You breathe fire and destroy as you conquer. You get arrows and swords thrown your way, and you deal with them as they come. You do not whimper in darkness."

"I just want to find out who did this to me so I can smash their face in."

"And I would expect no less from my own son." The Captain walked around the room to where the light switches were. "You don't have to go back to school. You don't have to put your varsity jacket on again…if you don't want to. You are an heir to a legacy and I will not allow you to crumble because of some misfortune. How would you feel beginning your career early with me? Hmm? Samantha or one of your cousins can be the face of NRG after I pass, but you can learn the work that keeps food on this table."

"Work at the power plant?" Dax's tone changed slightly and seemed less aggressive. "Doing what, exactly? I don't think I'd wear a suit very well. Plus, they could make Halloween masks of my face."

"Yes." The Captain smiled in the dark. "You will 'work' at the power plant just like your Uncle Benjamin, Leroy Watson, Larry Johnson, and now Gregory McArthur. None of them wear…suits. You will join them, along with my other workers. We will even tell your mother you are working in the power plant and give her some mental comfort thinking that I have you on a path. But you won't ever step foot in the power plant. Your jobs are of a nature that have nothing to do with that NRG building, but with a whole different type of power. You actually begin work tonight. I figured you didn't want to join in your aunt's little dinner party."

"Didn't even know there was a party here tonight."

"Now." The Captain put his finger on the light switch. "Go shower and face yourself in the mirror. You are going through a change, Dax, but I can help you channel that aggression, that rage. I can give you work that'll give you an outlet for what you won't find in this room. Do you understand me?"

"Yes."

"Meet me in my office in twenty minutes for your first assignment. I want you out of this house before the guests begin arriving."

The Captain turned and flicked the light switch. He began to walk toward the entrance to the bedroom door and then the roaring began. Dax was surrounded by mirrors and each of them showed him the same person...the same monster.

He flung a thirty pound weight like it was nothing and smashed the first mirror, picked up a kettle bell and swung it at the second mirror, and the third mirror was destroyed by him throwing his body up against it.

Good, the Captain thought to himself. *The more rage in him, the better.*

His son might not be attending an Ivy League college or have a family, but he did have exactly what The Captain needed to get some work done. He would help his son out of this rut and show him new ways to channel rage and emotion; he'd lead him down the exact same path his father had led him down, as his father did before him and so it would continue onward.

Dax Thorne wasn't the only member of the family who was broken.

Samantha Rose wasn't quite sure how she got home. Wasn't quite sure how she managed to get into her shower in her suite. But she had been there all day. Just letting the water run over her naked body.

How long she was held to that mattress was unclear. But the cocktail of ketamine and drugs had worn off and by that time she was too beaten up to even try and fight it. The same fate she had planned for Felicia was bestowed upon her.

How many guys...

How many hands...

How many lips...

How many fingers...

Samantha hated to be hugged by her family, let alone touched and...entered by strangers. They had shared her. All drugged out beyond belief. They had passed her around. She had been a toy for boys who had never touched a girl before, who didn't know what they were doing...which made it hurt even more.

Samantha had wept the entire day as the water rushed over her body.

"You are the reason we have no hot water." Her mother was at the bathroom door, Samantha jumped. She normally knocked. "Get dressed. Company will be here soon."

Athena Rose, the gazelle of a matriarch, dressed in her best—a jade dress that swished as she moved. Her eyes glowed, her skin was tanned, and her blond hair was in a predator's tail that whipped at her back and was held with a beautiful green stone clasp that had to be of emerald. If it wasn't, it didn't matter. It was Athena Rose who made cubic zirconium look like the Heart of the Ocean.

"Mommy." Samantha looked to her mother. She was balled up in the shower. "Help. Something horrible happened…"

"Get dressed." Her mother's voice had no care to it. "You look like someone's leftovers. I laid out the Chanel for you. Now get out of the shower and get yourself together."

Athena went to leave, but Samantha called after her. "Mommy…last night."

Athena ran her fingers along the doorframe and didn't even turn back, thinking for a second. "Where is the key, Samantha."

"I don't know what you…"

Athena turned at the lie and was back in the bathroom, standing over her daughter. "Ketamine and drug mix. You've been drugging people with a drug concoction. From this house. From that locked basement. As your mother, it pains me to think about where I went wrong or why…but this is a conversation for after our guests leave." Athena leaned in as close to her daughter as she could, who for some reason, at that moment, feared her mother more than she feared anyone else. "The key."

"Bottom shelf...under a wooden covering...next to the box of condoms."

"Right, and next to the weed and heroin while you are at it." Athena went over to the drawer, tossed the fall jeans back into the room, and took off the wooden covering that hid all of Samantha's dirty secrets. She kneeled down and grabbed an old key, one that had never been duplicated... archaic and rusty. A key that had more power in it than most objects did, more power than a diamond, or even money. Athena curled the key in her hand and, lifting a leg, her dress flowing with her, she smashed her heel twice into the drawer. Glass smashed and sounds echoed of other things being crushed; Samantha's hidden drawer of drugs and pipes and condoms was now destroyed. Athena turned and returned to the bathroom where her daughter was still sitting in cold water that ran over her bruised and scratched, naked body.

"You've learned some things from me, all right." Athena raised her chin and her eyes tore down upon her daughter. "But it wasn't kindness. It wasn't tenderness. How to be a decent friend, or even how to be a good person. You learned about the mask."

"Mask?"

"The one we all wear one day in one shape or another. The one that hides what's going on in here." Athena grabbed her daughter's arm, her jade jewelry clanging as she brought her naked daughter's arm and hand to her heart, smacking it hard. "But what you did was mask cruelty. You used a smile to hurt. A hug to kill. My work on you hasn't even begun yet; at the end of dinner, you will meet me in this room and we will discuss…you. Figure out where I went wrong and then fix you. Before you become completely lost. I will not allow you to continue down this path that you are on. You will not grow up to be a monster."

All at once, the bells from the time of slavery went off —someone was at the front door. The guests had begun to arrive.

"Get out of the shower. At this point, the victim act is pathetic; look up karma and understand what you are going through. Get dressed and smile and be polite to each of our guests. I expect you at dinner, on time."

Samantha reached her hand out to her mother. Her mother reached her hand out and turned the shower off and chucked a towel at her face.

"Do. Not. Make. Me. Repeat. Myself. Young. Lady."

With that, Athena was out of the doorway.

Samantha straightened herself as much as she could and began to get ready for dinner, weeping the entire time.

Rosaletta answered the door. The first to arrive was Andrea Watson. In a lovely, yet simple blue dress with real silver buttons. It was her favorite dress and she saved it for the best of occasions. With her, in his wheelchair, was Leroy Watson. He was on a ventilator and had a tube in his mouth.

"Rosaletta! Dear!" Andrea leaned in and kissed the maid on the cheek. "It's been ages. You look lovely."

Rosaletta smiled and offered her hand for Andrea's coat. "Always a pleasure to see you, Mrs. Watson." Rosaletta bent down and gave Leroy a kiss on the cheek. "Hello, Mr. Watson. He…he can hear me, yes?"

Andrea looked at Rosaletta without even giving a look at her husband. "Oh, he can hear you, all right." She pushed the wheelchair, perhaps a little too hard, over the threshold and into the grand foyer. "Place looks fantastic. Athena's work, I'm sure… That girl always had a flair for making things shine. I know, I'm early…but I just had this feeling it would be one heck of a night."

"I'll tell Athena you have arrived."

Andrea Watson waited until Rosaletta left the room and bent low and whispered into her husband's ear, "Hear that, Leroy. You actually get to see some old friends tonight. Been nine years since I brought you out of that house. I have me a feeling that tonight will bring all those memories right back." She kissed him on the cheek. "It won't change anything, though. Once a liar, always a liar. I like you quiet and where I can see you."

- -

As Susan McArthur was applying the final touches to her makeup, her twin girls had somehow appeared behind her. She turned to them and they returned her smile.

"You look pretty, Mommy," Katie said, her arms wrapped around her sister's neck, one identical head rested against the other. "You look like how I remember."

"You look like a magazine model." Kat smiled.

One day these girls will break hearts, Susan thought, *but with kindness and care*. Priscilla's visit showed something to Susan: the only way to ensure a child grows into a good adult is to set a good example. Care and love creates the kind of people this world deserves. You show kindness and kindness will grow; you show cruelty and it, too, shall grow.

"Thank you both for what you did." Susan smiled at the two girls who in a few months would be turning seven. "Sometimes you are smarter than I am. Stay young and pure for me, won't you?"

They all hugged. And Katie whispered to Kat, "When we flushed her vitamins…"

"I know."

Susan laughed and tossed herself on the bed and the girls tickled each other for a minute. The twins and their mother rolled around together, one of those moments you need to capture because soon the children will be teenagers and will not even notice you. But they come back... Susan could wait for Matthew to need her again. But, for now, these little girls needed all of her—not half of a mother who pops pills to escape reality, but a woman who shows them the beauty in the world and helps to create an everlasting glow around them.

Susan would do so.

"Uh." Matthew was at the door. "There's a woman at the door who kind of scares me."

"How's that for honesty." Susan smiled at the girls as she got off the bed and gave herself one more look in the mirror. The pills completely out of her system and a couple of trips to yoga along with some running through the gardens had refreshed her. "Matthew, what time do the girls need to be in bed?"

"Midnight, tonight," Katie spurted.

"You wish." Susan flipped her phone closed and put it in her purse. "Have them in bed by nine. Okay, fine, ten."

Susan put her hand on Matthew's face and looked him in the eyes for a second. They'd changed since the family had moved here. The past four years, he had grown, done things Susan was sure she didn't want to know about. But one day, when he was an adult, he would probably tell her, and they would laugh about his mistakes as a youth.

The circle of life.

She ruffled his hair.

"Ma. C'mon."

"I don't know when I'll be home. I honestly have never been to a dinner party like this before. You sure you don't want to come?"

"No." Matthew looked down at his feet at the thought of seeing both Felicia and Samantha at the same dining table. "I'll watch those monsters."

"Hey, now."

"Those little angels," he said with the right amount of sarcasm.

Susan even laughed. "Now, all of you go and show Mrs. Primm how good a job I've done of raising wonderful kids. Go. Go."

Susan McArthur waited for her kids to clear the room and then went to her dresser. Out of the underwear drawer she removed what she had uncovered the night before with Priscilla out back.

Susan had no idea when she would be home because she had no idea how the Thornes and the Roses would handle what she had found.

How they would deal with her.

Todd Mayfair, April Mayfair, and Leonardo Mayfair were at church. Even though it was empty, they took up a pew and quietly prayed.

Todd Mayfair prayed for his new and old friends, for righteousness upon all who had committed sins and hurt people, especially on those who'd hurt children. He also prayed for his mother and his little sister, Grace; he prayed that one day they would find her. He also prayed for the person who took her, for neither Todd nor April would allow them to ever live a normal life again.

April Mayfair prayed for forgiveness. She prayed that she was doing right by the Lord and that she continued to live His word through her actions. April prayed for her son, Todd, who had been violated in such a terrible way to save so many. April prayed for what she and the families of the children did to the dean of that prep school, but only for a moment, for she believed the Lord shared in her enjoyment at the man's ongoing pain.

Leonardo Mayfair prayed for his family. He prayed that his daughter Grace would be found so his wife's suffering could end. He secretly prayed that they would just discover her body already; he would never utter it out loud, but a part of him knew she was no longer on this earth. He prayed that his son, Todd, would grow into a strong man and that he was setting a good example for him. He also prayed for pizza because he was starving.

The Mayfairs had chosen to decline Athena's dinner party invite. For it would not have been appropriate to go to an event on the anniversary of the day their six-year-old girl had went missing so many years ago.

"Salome," Felicia regaled. "You look…fabulous. Are you going somewhere tonight?"

"Why, honey," Salome let out innocently. "The invite said plus one. I assumed it was meant for me. Oh, how foolish of me. I'll undress and take this silly makeup off…"

"No." Felicia ran to her. "You can absolutely come with me. I'd appreciate it. Matthew hasn't returned any of my phone calls. Plus…Cynthia Thorne…"

"Just as well I come, then." Patience in revenge. Patience. "I'll ensure that thorn doesn't prick you. Let's take your Mercedes; I don't think I've ever driven with you. Have to make sure you're not a speed demon like I was."

Both Salome and Felicia had spent some time getting ready this night. Felicia had spent hours on her hair and makeup, lining her eyes and lips, blending colors and perfecting strokes to ensure perfection. It had come down to two dresses: a red one and a green one, but the minute she put the red one on she could only imagine Cynthia's comments about her wearing red. The green one was just as beautiful, and fell to just below her ankles; she only owned one pair of high heels and they were black and surprisingly made the outfit come together well. If Samantha even glanced at Matthew tonight... Felicia put that rage in her box and thought about the night Samantha must have had. Part of her actually felt some remorse, which she was glad about —empathy showed humanity. An emotion Samantha had seemed not to receive. She had been nervous about tonight from the moment she'd received Athena's beautiful printed invitation, but having Salome by her side, any anxiety was relieved.

Salome Legree had gotten ready in less than an hour. She applied her finest makeup in under ten minutes, dark eyes and dark lips, smoky cheeks and purple-lined eyelids. She was trying to be patient. It had been nine years, and it was time to make a reappearance in society. Though it would be to no one's liking.

Mayor Neil Wolf closed the door that led to his attic, locking it. In a fine pin-striped suit with a red tie, he hadn't spent much time getting ready for this dinner party. He was too busy tinkering with his toys upstairs.

Neil was going on eleven years of being mayor. Eleven years of dealing with this town's lackluster *suburban* needs. He and the Captain had an agreement, one no one else knew about, and they were currently at odds.

The only reason Neil agreed to this dinner party, apart from the excuse to see his beautiful cousin, was to get the Captain alone.

The mayor's mansion wasn't as big as Thorne Hall, but 16,000 square feet was quite enough for him. Each room was gilded and he filled the place with expensive furniture that children could easy hurt themselves on or break. Lots of glass and steel and pieces with sharp edges. Large vases and giant delicate sculptures were in every room. It gave the house a vibe, as each room was decorated with the same type of furniture; the walls were all painted gray, his favorite color, and the portraits he chose to hang were of various wars in various countries throughout history. Each painting was more violent and brutal than the last. He favored the old ones, the ones of the demons and angels at war over heaven. Or Michael striking Lucifer down. Even his assistant got the creeps from coming to his mansion and had found ways to avoid it, which was the plan.

He had no wife, no kids, no friends, no parents he would take care of; he had the entire place to himself.

He snorted a line of white powder off a glass table and looked into the mirrored cabinet in front of him. He was in one of the six bedrooms. He was a handsome man, a gaunt man, but handsome. He shared his cousin's blond hair and emerald eyes, but where she was luster, he was faded. Those before and after pictures of presidents could spring to mind.

His phone vibrated and he knew that meant the limo was waiting for him. He snorted the rest of the line off the glass table and rubbed the residue on his teeth near his upper lip. He was dinner-party ready.

"Rosaletta. It's been ages." Priscilla bent forward and kissed the confused maid on the cheek. In a conservative pink dress with subtle designs of swirled stitching, her red hair was tightly wound and pulled back. The maid looked shocked to see Priscilla walk freely into Thorne Hall, eying everything as she walked around the grand foyer. When the maid wasn't looking, Priscilla even ran a finger over some molding to check for dust.

"Hello, Rosaletta." Susan smiled as she handed her coat to Rosaletta, topping Priscilla's. "The house looks fantastic."

Susan had never been to Thorne Hall. April had told her that Athena had stopped attending her own book clubs and teas months after her husband committed suicide, and Cynthia obviously hadn't planned on taking them on. She wouldn't have wanted to live here. It felt like some medieval castle, complete with the suit of armor glimmering in the corner; some haunted house at Disney World; this wasn't

Suburbia. This was something else altogether. Hallways seemed to go in every direction and she felt nothing but cold energy coming from each of them, except…

"Priscilla?" Athena had breezed into the foyer. "My word. How long has it been?"

"My dear friend." Priscilla and Athena embraced each other and Susan watched a reunion before her eyes. Honestly, she hadn't known what to think of Priscilla wanting to come tonight, but this is what she was hoping for. "Susan had a plus one she needed to use, and I figured why not surprise you."

"It is a welcome one." Athena and Priscilla's hands wrapped together, as Athena's eyes turned toward Susan. "You look like a whole new woman from the one I helped out of her car four years ago. I would have worn a different dress if I had known you'd look so stunning."

"You are too kind."

"Never kind. Athena smiled and turned in her green flow of a gown to lead the ladies into the dining room. "Only honest. Almost everyone is here. Lorraine and Lexi Scopello arrived just moments ago and the mayor has decided to grace us with his presence tonight. Cynthia, the Captain, and Dax should be joining us soon, and, of course, Samantha will be in attendance. Although she's gotten such good grades this year, she was actually invited to finish her senior year early at some higher education school out of country. She's leaving us tomorrow. I will miss her, but opportunities like this…you have to grasp them. What they can't learn here, they will learn elsewhere."

Did the room get warmer? Did Thorne Hall all of a sudden seem like it belonged in this *suburban* town? Priscilla was not joking—Athena had a gift, one that had been suppressed for too many years. Susan could see kids playing on the streets without worry, could envision neighbors not locking their doors, dinner parties at a minute's notice, knocks for cups of sugar as excuses to pleasantly gossip.

Susan hoped that what she had in her purse would help. A team was forming, and it was time to restore this neighborhood back to a place where good children were raised. Where nightmares didn't linger in the shadows.

Susan had defeated her inner demons; she could lend that strength to help destroy whatever threatened this town.

"I think it's time we go downstairs." The Captain was at their grand master suite bathroom door, peering at Cynthia through his dark glasses that he rarely took off, for he'd be blind without them. Cynthia had the entire bathroom tiled like some European bathhouse complete with a vanity that took up half the room. Her makeup products were all aligned and in order, and her knickknacks and Fabergé collection, all perfect. "All the guests will have arrived by now."

"Why is she doing this?"

"What?"

"Abraham." Cynthia turned, dressed in a long silk red dress that cut to above her knee at a point; her hair was pulled back and she looked worried. "Athena is gathering the entire town together."

"She's invited a few people for dinner, Cynthia. If she had something on us, she would have brought it up at dinner last night, right?"

"Right." Cynthia felt her hand want to scratch her nose, but she controlled it. "It was just an excuse for sisters to get together, as you said."

"You made sure to mention that she tell the mayor." He tapped his fingers on top of the cane's grand marble and gold top. "That we are all good to go, correct?"

"Of course. All just paranoia. I'm sure tonight will be just fine; let's go and get this over with. Where's Dax?"

"Oh." The Captain loosely waved a hand as he made his way out through their master suite. "He's on a job for me tonight. I've decided to start him early."

"A job?" Cynthia gripped at her leg. "He won't be at this dinner party? What job? What do you mean?"

"He won't be at any dinner party, Cynthia. He won't be returning to school; he will be doing odd jobs for me and learning how to run the foundation. It's his time to learn from me and not from some school. His time has come to take a place next to me."

Cynthia sat there for a second. Her son. Her poor son. Neither she nor the Captain had been good role models and her son had risen like he had. As a bully and a brut. Strong exterior mixed with the right amount of good looks and cockiness to get you through society. It wasn't until his accident that she realized just how vain he was. And it was her visit to the school that had opened her eyes to how much of a terror he was to other children; this wasn't the son she thought she had. She had not done her duty as a mother—she had raised something else altogether. He worked out in his gym in darkness. He ordered food and he brooded. Cynthia felt like she'd failed as a mother, and now she felt like she was losing her grip on their little family all together.

The Captain would destroy him. Cynthia gripped her leg a little harder. She couldn't allow that.

"Are you ready, darling?"

"Of course, darling."

The silver clock ticked from the corner of her vanity, a ticking bomb time, and tonight it had begun. Something, she felt, was starting that could not be undone.

"I stare in envy every time I see your garden, Mrs. Primm," Andrea Watson said, laughing from across the table. "It's just beautiful how you get those roses so perfect."

"I do enjoy pretty flowers," the mayor said from his seat a few over from Andrea Watson, and where Athena Rose would be placing herself as the head of that end of the table. "All you ladies have such pretty gardens. Makes driving around the town nice and I'm sure it's good for our image. Gardeners know how to do the jobs they are paid for. Happy citizens. Happy workers."

"I tend to them myself, as you do, Andrea. Not all of us need gardeners, Mr. Mayor." Priscilla smiled and then looked at the woman who was sitting next to Andrea, the seat over from where the Captain would sit. "Do you do a lot of gardening...I'm sorry, but have we been introduced?"

"Lorraine," Susan offered, who was seated to the right of Priscilla. "This is Priscilla Primm, my neighbor from behind."

Lorraine Scopello was in a dress that looked like leather, but it wasn't real, a rough snakeskin pattern and reached above her knees. If anyone dropped a napkin tonight, they would be seeing more than they'd bargained for.

"Oh my goodness, we haven't met." Lorraine lifted an arm and cocked her hand in a wave from across the table. "Lorraine Scopello. I live on Sun Drop Court. I've been here for a few years. I live in the old…they had some weird name…"

"Yes." Priscilla was smiling, but her tone had changed. "The Bixbys. They moved out in 1996. The Captain bought that house, was wondering who he was renting it to. I have cousins from the South as well."

"Ah, yes, my accent," Lorraine quickly replied. "Can't hide it."

"You are very beautiful," Priscilla continued. "So is your daughter…Lexi, is it? What part of the Carolinas are you from?"

"I've been to the Carolinas once," Neil said. "I think."

"Thank you." Lexi reached for her crystal glass of water, amazed at how heavy the glass was and sipped from it. She just wanted this night to be over.

"Lineswood." Lorraine unfolded her napkin. "You've likely never heard of it…it's a…"

"Susan." Priscilla turned her head to the right to look at Susan, perfect posture, poised. "Lineswood is a large trailer-park community. I have a thing for accents; can normally place exactly where someone is from. Now, I say largest trailer-park community because it's the cheapest you can get down there."

"Excuse me?" Lorraine went to retort.

Lexi coughed on her water.

Andrea Watson sat back and smiled, giving her husband a couple slaps on his leg, as if to tell him she was right about tonight.

Samantha entered the room that minute, Athena behind her. Athena had actually waited outside the door for a moment as she listened to this exchange. She would have let it continue, but her daughter had appeared.

Bless the angels, Athena thought. *I thought I'd never see Priscilla again. If this is to be war, she is a colonel.*

Samantha was pale, in a silver Chanel dress. Her hair was half-done and her head was lowered. Athena motioned her for her sit next to Lexi.

At that moment, Cynthia and the Captain entered the room.

"Welcome to my home, everyone," the Captain began as Athena stood at her chair with her eyes The Captain. "I hope tonight is as pleasant as we planned it to be. I know my wife and, of course, our host, Athena, have been hard at work to make sure everyone is happy." He pulled out the chair for Cynthia, next to Priscilla, who just smiled at her.

"Cynthia."

"Priscilla."

The Captain went to sit at his chair and eyed Athena from across the room; she was standing at her chair. Her jade gown just slightly swishing, her eyes on him, he felt goosebumps as she pulled out her chair and sat at the same time he did.

This isn't good, he thought. *This is not good.*

"I thought you'd put us boys next to each other," Neil said, looking over at the Captain. "I need to talk to you, mister."

"After dinner." The Captain's eyes were still on Athena from under his dark glasses, her jade eyes so calm they seemed cold. "Us gentlemen will have to have a cigar."

"I'll settle for that." Neil looked over Priscilla. "You were saying something before I interrupted?"

"Oh, yes." Priscilla turned back to Lorraine, "Lineswood…"

"Priscilla Primm," the Captain slipped in, knowing exactly where she was going with this. He had plucked Lorraine from the cheapest and lowest trailer-park community. One didn't have to write so many zeroes on a check when someone was already so down and out. "Out of all the houses I've bought up around town, yours has always been one of my favorites. Ever consider selling?"

"I plan on dying in my house, Abraham." Priscilla smiled. "But thank you for the offer. My husband says hello, by the way. Was wondering if you were going to ever call him about your stock portfolio."

Cynthia coughed.

"Tell Peter hello, and we should go golfing some time." The Captain sipped a glass of red wine while Rosaletta had begun circling the table with appetizers. Wine was being poured and conversation was beginning to break off into smaller groups. The table sat sixteen and there were missing chairs.

Samantha looked over at Lexi, who just shook her head at her.

Athena and the mayor were talking about expanding the school's after-school programs with Priscilla chirping in. Andrea was talking to the Captain and the mayor about Leroy's health, as he was once a worker for the Captain and the Captain's father. One of the first.

Susan wasn't involved in any specific conversation. A word was said here and there, and she listened in on chatter, this seeming almost pleasant. Cynthia was even talking to Lorraine as if she wasn't a quiche.

Then the doorbell rang. A tapping at the door, the sound of the end of a cane. A ghost chill came over the room.

"Are we missing people?" both Cynthia and the Captain said at the same time. To them, the night had been going perfectly. Appetizers and entrees were served.

"Yes." Athena stuck a fork into her steak and took a knife through it; she had purposely put a start time of an hour later on Felicia's invitation. "Allow me."

"No…" The Captain felt it and moved to get up. "I can get the door."

But like the gazelle she was, Athena was already past the dining table and heading for the front door, her blond braid swinging behind her and a small smile on her face.

Athena opened the door to Salome and Felicia.

"Salome." Athena smiled and leaned in to give her a kiss. "How great for you to join us. Felicia, you look beautiful tonight. Please, come in. You are both seated next to me."

Both Cynthia and the Captain heard the sound of the cane ricochet off the marble floor. Ten steps away, nine steps away…five, four, three, two, one.

"Our final guests." Athena opened the door to allow Salome and Felicia to enter. "Everyone, this is Felicia Johnson; she once lived on Sun Drop Court. And may I present Doctor Salome Legree…"

"Mother?" The Captain dropped his fork and his eyes widened under his glasses. He shot a look over at Leroy Watson, but Andrea just smiled back at him. "I thought…I thought…"

"Holy shit," Cynthia tried to whisper, but it was loud enough for Priscilla and Susan to hear it.

"Hello, darling Abraham." Salome made her way over to the Captain and kissed him on the cheek, leaving a mark of purple and black lipstick. "It has been too long."

Felicia looked at Athena, confused, but Athena had her hand on Felicia's back and brought her to the other end of the table, sitting her next to her as she sat at the head of the table and whispered over to Felicia: "Everything will be explained, my dear. Just…let this play out. I am right next to you."

Salome eyed the cane Abraham held, as he looked at the cheap version she held,

"May I have my cane back? This one is just not as…sturdy as that one." Salome grabbed the cane and switched them. "At your age, it's sad that you need one. But use the one I've been using for the past nine years. I'm sorry if we are late, Athena."

"It's okay, Salome. Take your seat, next to the mayor."

"It's just a surprise to see you after all these years, Mother." The Captain's eyes never left Athena, but if they had and he'd seen Felicia, something else might of clicked, but his mind now was spinning.

"You don't call. You don't write. A surprise at a dinner party. Not a bad way to reconnect with mommy dearest." Salome sat in her seat. "Heard there's been quite a stir going on these days: kids burning each other, girls getting roofied."

Salome slapped the mayor's leg. "You are doing a good job, aren't you?"

"Thank you, ma'am." Neil smiled, too high to notice the sarcasm. "What is this about burning and kids getting drugged?"

"My son got doused in gasoline and burned at a field party." The Captain tried to contain the look on his face. "He is permanently disfigured."

"I got roofied," Lexi freely said, her mother shooting her a look. "By someone who I thought was my close friend, but is just a phony who can't even meet me in the eye anymore."

Samantha Rose's head had remained down the entire time—what was one more wound.

"This is going on at the high school?" Priscilla put her hand to her chest. "That's outrageous. What kind of a community aura are we setting for our children to act like this?"

"I'll look into these matters immediately, madam," Neil said, rehearsed lines and speeches always flowing freely from his mouth. He'd learned many of them during his election years. "I'll make sure someone is on that."

"My son didn't deserve what happened to him." Cynthia looked at the Captain. "He should also be at this table tonight, Abraham."

"Did my daughter-in-law just say I am right?" Salome slapped Neil on the leg again. She could tell he was high; after all, she was a doctor and a scientist. His pupils were gigantic.

"If you ever get married, Mr. Mayor, that's something you can take to the grave with you."

"It's kids being kids." The Captain sturdied himself and his smile fell. "We don't all have perfect households in crime-free neighborhoods. There are bad people out there; people make mistakes; there are situations we cannot control. Life is like a pool: you either swim or you sink. You can't blame the mayor or me for how this community is turning out… If you want a perfect *suburbia*, go find it. You won't because it doesn't exist."

Athena Rose slowly raised herself with her arms crossed before slamming them down on the dinner table so hard the silverware shook and a few glasses fell over to shatter. "Let me tell you something." Her eyes ablaze with fury, in her feral nature she looked more beautiful and ferocious than ever. "These aren't just a bunch of houses in the same place. This is not just some town, some community; we are not just ants in this big wide world. We aren't some analogy of what life is. Each and every life has a purpose; we don't all make it to the big screen and we don't all become Oprah or Bill Gates. But in these little boxes that stretch these streets like spider webs are people whose lives are connected, individuals with feelings and emotions and love. We care about one another. It is our responsibility to set examples and control them. Not buy up houses and fill them with middle-class citizens that you have bought to work for you. What even goes on at that power plant, hmm? Why did my beautiful husband turn into this gaunt ghost before my very eyes; is that something you can answer? You, the great Captain."

Athena's finger slowly rose and pointed across the long table at the Captain who sat in silence. He held his posture though there was fear in his eyes as he slowly weighed the energy that was being thrown around like a flood of fury. He could have been drowning, if this was real water. But this was not real water, so composure would remain.

"And…" Athena turned her eyes on her sister. "*You.* How much of what you know and don't will remain a mystery to me. Look, you are the Queen of Stepford, ruling over a community that wants to be happy and have their kids playing soccer on the streets and biking around. Instead, they are poisoning, burning, and raping each other. That's not completely on them; that's on us as well. You think Dax hasn't left this house for days because of his scars, but it's because he doesn't know where he went wrong. Because you never taught him right from wrong. Because all you cared about was money, greed and, apparently, Maxine Johnson."

Lorraine Scopello looked over at the Captain for the first time that night, breaking her mask of smugness. "What does that loon have to do with this?"

"Athena." The Captain was calmly staring across the table of guests who each had their parts in this tale. "I think it's time the men go for cigars and the women tea, but if you could give me a moment with my mother, I'd appreciate it."

Athena looked over at Neil and whispered, "Have a police car outside Salome's house."

"As you wish, beautiful darling dearest cousin." Neil opened his phone and sent a text. "Done."

"Shall we go have cigars?" The Captain calmly looked over at Neil, who nodded and smiled. Finally, the mayor was going to get what he wanted. "I'll roll your husband in with us, Mrs. Watson; only fair you ladies get some quality time together."

Dr. Salome Legree and Abraham Thorne stood in a room adjacent to the foyer. It could have been used as a living room, but it was one of the many spaces in the house that no one used, though it remained clean.

"I thought you were dead." The Captain looked at his mother in disbelief.

"Call me a cat, then." Salome looked over the cane the Captain had been using for the past nine years. Her cane. It was fine oak and the top was finished in European marble with speckles of gold that matched her son's eyes. "You took good care of this. You know serial killers keep trinkets of their victims."

Cynthia stood at the door, had decided on not joining the ladies in the adjacent fireplace room for tea; she had remembered that night back in 1996. The night her husband had told her that his mother had died of a heart attack...

"You didn't think I'd keep your secrets?" Salome was standing firmly in front of her son, both hands wrapped around her cane. The Captain removed his glasses and rubbed his eyes, his amber eyes with their golden flecks, a trait in their family. "You tried to have Leroy Watson push me down a flight of stairs? Ha. I spent years in Africa and Europe researching and studying; we encountered things there that had more of a chance of killing me than him. What? Did you think when he never reported back that the job was just done?"

"All I found at your house was blood and your cane." The Captain didn't look like a man in his late fifties anymore; he looked like a child who had messed up and now was answering to his mother. "I figured you had given him a good swift hit to his head or something, and that's what put him in that wheelchair."

"When Andrea found out what her husband almost did." Salome raised a nostril at him. "We put him into a coma. That's why you kept me close in the first place. I'm the only one who can cook the potions you want and procure the drugs you asked for. I mixed a little of this, a little of that. For as long as Andrea wants, Leroy will remain in that wheelchair. That old coon doesn't have much life left in her, but let her enjoy it. Not worrying what jobs you have your 'workers' out on. Did they ever find Maxine Johnson?"

"I had nothing to do with her disappearance." The Captain looked away from his mother and couldn't find a place in the room for his eyes to land, so he just looked at the floor. "For God's sake, Mother, I loved her."

"Your idea of love is a sick one." Salome smacked the bottom of her cane against her son's leg. "I'll never forget that night. Nor forgive you for trying to kill me. But the fact that you didn't think I could keep your secrets, after all the ones we have in our family, from all the generations of Thornes. Well, I cannot trust you. You won't have another chance like you did in 1996; I will live until it's time for me to go to heaven, Abraham. Your judgment has not even started. Tonight is only a drizzle compared to the storm that is coming. You cannot kill me again for I am already dead."

Cynthia gripped her dress at the leg and felt her ulcer burn. Her husband had told her that his mother had a heart attack; she'd attended her funeral. But all this about Maxine, this she had known. This was old news that she tried to forget every day—their marriage wasn't conventional, but rules had been drawn. He had crossed that line. She had known about his actual love for Maxine and...

"I think I'd move this coat of armor." The Southern accent rang through Cynthia's body like an itch. "Replace it with something more modern. What do you think, Lexi?"

"I think I want to go home."

"Soon this might be our home, remember?"

Cynthia closed the door, allowing the Captain and his mother to go over...how he'd failed to kill her and had turned on Lorraine.

"What are you talking about?" Cynthia moved about the grand foyer, only inches away from Lorraine who truly had terrible taste in how to dress for the occasion; who wore snakeskin pleather? She also smelled like cheap perfume. "Why would I move it? That coat of armor dates back to the beginning of the Thorne tree."

"Well." Lorraine bumped her hip, the fabric of her dress making the most annoying stretching sound. "I think that is something you and your husband should discuss. I don't feel it's my place to tell you who he loves and who..."

"Oh, shut up, you stupid bimbo." Cynthia shook her head. This dance was ending now. "The only reason my husband moved you into this town was because he needed a new blow-up doll to play with."

"You know...about our affair?"

"Affair. Affair?" Cynthia laughed and the sound bounced off every wall in the house. "Lorraine Scopello, an Italian woman from a big city who lost everything and had to flee to the Carolinas, where she and her daughter were abandoned by the one-night stand who'd produced her. I'm the one who found you on match.com; I'm the one who picked you out for him. Maxine caused…so much trouble. For she was intelligent, bright, and actually had an ounce of common sense."

"The loon who shot herself?"

"If that's what you've been told, then sure, the loon who shot herself." How that rumor started, who cares. But it was so far from the truth. Cynthia went to the front wall and rang the bell for the kitchen, where she knew Rosaletta was. "You will never live in Thorne Hall. You will never inherit anything more than upgrades. You like your new kitchen? The pool in your backyard? Diamond earrings were going to be my next suggestion. You are a pump."

Lorraine stood with her mouth agape. Lexi was trying to hide her smile and Cynthia caught that with amusement… then realized that Lexi might actually hate her mom. The lessons she was learning at home, Cynthia could only imagine. Lorraine Scopello was no example of what a parent should be.

"You know, Lexi." Cynthia had turned her attention to Lexi and softened her tone as much as she could. "There is a great boarding school just an hour's drive south of here. I debated sending Dax there after middle school, but his father insisted on him remaining local. Would you like to go there?"

"You can't send my daughter…" Lorraine began, but Cynthia held her hand out at her. Lorraine looked at her daughter with a 'we are a team' look, but Lexi looked from her mother to Cynthia for a moment.

"I'd like that," Lexi said quietly, but Cynthia had heard it and so did Lorraine.

Rosaletta had appeared.

"Get their coats," Cynthia snapped at the maid who bumbled off to grab the coats. "Great. I can make a phone call tonight and you can leave tomorrow. Are you a good student?"

"Straight As…and a B in chemistry. Science isn't my strong suit."

"Math was my weakness." Cynthia rubbed the area of her dress she had been gripping at all night to try and smooth the wrinkles out. "They offer fabulous scholarships to all the Ivy-League colleges, or wherever you want to go. When that time comes, write me and I'll help you."

"What are you doing?" Lorraine's face was contorted with various emotions. Rosaletta had returned with their coats. Lexi put hers on and Lorraine just stood there, loosely holding her fake fur; it wasn't even a good fake. "This is my daughter. You can't make these decisions for her or for me. I'm going to live here one day."

"For Christ's sake. Lexi, darling, I'll be in touch tomorrow. If you'd mind waiting outside? A word with your mother is necessary before I let her leave my house."

Lexi smiled and with a skip in her step kissed Cynthia on the cheek. Cynthia was caught off guard by this affection and a part inside of her that had been dead for some time lightened a little. She waited until Rosaletta closed the door behind Lexi. Cynthia didn't care if the maid or the whole world heard what she had to say next.

"Lorraine, you are an unfit mother. I know what happened in the big city. You made stupid decisions on ridiculous business deals and wasted all of your family's money. You could have been something, but instead you chose sex and partying. How many nights did you leave your daughter home alone? How many men could possibly be her father? So off you skip and dance to a dreadful trailer-park community in the Carolinas and do nothing there. Nothing. My husband has needs, and, frankly, that wasn't part of our arrangement when we got married, so I picked you. I knew he'd never fall in love with you. For that was not allowed. Does it ruin it that I know? That key you're going to use to open your house? I had it cut. Every time you open that door, remember: I've known all along. Your daughter is a good person, you are not; she will go to that boarding school and she will learn how to be a good member of society. Not turn out like you, that is, if you want this arrangement to continue. I can simply have you sent back to where I picked you from."

Cynthia motioned for Rosaletta to open the door. Lorraine's mouth had closed slightly, but shock was still on her face. Cynthia looked at her to give her a chance to say something, but she had nothing left to say.

As the door closed, the voice behind her ran goosebumps down her spine. "That wasn't kind, Cynthia." The Captain was standing there with his mother, whose face was all winnings. "How am I going to fix that?"

"Fix what, Abraham?" Cynthia snapped back. "Nothing has changed. If anything, now you don't have to worry about her daughter when you go to her house. She is an unfit parent, and I just gave her daughter a chance at life. I think I fixed the issue."

"I think your wife is right," Salome said in her therapist's voice, one of the many roles she played as doctor, scientist, and psychotherapist. "You want an arranged marriage like that, so be it. But don't tarnish the children."

"Listen." The Captain put his glasses on over his amber-and-gold eyes and looked at his mother. "I don't think I'm ready for motherly advice from you quite yet. I am going to join Leroy and Neil in the smoking room. You ladies...let's stop causing commotions tonight, shall we?"

Salome looked to Cynthia who offered her arm to her mother-in-law. Salome raised an eyebrow, but took her arm and was led down the hallway to the tea room. Where all the ladies were waiting. The doors closed behind them.

Athena was standing next to the fireplace, staring into it. Felicia was on a chair close to her, and Samantha was in the back of the room with her arms folded and her head down. Andrea was sitting on the couch making small talk with Priscilla and Susan when Cynthia and Salome entered.

Athena turned her head. "Where's Lorraine?"

"I sent her home," Cynthia said in a monotone voice. She walked over to the liquor cabinet and poured herself a huge glass of vodka. "Anyone else? Children included?"

"Yes, please," Samantha said for the first time all night.

"No, thank you." Felicia shot a look at Samantha. One would think she would be amused at the mess she was, but Felicia pitied her. She had tasted her own medicine, literally, and crumbled under it.

"Absolutely not," Athena shot at her daughter whose head fell back down. "I don't quite know how to go about this. I've been envisioning this night in my head for quite some time now... Salome?"

"My delivery is not as pleasant as yours, Athena." Salome looked around the room, "but...fine. Felicia, darling, it wasn't random that I adopted you...I'm your grandmother."

"Okay, you're right." Athena looked over at Salome. "Let me do this. Felicia, we have half a journal of your mother's; she was a patient of Dr. Legree's many years ago. Started seeing her after she began losing periods of time and experienced sudden bursts of rage that, as I've read, she took out on you."

Felicia's amber eyes with their gold speckles just stared back at Athena, then over at Salome. "I don't understand. My father is your son?"

"Larry Johnson is not my son, but Abraham Thorne is. I kept my maiden name as my practice had taken off on a level I never expected. His father, him, and you all share the same eyes. I had your DNA run after I adopted you...you see...in therapy, your mother confessed things to me."

"Should we be here?" Susan said to Priscilla, feeling incredibly uncomfortable. "Maybe it'd be best if we left."

"No," Athena said, a slight force to her voice. "Tonight isn't just about piecing Felicia's past together; it's about us moving together as a community. Stopping from what I am suspecting happens every time the foundation ball comes around... Priscilla and I remember a time where we didn't have to lock our doors or worry about our kids, instead letting them play outside till after dark. But, not to be poetic, some thorns have been busy pricking everything they have come in contact with. Cynthia, maybe you'd like to leave the room—we know how you feel about Felicia, so you must have known…"

"I didn't." Cynthia swung the glass of vodka back and sank into the couch next to Andrea and Susan. "My husband currently has my son out on a 'job.' Dax is eighteen years old and my husband has him…I don't even know. Maxine Johnson caused a lot of drama on this street… I knew of my husband's affair with her…but it wasn't until I realized his obsession and love for her that my hate started for the both of you. I'm…. I'm… I'm sorry Felicia. I mean that. I also thought Salome was dead! I attended her funeral and services! I'm… I'm…anything said in this room will not reach the Captain's ears, okay? I was on board with the Captain until my son was sent out into the dark of the night. Until his mother seemingly rose from the grave. Until he started shutting me out. I don't even know what is going on around here."

Susan, Priscilla, Salome, and Andrea all looked to Athena, who nodded.

Felicia took a deep breath, a tear rolling down her eye and looked up,

"My mother was having an affair with….

"Can I leave?" Samantha let out from the corner. "I'm exhausted and would like to get some rest."

"Wow. That's right." Athena smiled across the room at her daughter. "You leave tomorrow, look up empathy while you are packing."

"Leave? This room? What are you…"

"I said we'd talk after dinner, but it seems this is an open forum. I'm sending you to Europe to an all-girls Catholic boarding school to finish your years. They continue as a university as well. Get a job, this is a working school, I hear Dean Schatten is quite the peach. "

"Mom."

"Samantha, go to your room and pack. You are excused from this dinner party. Say goodnight to everyone and show some manners."

Susan looked over at Athena, shocked. She had always assumed Samantha was the popular girl with the good head on her shoulders. But she had never actually spoken with her, or spent time with her; just assumed she shared the same graces as her mother.

But from the exchanges she saw tonight, Susan knew Samantha was far from what she appeared. Besides, Samantha had not spoken a word at dinner and had a look on her…that could use some real therapy.

"It was a pleasure to see you all." Samantha tried to smile as best as she could, and met her mother's eye to assure that was enough. Athena nodded at her. "I am off to bed."

Athena waited for her daughter to leave the room before turning her attention back to Felicia. For a second, Felicia wanted to go after Samantha and just try and get a 'why' out of her one more time. But...her leaving the country was better. She looked to Athena with a questioning look. "The Captain was having an affair with my mother?"

"Yes," Cynthia answered. "He was obsessed with her. In love with her. Had your father working late nights and doing all sorts of things so he could be alone with her. But I don't think he even knows you are his daughter."

"And he shouldn't." Athena had her eyes on Cynthia.

"Why?" Susan inquired. "After all these years, what harm could it do?"

"He might not accept her," Cynthia said as kindly as possible. "I'm surprised Salome is still standing right now. You know he told me you had a heart attack. We had a funeral for you and everything."

"Closed casket?" Salome joked. "I don't think now is the right time for my son to learn he has a daughter running about. Nor, no offense to Susan or Priscilla, do I think Athena and I should share everything we know... See, your mother kept a journal. A day before she...vanished...we had a session in which we tried hypnotherapy. It was our third attempt, but it opened her up. The next day, she came by and left me the first part of her journal saying something about how it was done."

Susan looked to Priscilla, who looked to Susan and nodded.

"I found something last night digging," Susan said and went to open her purse. "Priscilla and I...well...we read the entire thing. It's the second half of Maxine's journal."

"Are you burying bodies, too?" Salome inquired. "We have enough secrets in this town."

"She's digging quite a lovely coy pond." Priscilla let on a small smile. "Susan shares our wishes for this town to return to normalcy."

"As much as I'd love to read the entire thing as if reading a novel," Athena spoke up from in front of the fireplace, "I think, Felicia, you are old enough to read what your mother wrote. I read the first half and it might put some peace to what you went through in your terrible childhood."

"Yes," Susan spoke up, handing over the second part of the journal, which had been wrapped in a red scarf before its burial. "I think you might want to read these on your own, dear."

Salome walked to her granddaughter and put a hand on her shoulder. "I'm sorry it took us this long, that you were kept in the dark. But first I wanted you to be of an age that you could process some of this. I had the journal in my possession for so long, I sent it to Athena and we began communicating again. This dinner party was the best excuse we could come up with to get us all in the same room. I wanted you to see your father, see the man you luckily avoided being raised by. I will continue to keep you safe…if you can forgive…"

Felicia stood and wrapped her arms around Salome who, slightly shocked, let her cane fall and hit the ground. The marble top echoing a sound through the silent room.

"So," Cynthia said, directed at Salome, "that is my old Mercedes, then. The one I got rid of some nine years ago."

Salome smiled at Cynthia. "Yes, dear. Still a nice car for Felicia to drive, but that is also a talk for another night. That stain…"

"Of course it is." Cynthia swirled the contents of her glass. "So happy my mother-in-law is back in my life for conversations and visits. Digging up the past."

"Sarcasm, dear." Salome reminded. "Must be hard to sell houses when you can't even pretend to be pleasant."

"I've actually obtained a real-estate license." Priscilla Primm was busying herself with her purse and checking her phone. "I am going to start filling these houses with families again. Tonight is just a start to restoring our community. But…this reconnection has reminded me of the good days. How they should be restored. It seems like everyone in this room is on the same page…Cynthia?"

Cynthia Wolf-Thorne stared at the enormous diamond on her finger, the one Abraham had let her pick out. He never had actually proposed; from the beginning their arrangement was a business deal. Cynthia got a new Mercedes whenever she wanted, the newest of fashions…and then they'd stumbled financially in the 1990s…until the next foundation ball when, all of a sudden, the checks increased and money seemed to be pour in like a waterfall. Cynthia never questioned it, but now she needed to know why.

"Yes. You have my full support; whatever that is good for." Cynthia swung back her glass again. "If everyone else wouldn't mind, it is getting late and I think my sister and I need to have a heart-to-heart conversation."

"Do we?" Athena looked shock at the notion. "Caught me off guard."

"Susan?" Priscilla smiled pleasantly at her neighbor. "Come over for some tea and cake. We had a birthday celebration a few days back for one of my grandchildren and there is still enough cake to feed an army of kids. Andrea, if you would care to join us?"

"Another time, Priscilla. Truly. I have to make sure Leroy gets home and put to bed properly. At almost ninety, it's amazing he's still breathing."

"I don't know how you do it," Cynthia blurted out. "It's been nine years and you've been taking care of him like some saint."

Salome and Andrea exchanged looks. Andrea shrugged. "It's just a wifely duty."

While Priscilla Primm was entertaining Susan and ending the evening on a high note, Matthew McArthur had seen the light in Todd's room flash on and felt like he needed to make sure he was okay, and not just because of the anniversary of his sister's disappearance. But after everything he had told him…a part of him felt like he just needed to give him another hug. He had never heard such a terrible story, and he loved his best friend. The girls would be all right for half an hour. Just one more hug.

Katie and Kat were sound asleep and Matthew knew he wouldn't be missed. They had so much energy during the day that at night they slept like the dead. He tossed on a hoodie and went to head across the street.

From the bushes, Dax watched as Matthew left his house and left his door unlocked. He dropped a rag he was going to use to break a window and slowly crept toward the front of the house. As Matthew knocked on Todd's door, Dax quietly slipped into the McArthur house.

The beast of a boy was just eighteen, but through steroids and the time he spent at the gym, he was over six feet and weighed a good 230 pounds. But thanks to years of football and even ballet recommended by the coach, something he'd admitted to no one, he was silent on his feet.

He had never been inside the McArthur house before, but it was *suburban* wallpaper. All these houses seemed the same. They were pictures come to life from some magazine, perfectly arranged rooms and photos of smiling families on the fireplace and spotless kitchens with empty sinks. Clean. The carpets and drapes all matched and the colors all flew in a constant. Boring. One day, he would build a castle like Thorne Hall and fill the rooms with dead animal skins from hunts he had fantasized of going on.

But tonight was a different type of hunt.

He slowly crept up the stairs and immediately knew which room he had to go into.

Their door had double pink Ks on it. He removed the other rag from his sweatshirt and the small bottle, doused the rag, and slowly walked to the middle of the room.

Katie McArthur opened her eyes to a monster carrying her sister Kat. It was bigger than anything she had ever seen and its body was humongous, its skin covered in scars and burns.

Monster.

"A monster!" she screamed as it took her sister. "Help! Help! Help! Help!"

Katie got out of bed and grabbed at the monster's leg. "Let go of my sister!"

She bit her tiny teeth into its leg, causing it to groan a terrible sound. "Let go!"

But it just kicked her off; she wasn't a percentage of its size or weight. As the monster made its way quickly down the hallway, she grabbed a baseball bat out of Matthew's room that was the size of her, and as the monster was going down the stairs, she gave it her all and swung it and met his head.

The monster roared and Katie screamed again. "Kat!"

But the monster continued to head toward the front door and Katie stumbled down the stairs. "Matthew!" she screamed frantically, trying to swing the bat at the monster, "Mommy! Daddy!"

But the monster had left their house and was out in the night. Katie was too terrified to follow him, and felt, for the first time in her life, alone. She crawled up into a ball and began to sob.

"He's not much of a talker," Neil Wolf said to the Captain as they puffed on cigars, motioning over toward Leroy. "Cancer? Dementia? Old people's disease?"

"He is almost ninety. I sent him awhile back" The Captain was sitting in his oversized chair looking at a boar's head on the wall, something his grandfather had hunted down years ago. "I thought he completed it, but he didn't, and those involved have been punishing him for it ever since."

"Your mother seems…lovely." Neil rolled his eyes. "I do see the family resemblance. Though didn't I attend a funeral for her, like, ten years ago or something?"

"Neil," the Captain said to the mayor. "It's been a long night. Cynthia told me she had a message relayed to you."

"What message would that be?" Neil took a puff of the Cuban cigar, made a face, and put it out in his whiskey glass. "Gross. Your little foundation ball just passed and I played my part. Every cop in town was elsewhere. You had your little parade go on…if I don't get what I want…this next one… well, you certainly won't be raising as much money as you did if I have the police…"

"When you get home tonight." The Captain was exhausted and just wanted this over with "What you want will be at your house."

"Just like last time, and the time before?"

"Yes." The Captain met Neil's eyes and was trying not to appear disgusted. "Just like before."

"I hope we have an understanding then," Neil got himself off the seat he was sitting on. "If you want things to run smoothly every time for your foundation ball…well, I'll be needing consistency. Not arguments on the phone and disputes over morality. What you are doing is comparable to what I want anyway."

"I would disagree," the Captain said, staring at the boar's head, wishing he was more of a hunter, "but…you have a present waiting for you at the mayor's mansion."

"Life is not a metaphor." Neil patted the Captain on the shoulder. "You sound idiotic which each one you make. Life is what you do when you want to do it. I get what I want."

The mayor flipped his phone open and called his limo driver as he exited the room without even saying goodbye to the Leroy, the Captain let out a heavy sigh. He looked up at Leroy Watson, a tube in his mouth for feeding, the IV stand pumping who knew what into his arteries and veins… His mother…

"It looks like I have to finish a job that should have been finished nine years ago," the Captain said, fondling his mother's cheap cane in his hands. "My mother or not, that woman cannot be allowed to walk this earth. She may appear a saint in her old age, Leroy, but almost eighty years on this earth…we can go from devil to angel and back to devil again. Circumstances change us. Mistakes and lessons twist us. Things are changing again, and I wish you could be here to help me. Truly. I wish you were still with us, old boy; you were one of my favorite…"

"Workers?" Andrea Watson was at the door with Salome and Felicia next to her. "Are you two fine gentleman done catching up?"

The Captain looked at the floor and motioned, half-drunk, for Andrea to wheel her husband away. "Thank you, ladies, for an unforgettable evening. I hope you all make it home safe." He gave a quick glance at his mother, his glasses back on so she couldn't see the look in his eyes. "I'm assuming I won't be seeing you anytime soon."

"Oh." Salome smiled as she put her hand on the small of Felicia's back to turn her away. If he saw her eyes, he'd know, and it wasn't time for that. "I'll be around."

The Captain listened as Rosaletta got all their coats and everyone exchanged pleasant goodbyes…as if this hadn't been the dinner party from hell…and the doors to Thorne Hall were closed.

He sat in his chair for a second and walked over to the cabinet filled with ancient guns. *Athena*, he thought. *What to do about Athena.*

"You said we needed to talk." Athena and Cynthia were alone in the adjacent room to the dining hall, desserts and coffee and tea and liquor all on the table in front of them. "I'm here to talk. But let's also take a walk."

"A walk?" Cynthia looked confused. "A walk where?"

"Amuse me, sis."

Cynthia followed Athena down the hallway to where Samantha's room was. Athena pushed the door open and Cynthia peered in. Samantha was packing her suitcase, tossing various clothing inside, clothing that cost more than it should. Samantha treating each article as if it were meaningless, the girl truly had no concept of value, worth, or care.

"Your plane leaves early," Athena said with no tone in her voice. "Four a.m., I want you out of this house; is that understood?"

"Yes." Samantha didn't even look over as she continued to pack. "Mother."

"Good. Cynthia, have her door locked. I want to make sure she doesn't escape. Or try to drug anyone else tonight."

Samantha shot her mother a look, but it quickly fell away from her face; she didn't have any energy left in her to fight, and she didn't know why she fought so hard in the first place. She had no friends left, she had no prospects here, so she packed.

Maybe…a change would change her.

Samantha's door was closed and locked.

"Wait. Where are we going?"

"I found this key in her drawer." Athena unlocked the basement door. "I know what's down here from those files I was given and I can make assumptions about the journal entries. But I've never actually been down here; have you?"

"Once…" Cynthia admitted. "Years ago."

"Why the change of heart." Athena turned her back against the door she'd just unlocked. "Your entire attitude has changed since our dinner. I was planning on keeping you out of most of tonight, but you seem to be on the same page as me. Why?"

"Recent events." Cynthia looked down at her thousand-dollar shoes. "Have shown me that I've been blinded by money and power for quite some time. I thought I was happy with this arrangement, but I took a busboy home last night and paid him for sex. That's how happy I am."

"I called you a cab before I left you last night." Athena raised an eyebrow. "You stayed?"

"That's not the point." Cynthia looked to the other end of the hall to make sure no one was listening, not even Rosaletta. "I'm beginning to sound like a broken record, but he sent my son out on a 'job' tonight. I never ask where, why, who, how. I don't know how the money keeps coming in like it does, nor do I know why our last couple of foundation balls have raised quadruple the amount of money than the previous ones. But I do know that my son…has crossed a line tonight. I figured his scars and burns would heal and he'd return to school, graduate, and go off to college. Perhaps even get a good job. I didn't know he was some awful bully; I didn't know any of these things. It seems my husband has been keeping me in the dark about him…under no circumstances can he know Felicia is his daughter. I honestly thought Salome had a heart attack. I didn't realize he'd sent Leroy Watson to kill her. That list of women you showed me last night. As of now, everything I've been blinded by, my new cars and diamonds and dresses, I've just been a pawn in his game. Handing houses over to his sluts and workers, who haven't been bringing anything but terror to this community. That's why now…also…I need to confess something to you…and I need you…"

"Let's venture downstairs," Athena said. "I feel like the 'also' can wait."

They opened the door and a sound of pressure was released. It had been awhile since anyone ventured down these stairs.

A part of Thorne Hall that remained true to its original building. The stone steps were bulky and uneven. The lighting, from a decade ago, flickered madly and could use rewiring. The switch even clicked on with an unwelcoming sound.

"Ghosts live down here," Cynthia said. "I can feel it."

"So can I." Athena wrapped her hand in her sister's and together they slowly made their way down the twenty or so steps.

As their heels echoed down the damp and gloomy steps, they finally hit the bottom. Athena reached her hand along the wall and felt a switch that needed to be pushed in to ignite the electricity. She pushed the switch and, from above, fluorescent lights turned on.

The room was empty. Completely empty apart from a cabinet across from them, about a yard away. Athena walked directly over to the cabinet and opened it. The shelves were lined with various bottles of ketamine and other glass bottles of various colors and sizes.

"Help me," Athena said as she ran her hand over the outside of the cabinet.

"Do what?"

"Move this. There is air coming from behind this cabinet. I can feel it. There's another room back there."

Cynthia hesitated. She had only seen this room nine years ago; the only time she had ever seen the door unlocked, and seeing the cabinet of drugs was enough for her to figure out how her husband was attracting Maxine's love…by drugging her…

"Wait," Cynthia said. "I need to tell you something. It needs to be now."

Athena turned toward her sister and rested her back against the cold stone wall. "Fine." Athena had her hand on the cabinet, ready to push it aside and reveal whatever lay behind it. "Go ahead."

"I can tell you what happened to Maxine Johnson. I can tell you what happened to your best friend. I can't tell you what happened to Grace Mayfair, as I don't know that myself. But I can give you some closure regarding your best friend. I would ask forgiveness before I begin this story, but, at this point, I deserve the karma that comes my way," Cynthia began.

Salome and Felicia sat together in the living room of Salome's grand Victorian. A police car sat outside; they were going to take shifts sitting outside the house. Salome had made warm milk for Samantha and had poured a hefty glass of wine for herself. They had finished together the first part of Felicia's mother's diary.

"Are you okay?" Salome asked, handing over the warm milk. "We don't need to finish the rest of this tonight. We can wait until tomorrow."

"No," Felicia said. "That was your name redacted and blacked out?"

"Yes…" Salome confessed. "I didn't know whose hands this journal would fall into and I couldn't chance getting involved. I've been trying to figure out and stop what was happening to your mother for years. Her coming to see me for therapy was a blessing."

"I'm ready... I can't read these out loud anymore, though. Do you mind?"

"Not at all, darling." Salome crossed the room and sat down next to her granddaughter as they unwrapped the red scarf that held the second journal of Maxine Johnson. "This is cashmere."

"My mom used to wear this." Felicia began to tear up, which had been happening the entire night; she had short sleeves on and throughout reading about her mother's unknown hatred toward her each burn, each scar, each slice on her skin had felt fresh. "I'm sure if we clean it..."

"It will be as good as new. You do know your mother loved you, Felicia."

Felicia's head remained lowered.

"Listen. I am no saint in all of this. Your mother was being drugged almost nightly by your...father. The Captain wants what he wants, and he wanted your mother. She didn't begin writing in her journal again because she was lonely. She was losing time and going through severe withdrawals on the days she wasn't getting drugged by the tea. That causes aggression and anger that comes from a place that isn't us." Salome put her arm around Felicia. "You don't need to forgive her. You don't need to do anything. But understanding what happened, well, it might help you move forward."

"Just read, please."

"Winter, 1996. *The things we must do. The things we must see. The things we must endure to find out the truth. To find out the shadow monsters that haunt me in the night. I've been pouring the tea out into a plant in our bedroom, which is now dying. Last night, when Larry brought me my tea...*

"Thanks, Darling." Maxine smiled, Larry pulling a strand of blond hair away from her face and putting his hand on her her lovely face. "Why don't you sleep up here? I know you blame it on your snoring, but I've handled it for so many years. Why the past couple of months has it bothered you so much?"

"I just want you to sleep well." Larry looked shocked by the question and scratched at his head in worry. "You take care of Felicia all day, and this house; I just want you to...I need you to...please sleep."

That wasn't true. The side effects of the drugs in the tea, and this was no excuse, had caused Maxine to take out anger on her child during withdrawals. She hadn't properly cleaned the house in months and spent all her time building the gazebo. Larry knew what he was doing was wrong, and unforgivable, but the choices the Captain had given him on the matter were not easy. Why his wife? Why did this man need his wife so badly?

"Of course." Maxine kissed her husband on his lips and he shivered like a boy who had just beaten a girl and was being shown affection. "I love you so much, Larry. We were once so happy. Remember? When Athena and Benjamin brought the children over, when the entire Bixby family would come by just because. The Primms having us over for dinner on Iris Lane. The Hendersons and us would be kicking soccer balls with the kids on the street in the night…"

"Years ago. People change. So much has…"

Maxine placed a hand over her husband's mouth, "Hush," she said, faking a yawn and pretending like the drugs had begun to hit her. "I'm feeling sleepy."

Larry got up from the side of her bed and stood there for a second. For a minute. Forever. Looking down upon his beautiful wife. You can't explain the type of agony his body radiated. His stunning wife; tonight he saw a glimpse of the woman she once was. A glimpse of a past memory of a woman he'd once married and promised to protect. He'd failed.

As he left the room and closed the door, tears began to swell in his eyes. It had been five years now since it had started. He had almost forgotten who was in that bedroom, who he was supposed to be sleeping next to.

Maxine and Larry Johnson had been high-school sweethearts. She was a new student her sophomore year and as her books fell in front of the entire cafeteria, Larry had sprung up from the table of his football buddies and helped catch them. He went a step further in that first moment and had brushed a strand of golden hair away from her face as he realized he'd never had seen her before; that he had never seen anyone so beautiful. Anyone so beautiful and lost. Maxine had smiled at him in a way that no one had smiled at him before, and whatever the reaction on his face, they wound up eating lunch alone together that day. He was on the football team and she was a cheerleader. They were on prom court together. Joined sister fraternities and sororities. Not once had anyone else touched her besides him, and never had he let another girl or woman lay a hand on him.

But life isn't cuddling in bed till noon and making love till the sun rises. It's not playing footsie while studying for finals or playing strip flash cards for big tests. No, life comes, real life comes when bills are thrown at you like glitter. Where you make choices each day that may lead you somewhere happy and may lead you somewhere dark and unforgivable. You meet people and you make deals. A Captain shows up one day and tells you he'll take away all your financial trouble if…

The rapping was at his back door. That single knock on the window that made his stomach lurch. He approached the back door and Benjamin Rose and Leroy Watson stood there with dead expressions on their faces. These were also once family men. Handsome men. Great examples and fathers they could have been. But they had taken the wrong deals and jobs. Larry waited at the door as they went and got his drugged and passed-out wife.

"How long is she going to be gone this time?" Larry asked. "How long…"

"You ask us that each time," Leroy said, his voice as empty as his eyes. "And every time my answer is 'when the Captain is through with her.'"

Larry didn't know what else to say. He scratched at his head as he watched his wife get carried away.

Maxine had taken some improv classes when she was in college, but it wasn't hard to fake being asleep. She kept her eyes closed the entire time, her mouth slightly ajar, assuming one would drool a little if they were so heavily drugged. The two men placed her body in back of what felt like an SUV and slowly drove up the street with the lights off. They reached the gate at Thorne Hall and Maxine heard it slowly open.

But they didn't pull around the main entrance; instead, the car lurched slightly as they pulled onto the lawn. Maxine had been to Thorne Hall before. Athena held book clubs there at times. She was being brought in through the back door.

The door opened and she heard Abraham Thorne's voice, the voice of a self-proclaimed Captain. Men who needed to give themselves titles normally had egos that could never be satisfied.

It wasn't until they were inside, that her body was passed over to the Captain's arms.

"She is so beautiful when she is asleep. So much personality and spark when she is awake, but when she is asleep, like an angel. Wouldn't you agree, Leroy?"

"Yes, sir," came Leroy's monotone reply. "As you say."

Maxine Johnson was carried down a flight of stairs, a door shut behind them. She opened her eyes just enough so she could see blurry images but still appear to be asleep.

Leroy Watson and Benjamin Rose were moving the cabinet and sounds of glass clinked together.

"Careful," the Captain snapped. "I need every drop of what's in there."

She felt her body placed on a mattress on the ground.

"You, men," the Captain said, a hungry sound in his voice. "Wait outside. I'll bring her to you when I am done."

Maxine debated her next option. The Captain stood at easily over six feet and had a good two-hundred and something pounds to him. She was thin and petite, and the drugs didn't exactly help with her muscular strength.

Her dress was lifted. She could give him one fair shot to the groin, but what would his workers do? She didn't have it in her to kill him. Did they have it in them to kill her? She heard the sound of his belt being un-looped from his pants.

Would she allow this. Go home and leave her husband and take Felicia far away, find an actual *suburbia* to live in. If she could endure this, she could endure being a single mother.

Then came the sound of his jeans being unzipped.

"Abraham!" a voice called from outside the room. "What in God's name?"

Maxine knew that voice. It was the voice of Dr. Salome Legree, the woman who she had passed her last journal to. The woman who she had discovered this entire horror with —had she known? Had she...

"Get off her immediately!" The sound of a swishing came through the air as Salome smacked her son on the side with her cane. "Cynthia! Cynthia!"

"Are you insane?" The sound of a squabble followed by another sound of thumping of the cane against the Captain. "Go home, Mother. Go home now."

"You bring this poor woman home," Salome spit. "I never questioned why you had me cook up so many different types of drugs. I figured it was for the foreign whores, but this...this is my neighbor. This isn't a Russian mail-order bride!"

"Go home...now."

Maxine let her eyes open slightly as she noticed a video camera against the wall, the red light recording, and the Captain leading his mother out of the room and up the stairs.

The room was set up like a bedroom, mattress on the floor, a nightstand filled with sex toys and other obscene objects. Also, in the darkness against the wall, was a large bookshelf, but it wasn't filled with books; it was filled with VHS tapes. Hundreds.

She had to shut her eyes as Leroy Watson and Benjamin Rose returned to the room.

"My mother saw both of you," the Captain said, as if this was all their fault. As if they were the ones to blame for the raping of Maxine Johnson. "Leroy, when Maxine is back in her bed, go deal with my mother. Bring me that cane of hers when you are finished."

"Yes, sir." No emotion in his voice, no care. "Whatever you want, sir."

I was brought back home and placed in bed. Today I called Salome at least a dozen times with no answer. Felicia, my darling daughter, if this has been going on for as long as it has been, I believe the Captain is your father...I believe my subconscious knew that... I don't expect you to forgive my actions. But from here on out, I will treat you better; we will get out of this town. I will find us a home where we can be happy. A place where you and I can be a family, for your father is lost and the man who is your actual father...is a monster.

Do I feel bad for what I did to your father? No. I dare not call the cops in this town, so I handled him on my own. Rat poison does the trick, if you are ever in such a situation.

We shall leave today…as I am writing this…there is a rapping at my door. I heard the sound of an expensive car pull up the road. I didn't realize it stopped here. I know those heels. Cynthia is at my door. I have to answer…"

Salome looked up and then back down at the journal and flipped; the rest of the pages were blank. She scratched at her arm as she stared at the blank pages. This wasn't what she was expecting, she had thought…the Mercedes…that blood stain…

But Felicia no longer looked upset and Salome got a chill from the look on her face. Salome would of taken upset, this was dark. Cold. Unforgiving.

"Darling," Salome asked, a tinge in her voice. Something had shifted in Felicia. The serenity that she had worked so hard for, gone. Maybe it was too soon. Maybe this wasn't a good idea. "Are…are you okay?"

"I will be," Felicia said, staring into the flames of their fire, her voice raspy. The rage box was no longer on the shelf —it was open; it was wide open and it was encompassing her. "Trust me. I will be."

"He got messy," Cynthia said. "I was coming down here as his mother was roaring and storming out of the house. I can remember it like it was yesterday. I watched as

Leroy and your husband carried Maxine Johnson out of this house, drugged. He wanted her so badly that he was having her husband drug her at night, and taking her while I slept. We have always had an open marriage, always seen other people if we wanted, but he has never hidden anyone from me like this. He has never…"

Cynthia grabbed at the dress leg again. "He loved her. I thought his love for her was driving him crazy. That car, that Mercedes that Felicia is driving around in, is the one I had in 1996. I took that car the day after I caught him…doing what he did to her. I went over to the Johnson house and waited for no one to be home but Maxine, waited until nighttime. I don't know what made me so angry, it wasn't that he was having sex with her. Fuck, I'm the one who found Lorraine online and moved her in so he could have a toy to play with. But he loved Maxine. He loved her so much that he was getting sloppy, drugging her and taking her in the middle of the night. After I saw them drag her out of here, I slipped away to our bed, and he returned to it as if nothing had happened. He could actually just brushed aside what happened, as if it was nothing; that's how much he obsessed over this woman. I knew I had to do something. So…I knocked on her door and when she answered it I stepped inside her house and pushed her, hard. I saw Larry's face head down in a cereal bowl, and I knew she had poisoned him. She fell to the ground and I took out one of my husband's guns and I shot her. I have terrible aim and only got her shoulder."

Athena stood there, didn't flinch an inch, her eyes on her sister.

"The whole thing was such a mess. She was writing in this journal about what happened here the night before. I took the red scarf she was wearing, wrapped it around the journal. I buried it in her backyard and then I dragged her out to my Mercedes and put her in the back of the car. The shot didn't kill her, and for a moment I debated bringing her to a hospital. But…"

"You didn't."

"No…I took her to the swamp near NRG. The one behind the buildings where all the kids go and party. I buried her body in the muck and murk and beat her down with a rock." Cynthia looked to her sister for a response, but Athena's face hadn't moved. just…something snapped in me, sister. I couldn't bear him loving another woman, even though he didn't love me. Ha. I could probably use all the therapy and drugs Dr. Legree can conjure up, can't I?"

"I shot my husband," Athena said, her face not moving, her voice soft. "He didn't commit suicide. That day you moved the McArthurs into their home, Lucas was home for a visit from college. Apparently Benjamin had let him in on what exactly goes on up here, some of the work he did for the Captain, and how the Captain wanted him next as a protégé. Your sick husband wanted to pluck my son out of his Ivy-League school and have him do…his biddings. I came home to them arguing. But when I heard Lucas repeat the things that my husband was saying to him, I saw that the man I married, the beautiful man who used to surprise me with gifts and wait for me in bed with champagne, was dead already. Your husband had killed him. As they argued, I walked past them and upstairs; I removed my pistol from the closed case I kept it in, walked down the stairs, and shot him directly in the head."

"Athena!" Cynthia's hand went to her mouth. "I…"

"Now we both have shared secrets." Athena went to push at the cabinet. "Confession time is over. What happened nine years ago cannot be fixed, but the future can. Help me move this."

Together, in fine silk gowns, with their hair done and makeup perfectly applied, the ladies of Thorne Hall moved the cabinet away. An even older light switch was hidden behind.

"This could have been an Underground Railroad stop at one point," Cynthia said. "I didn't even know there was anything behind that cabinet."

"Do you really think, knowing your husband, they would have helped any slaves escape back then? They have the bells all over the house."

"The ones you ring at night to freak me out."

"Yes, I confess." Athena shot a look of amusement at her sister. "Why can't you leave Rosaletta alone?"

"I don't know," Cynthia admitted as they searched for a light switch. "After everything that's come out tonight, I think we can tell I have some unresolved anger issues."

Cynthia's long nail found the little button and pressed it, light bulbs older than them flickered on with the sound of threatening to pop off.

The room had a mattress in it, a nightstand filled with sex toys and metal objects, and sheets that were faded and old. A camera in one corner, a camera in another corner, a camera on the ceiling. Filing cabinets on one wall, but on the other, a bookshelf filled with VHS tapes. A small bench with an old TV and VHS player.

Athena ran a finger along the tapes, which all had women's names on them and specific dates.

"This might as well be called a rape room," Cynthia said as Athena mentally thought the same. "What are all those VHSs? All those names on them."

"The same names that were in the folder I gave you last night." Athena shot Cynthia a look. "Which is where?"

"Hidden in my purse; he doesn't look through my stuff."

"Well, here's Maxine Johnson...but let's take a look at Marcella Garcia first, shall we? Notice the date?"

"Our last foundation ball..."

They popped the VHS into the player and in bad color the tape began to play. A man of Asian descent was having sex with a Spanish woman who was passed out. Athena grabbed another tape, this one with the name Irina on it. An Arab man having sex with a Russian girl who was tied up, awake, and handcuffed to a bed. Then continued…various foreign names of girls and foreign men…each tape was slightly more depraved. Cynthia went to press stop as a man in a suit was heating a branding stick over an iron as a woman tied up in bed struggled. But Athena slapped her hand away; if they were going to dive into the deep end, they would dive all the way down.

"This isn't here," Athena said, as Cynthia couldn't remove her eyes from the tape. "These last few tapes. These weren't taken down here."

"Then where?"

"Cynthia." Athena turned to her sister and brought her hands into hers. "Where do all the men go during the foundation ball? You know. After the presentations are done and the cakes are served. All the women come inside and the men they go to…the power plant, right?"

"Right."

"I think you need to take a visit there. Immediately." Athena went to shut off the light, but not before putting a couple of the VHS tapes under her arm. "You need to find out what goes on there. You do see what's happening, right?

Your husband seems to be giving away women as party favors during your balls. That's why the amount of money increases each time…"

"But why does our cousin write the biggest check?"

"That is a great question."

Athena and Cynthia stood outside the room in which Maxine Johnson had conceived Felicia and had been brought countless times thereafter.

"One that I will figure out. I wish my son was home; he'd help us in a heartbeat. If we are to return this neighborhood to its former glory, he'd be a great ally."

"Holy shit." Cynthia looked over at Athena, her heart beginning to race and her ulcer burning with worry. "I completely forgot to tell you. Lucas is in town. He's at the motel. My husband knows. You need to…"

"Do nothing." Athena's expression didn't change. "Lucas is more capable than most of us. If he senses trouble, he will get out of there. I personally sense trouble here, so I'm going to move over with Salome and Felicia. Make sure Samantha gets in her cab at 4 a.m.; she needs the poison drained from her and that's not going to happen here."

"I feel like…I want to move with you."

"No." Athena grasped her sister by the shoulders. "Listen to me. Until the next foundation ball, I need you to stay…no offense…but awful. Exposing something like this shouldn't be a secretive thing. Our cousin will have a cop wherever I want at a single call, but if he's writing big checks to your foundation…we can't trust him either. We need to keep our distance from each other…you need to tell him…"

"She was just such a bitch tonight." Cynthia removed the large diamond earrings at her gigantic vanity. "I can't believe I didn't see this coming; plus, your mother? Did she dig herself out of a grave? Athena and her daughter will be out of here by morning, and we'll never have to tolerate a night like this again! After how hospitable we have been."

"Don't bother yourself with such things." The Captain was standing behind Cynthia as she began to remove her makeup. "All is well. Disagreements and a badly planned dinner party was all that tonight was. By tomorrow, the neighborhood will have different worries and problems to deal with."

"You sound so sure." Cynthia didn't like the tone in his voice, how smug he was, how confident after a night like this. She had never paid much attention to such things before, but now, she would pay attention to everywhere he went and to everything he did. "How can you be so sure? This truly was the worst affair I've ever been to."

"Oh, my darling." He placed his hands on her shoulders and she held herself firm. "Don't I always fix everything?"

"Of course, darling." She waited a moment so she could control her voice. "Has Dax returned? I haven't heard him come back in."

"No." The Captain's voice was still. "He won't be back till late. I'm just making sure everything runs as normal."

That's what I'm scared of now, Cynthia thought. *Tomorrow I make my first visit to the power plant.*

"It's nearing midnight, Susan." Priscilla smiled. "Tonight we pulled the mask off the clown and saw the monster underneath."

"That's for sure." Susan was gathering her purse up. "Though, I hate clowns. Your offer stands?"

"Of course." Priscilla lifted herself slowly off the couch and went to open the back door. "Let's save your husband before it's too late. My husband will get him a fine job at his financial firm. Enough that you will be able to afford this house on your own. Meanwhile, I will work to fill these empty houses with good families, with strong morals. I tend to be a good judge of character. Soon we won't have to lock our doors at night; soon there won't be strangers in the night—just friends."

"I'm truly glad I met you." Susan hugged Priscilla who, though typically stiff, returned the hug warmly. "You've shone a light on this town…and even on myself. I was lost in pills and a coy pond."

"Just concentrate on your family. Go home…" Priscilla's eyes widened as she looked over to the McArthur house. "Now."

"What?"

"Susan, look."

There were police lights in front of her house. She grasped Priscilla's hand as the both of them made their way through her pristine garden and through the mowed emerald lawn and the crunching fall leaves that would be raked away tomorrow.

As they circled around the house, the Mayfairs, and Matthew and Katie all stood outside.

"Where's…where's… Susan didn't even need to say her name to know. April grasped her other hand.

"A monster took Kat," Katie was crying. "A monster took Kat away."

"Where's my husband?" Susan looked around frantically, the entire neighborhood gathering slowly, but Gregory was nowhere in sight. "Where is he?"

Lucas Rose was slowly hitting the gun Gregory McArthur had pointed at him against his leg. He looked across the room at the man who he'd bound to a chair.

"You look like my father," Lucas said as he circled the chair one final time, ensuring the rope was tight enough around him. "Not in the sense of actual looks, but you look like he did before my mother shot him. You look like you've been ordered to be put through hell. Some could argue that the Captain is to blame for all of this, but we all have choices. My father made the choice to hurt innocent women and off people for the Captain. The same choices you are making. I think we lose a part of our soul every time we act on such... matters. I can see it in your eyes. Your soul has been lost."

Lucas flicked the gun and Gregory shuddered in his chair. "Oh, don't be silly. I'm not going to kill you." Lucas tossed the gun from hand to hand. He was just as attractive as his mother and sister. Just as smart, but where Samantha had used her intellect for bad, Lucas was more like his mother. "I'm going to call my mother in the morning and we all can have a little chat."

Gregory tried to make noises, but having a jockstrap stuffed in your mouth and a rope wrapped around it made it difficult for him to say much.

"I knew telling my aunt I was in town would reach the Captain's ears. I just didn't think he'd act so soon on having me killed. Thought he would send someone who would put up more of a fight. You are a pathetic excuse for an assassin. That is what he does. I might be Lucas Rose, but I will be a thorn in his side. And you..." Lucas tapped the gun against Gregory's head. "You are going to help us end all of this. Get some sleep if you can. My mother won't be as kind to you in the morning."

As Mayor Neil Wolf left his limo, he didn't bother talking to the driver or the two men who were at guard at his front door. They opened the door into his gray and glass and steel home.

He hummed to himself as he climbed the stairs, passing by all the bedrooms and to the end of the long gray hallway. Each painting more ferocious than the last, wars and demons and scenes from Biblical times and battles throughout history.

He went to put the key in the attic, but it was already opened. The carnival music still playing, he climbed up the stairs into a room full of color. A toy train set was moving along the floor, a track that circled the entirety of the attic, which was the same length as all of the floors in his mansion. Pictures of clowns on the wall, a ball pit off to one side of the room, a collection of dolls piled up in another corner. The entire room was a child's playhouse. Toys of every imaginable nature, pinball machines, even a few arcade games. Not the type of toys that you would buy happily for a child, though; these weren't your average toys. They were all antiques, nothing new from Toys 'R' Us. These were toys found at yard sale, and antique stores, toys that made rusty grinding sounds as they turned; the puppet from the jack-in-the-box's head was half-missing. These would have been collectors' items if he had taken care of them, but they weren't taken care of as they should have been. The dolls all had horrid looks and the clown painting on the wall was menacing.

Dax stood there and Neil sniffed at him, a monster all right. About three-quarters of his face had been burned so severely that half his nose was missing and he had no hair, eyelids, or lashes on one side of his face. He was gigantic, full of muscle, something from a DC comic.

"Aren't you just a wonderful addition! You are just… mortifying! I love it! Beautiful beast of a creature!"

"The Captain wants to make sure you are happy," Dax grunted, didn't even call him his father. "Are you happy?"

The mayor turned around and walked to the other end of the playroom, where the cages were.

"Hello there, new friend." Neil bent low and smiled at Kat McArthur. "You and I are going to be best friends. We are going to play a lot of games together."

"Grace?" Neil turned his head to a fifteen-year-old Grace Mayfair, who was dressed in little girl's clothes and had her hair done in pigtails and her face painted like a doll. "You've met Kat, yes?"

Grace nodded.

"Good." The mayor turned toward Dax. "Yes, go home to your father and tell him everything will be as peachy as ever for his next foundation ball. He can continue as he has planned. I am content for now."

Dax bounded down the stairs and made his way out of the house. There was a third cage holding a woman who looked to be about twenty. In a forth cage, a woman who had died some time ago, though she was propped up and dressed in girl's clothes and painted like a doll.

"Some of us are new, and some of us have been here for quite some time, but we shall all play together." Neil smiled at his new friend, Kat. "We shall go over our rules, now, shall we? Grace knows what happens if we don't follow rules."

Grace's mouth had been covered by duct tape, though red lips had been drawn on, and tears were forming in her eyes. Kat wanted to scream, but she knew she shouldn't. It was the oldest one, in the cage at the end, who began to sob.

The mayor got up and let in and out a fresh deep breath of air, excited, enthralled, high. "Welcome to my playhouse."

Epilogue
NRG Power Plant
The Next Day

Cynthia had the blue folder in her purse as her Mercedes pulled up to the NRG Power Plant. The guard at the gate recognized her at once, and the gate opened before her Mercedes even needed to stop.

I've never been here before, Cynthia thought. *Abraham must have assumed I would never care enough to come here. Will they tell him I visited?*

The Thornes, always in their cleverness, had named the power plant NRG and it had sat here, grown, and renovated for generations. Controlling the power of the entire town and then some. But, like Thorne Hall, it wasn't a pleasant structure. Two humongous smoke stacks in their hourglass shaped towered seemingly to the sky, growing larger and larger as she circled around to the main entrance. The entire building connected it with its outdoor stairs and darkened windows, making it truly an unwelcoming place. But the

Thornes never cared much for anything except power and wealth.

Cynthia left her car parked in the center circle of the empty area where the entrance was. Employees parked below. She walked across to the only double doors on the main level, assuming it the entrance. She opened the doors to a perfect white room. Perfect white sofa. Coffee table with flowers on it, a couch, her husband's office all the way down the hallway. Men in suits walking from office to office...maybe this wasn't as bad as she thought.

"Hi...Mrs. Wolf-Thorne," a front desk assistant squeaked nervously. "Over...here."

God, Cynthia thought. *Am I that notorious for being a bitch.*

"Welcome," the handsome male receptionist said and smiled, dressed as a receptionist should be. "A pleasure to see you. Can we do something for you?"

"How did you know my name?"

He motioned behind her; she had missed it, but above the couch was an elegant portrait that ran the wall. One she had commissioned some years back, when Dax was in middle school, a family portrait. They looked like the perfect family in their fine suits and her in a grand gown.

Presentation is more than half the game.

"I've just never been here before." Cynthia looked closely around the office section of the power plant. "Maybe a tour?"

"Sur., I'm Doug."

"Hi, Doug." She held out her hand and they shook pleasantly. "I'm Cynthia."

It worked for Athena—why not try treating people with a different angle.

Doug led her around the office where men were yelling on phones, gossiping about their wives, and conducting normal office work that she would approve of if she ran it. Her husband's grand office held photos of the family that covered every section of it. She walked around to his desk and it was obvious his chair was worn; he had spent a lot of time here. She had just gotten him that leather chair a year or so ago.

Then Doug brought her outside. That's when she noticed, off in the distance, past the swamp, near the woods. A building that stood on its own.

It was a larger building, no windows, a flat roof, completely dark, and had large metal bolts covering the outside. Almost like a gigantic fallout shelter, it had two floors and chimneys. But…it wasn't right.

"What's that building over there, Doug?" Cynthia smiled pleasantly. "I'm not exactly educated in the electricity business; my days are spent getting my nails done…and helping out with charities."

That was a lie, but whatever.

"That building over there, well that's where the electricity comes from."

"Wait, no." Cynthia brought her coat tighter around herself. "That's the power plant?" Cynthia pointed to the high, ominous smoke stacks and the NRG plant that was in full use. The thirty-something-year-old smile, and nodded his head and made an *'I'm about to teach you something sound.'*

"Mrs. Wolf-Thorne," Doug said. "Right, but in that building is the energy. It gets pulled from that building over there and sucked back into the power plant so it can be used. Then the building produces more energy and it gets sucked underground into the power plant."

Cynthia looked around her—was she on one of those new reality shows?

"Doug…where did you attend school?"

"The Captain hired me from out of town, Mrs. Wolf-Thorne. My family had no money; I never went to school. I've been working here…well…since I was seventeen. He scooped me up, gave my parents enough money to be happy for the rest of their lives. I've been working that front desk ever since; you know that."

Cynthia held her hand up toward the building in front of her; she didn't know why, but energy radiated from it. You could feel it. It was stronger than all the power actually being produced by the power plant. This building was radiating a type of energy that didn't supply people with light, but with darkness. It crawled her skin and made her want to run.

Perverse.

"So." Cynthia didn't turn her eyes from the building in front of her, the one with no windows. One singular bolted door and a single chimney pipe, but she needed to hear him say this one more time. "Because I'm not so bright when it comes to how power plants work, explain to me, Doug, how does it all work?"

"Well." Doug pointed at the terrible-looking building Cynthia was staring at and with his other hand pointed at the actual power plant. "That is where all the actual energy is stored, yah know, like from the air and stuff. It all bundles up in there and when it's full, it gets sucked into the building we work in to be used as energy, you see…"

Cynthia couldn't believe the building she was staring at, or how dumb Doug was for that matter…for she knew then…behind those closed doors was where all the horrors happened.

"Doug." Cynthia gulped, trying to remember the last time she was this scared. "Do you have a key for that building?"

Thorne Hall
The Captain's Office
Winter, 2005

The letter arrived at Thorne Hall just as fall had become winter. In another three years, there would be a grand foundation ball that would draw in men from all over the world. It hadn't always been that way, it had begun as a family tradition. A way to include the neighbors and make the town feel comfortable around so much wealth. Those were before the railroad times, back when society was still working out the kinks. Then the slaves, and railroad and power workers came in. The Thorne family's foundation ball had become a time to celebrate the power these men had achieved. The concept of this power had changed over the years. Hunts of a different nature, and unspeakable acts.

The letter sat on the Captain's desk and, as he sat back with a whiskey on the rocks, he stared at it. The handwriting seemed oddly familiar. No lights in the room were on besides the fireplace, which roared behind him.

It was addressed to the entire Thorne family, and was in an aged envelope. He used a letter opener that was in the shape of a sword and depicting his family crest.

In perfect cursive writing on the dull paper of his mother's ancient prescription pad was a poem. The Captain read the letter and dropped it on his desk like a bee had just stung him. A poem was written in a girl's handwriting, a poem Felicia Johnson had written before fleeing Salome's house in the midst of the night:

To Every Member of the Thorne Dynasty

Wicked twisted spider web
web you weave the life you've led
Wrangle tangle lies gone spread
Choices made, paths not tread
never clever eyes all red
Regret will make your final bed
Wicked twisted spider web
No cries for those already dead

Sing your songs, bang, joke, drum
Let spirits and pleasure slide your tongue
I have a harp and it is strung
Sounds from which you can never run
It's over now the bell has rung
In three years, I, death will come

Felicia Thorne-Johnson

ABOUT THE AUTHOR

Christian Jeremy Alecci resides in Bergen County, NJ. Christian splits his time between health and nutrition in the role of a certified personal trainer. In his free time he pursues his love and passion of writing, CEO of CFPublishing. He enjoys all things macabre, and finds inspiration from his favorite author Stephen King as well as high fantasy novels. Also is the author of Avon, Hush and Suburbia.

Fun Fact: CJ thinks he would be the first victim in the horror movie. Hopefully his writing is better than his chance of survival.